Praise for Miles In Time

"In Lee Matthew Goldberg's full-of-fun MILES IN TIME, fourteen-year-old Miles Hardy embarks on a time-traveling mission to save his brainiac brother's life. This madcap adventure finds Miles teaming up with his Past Self while trying to thwart an evil corporation from stealing the secret to his brother's time machine. You'll want to go back and read this again…and again…and again…for the very first time!"

Alan Orloff, author of the Anthony- and Agatha-Award winning YA thriller I PLAY ONE ON TV.

"Perfect for fans of Alex Rider, this time-travel mystery will have you flipping the pages to see what happens next. Readers will love wise-cracking Miles and his sidekick Kevin as they Sherlock in time, to find out who's after Miles' brother's time-travel invention. The best blend of mystery and adventure to keep even the most reluctant readers glued to the page."

Fleur Bradley, award-winning author of MIDNIGHT AT THE BARCLAY HOTEL and DAYBREAK ON RAVEN ISLAND

Praise for Runaway Train

"An engaging '90s pastiche with an earnest heart beating at its center."

Kirkus Reviews

"A mixtape of the 90s, paired with a beautiful story of love, loss, and finding yourself. I couldn't put it down!"

Raegan Revord, Missy Cooper on TV's
Young Sheldon and founder of the
#ReadingWithRaegan book club

"Raw. Riveting…Realistic and shocking, hopeful and satisfying, Runaway Train will keep readers turning the page.

USA Today Bestselling Author Rebecca
Forster

"Goldberg's storytelling is heartfelt, assured, and polished."

Book Life PW

MILES IN TIME

Also by Lee Matthew Goldberg

Wise Wolf Books Young Adult Starter Library

Runaway Train Series

Runaway Train

Grenade Bouquets

Vanish Me

Runaway Train: The Complete YA Contemporary Coming-Of-Age Trilogy

MILES IN TIME

Miles In Time
Book 1

LEE MATTHEW GOLDBERG

WISE WOLF
BOOKS

Miles In Time
Paperback Edition
Copyright © 2025 by Lee Matthew Goldberg

Wise Wolf Books
An imprint of Wolfpack Publishing
1707 E. Diana Street
Tampa, FL 33610

wisewolfbooks.com

Paperback ISBN 979-8-9908171-2-8
Ebook ISBN 979-8-9908171-1-1
LCCN 2025932627

"TIME DOES NOT CHANGE US. IT JUST UNFOLDS US."
MAX FRISCH

MILES IN TIME

Prologue

BANG!

The loud sound wrestled me from my sleep. I'd been dreaming about melting clocks. Watches on people's wrists. The alarm on my bedside table. Every possible way that time could be shown. Looking closer at each of those melting clocks, the hands all started going backward. Faster and faster they spun around and then...

BANG!

I shot up in bed with sweat dripping from my forehead. Was it thunder? A truck backfiring? Outside my window, the sky was blue and the street below empty. I figured I just dreamed of the sound.

I made my way to the bathroom to brush my teeth and splash some water on my face, but the loud sound kept ringing in my ears. Stepping outside, the air smelled a little like gunpowder. I recognized the smell from when I got to shoot a rifle once at summer camp. I went by my parents' room and saw that Mom was still sleeping and Dad had already left for work.

Half asleep, I stared at my brother Simon's door down the hall. The door had been left open a crack, which Simon never did. Even if he hadn't come home last night, I remembered shutting it when I left his room. The gunpowder smell grew stronger the closer I got. Faint puffs of smoke curled through the crack. My heart started slamming into my chest, feeling like the worst heartburn ever. My body went cold, fingers and toes going numb.

"Simon?"

I pushed open the door.

Nothing could possibly prepare me for what I was about to see.

Chapter One

I'd always thought of myself as a detective. Although, "aspiring detective" would probably be a better title. Back in junior high school, I even founded my own agency and put up flyers around town of me in a deer-stalker hat smoking from an old briar pipe I secretly bought off eBay with my parents' credit card like Sherlock Holmes used. But I still hadn't come across a BIG CASE yet beyond some old lady's missing cat, and I was about to give it all up so ass jerks at school would stop calling me *dick*-tective. The main problem for my lack of business was I lived in Frontier, Iowa, a sleepy town with a Main Street that stretched for three whole blocks, neighbors that waved when they said hello, and cornfields, cornfields and more cornfields—a place where nothing dangerous, and nothing truly terrible ever seemed to happen to require my services.

"I really hate corn," I was saying to my friend Kevin one morning. We'd recently started high school and were passing by walls of six-foot cornhusks like we did every day. I didn't know that in just twenty-four hours, I'd be opening my brother's bedroom door to discover that gruesome things actually happened in Frontier.

"Corn, corn. It's good for your heart. The more you eat, the more you fart," Kevin sang.

"You mean beans."

"Tell that to my mom's cornbread, Miles," Kevin said. He squinted until a small *toot* echoed through the fields.

I had to laugh. I'd woken up in a bad mood, which had been the norm these last few weeks. Over the summer, I'd given my agency one final shot by searching for a big case, but now school had started up and all I had on my plate were more missing cats. Besides, while in junior high kids may have thought of my "hobby" as adorable, as a freshman, I learned it was the fastest way to get shunned.

At least Kevin was good at making me crack up. Kevin had red curly hair like a clown. We'd been friends ever since the sandbox in kindergarten when Kevin picked up a Tonka truck and clocked me over the head. After many tears, his mom arranged a play date to apologize and we hung out in his mega tree house that became the initial base for my agency. He'd showed me how to fit an entire box of Junior Mints in his mouth and wound up puking through his nose. To this day, he can still find a gross way to make me feel better whenever I'm down.

Once we passed the cornfields, we arrived at Jeremiah Boonton, a butter-colored building that was Frontier's only high school since our town was so freaking small. Walking down the hallways, everyone was either glued to their phones or caught up in conversations about parties I knew wouldn't involve me.

The bell rang, causing a mob of kids to push past us. By accident, I bumped into this girl with freckles and blond hair. She gave me a smile, but my dumb ass was too embarrassed to smile back. Over the summer, my dad forced me to get metal braces for my teeth since we couldn't afford clear ones.

"Is that the girl you were swooning over last week?" Kevin asked, jabbing me with his elbow.

"Shut up," I said under my breath as she quickly looked down at the floor while passing us by. I'd first noticed her the other day in the cafeteria with her freckled nose in a giant book and her tray propped up against a windowsill because no one had invited her to sit with them. I knew that feeling all too well.

I usually clammed up around girls (and guys!) and hadn't really done too much yet. I know, I know—*Virgin Alert*, but I figured I had a ton of time to go further, and it should be with someone I really, really liked. My first experience was at a movie with Katelyn Fowler in seventh grade when our hands both reached for the popcorn and I looked into her eyes that seemed like they were begging me to move in for a kiss; but after we swapped some salty spit, she confessed that she already had a boyfriend and this could never happen again. My next time was right after I graduated junior high, and everyone was invited to Marin Franklin's farmhouse. Marin had rustled up a ton of wine coolers and a bunch of us had escaped into the cornfields at night. Under a winking moon, I watched Billy Cordy feeling up Allison Yeager while Jimmy Gaston and Ella Edwards frenched. I was left alone with Ella's cousin

Dave, who had wavy black hair that he liked to flip out of his eyes. He said I kind of looked like a *way* younger version of the guy who played Batman in the good *Batman* movies and I laughed. He made fun of my mushroom haircut with a part down the middle and said it made me seem like a little kid. The wine coolers were making me sway and when he licked his lips, I leaned in for a kiss. It lasted for about a second until he pushed me away, shook his head, and wobbled off. When I told the story to Kevin, he asked if I liked girls *and* guys, and I didn't know, like I hadn't thought about it before, but I answered that "I liked what I liked" and that was that. As of now, Kevin was the only one I told because people tended to be narrow-minded in Frontier and my business was *my* business.

Watching my cute new crush weaving through the hallway, I wondered what her name was, deciding I could still fall in love with her even if it was something like Sharyleigh (there was a lady who worked at the local Walmart with this name). She was wearing a flowery dress and sneakers that she had doodled on with a marker. Not with stars, hearts, or smiley faces, but with like really cool drawings of different kinds of clocks that reminded me of the Salvador Dali poster my brother Simon had hanging in his room. She walked kinda funny on the tips of her toes, like she didn't want to bother anyone by making a sound. It made her seem as if she was gliding through the halls. For a second, she glanced in my direction again so I quickly bent over and pretended to be tying my shoelace. By the time I looked up, she had already disappeared around the corner.

"She's new in town," Kevin said. "Don't even know her name."

"Mission accepted, I'm gonna find out," I said.

"Not if I do first," Kevin winked, but I wasn't worried about Kevin stealing her away since he thought the best way to get a girl to like him was by burping in her face.

We slapped hands with our handshake that involved snaps, claps, and a fake punch to the gut.

"Don't forget," I called out as Kevin began to walk away, "We're meeting Ms. Kissey after school to go over details about the case of her missing cat."

"Isn't she the one who offers to pay us in pies?"

Unfortunately, this was true. Most of the cases we still wound up taking were pro bono, or *pie* bono as I liked to say. In my mind, I used to think we were practicing, sharpening our skills until we'd get our BIG CASE, but I was probably taking a turn toward Deludedville. While it might've sounded as if we were bored kids messing around, this was legit what I wanted to do when I was like old and stuff, help people solve crimes that were ruining their lives. 'Cause I knew I'd be good at it and I wasn't good at much. So, Kevin and I kept putting up advertisements on telephone poles, in the rec center, on the school boards, and in the Made-Rite diner on Main Street. We even created a low-budget website, but so far it was mostly old ladies with lost cats who responded. In fact, twice we had to find the same lady's cat that was clearly trying to get away from her.

I'd dubbed my business *Mr. Hardy's Detective Agency.* At first, I wanted to call it *Sherlock's Sleuthing Agency*, but Kevin thought that was too on-the-nose. The *Hardy Boys* were my second favorite books and my last name also happened to be Hardy so the name couldn't be more perfect. Kevin wanted his name in the title as well, but I argued that Gooligy didn't have the same ring. Also, I'd been the one who solved every case while he usually tagged along.

"I know she pays us in pies, but they're home-baked, not with a crust from a mix," I reminded Kevin, trying to make the best out of the situation.

"Tell her to throw in a scoop of ice cream and she's got herself a deal," he said, turning around. "See you for food poisoning at lunchtime in the cafeteria, Hardy!"

I gulped and swallowed back some acid rising up my throat. As I slung my backpack over my shoulder and headed to class, my stomach was already rumbling from the abuse it knew would occur from the cafeteria's deadly food.

At least I was confident I'd find Ms. Kissey's cat again and have some pies to look forward to later, but I knew I was really itching for something horrible to happen in Frontier. Something bad enough to put the town on edge and only *I* would have the skills to solve the crime. Something that might give me reason for being.

I should've told myself to be careful what you wish for.

Chapter Two

While I struggled with most subjects in school because I didn't really care, during history, I actually soared. I had an uncanny ability to remember dates and facts and often pictured what it would be like to live in a time far more interesting than the one I'd been born into. Today Mrs. Neeley was talking about the Roaring Twenties. World War I had just ended, resulting in a booming economy and wild jazz parties with flapper girls. It fascinated me to think that back then everyone seemed to be having such a good time without realizing that the stock market was about to crash and the Great Depression would be right around the corner with World War II on the horizon.

During Earth Science and Pre-Algebra, I gave up paying attention to the boring lectures and imagined being my age in the 1920s. Back then with the success of *Sherlock Holmes* and the recent publication of *The Hardy Boys*, I bet my detective agency would've been way more popular while these days it seemed as if being on some lame reality television show and taking selfies was what everyone aspired to do.

The bell rang as I stuffed my books in my backpack and headed to the cafeteria. In addition to its awful food, eating lunch there genuinely sucked since seating was clearly set up by how cool you were. The jocks and cheerleaders had their corner by the windows that got the best light, the theater kids and the glee clubs were in another by the speakers, while the burnouts had their own section that often smelled like stinky pot. The last corner housed the Brainiacs, which left me without a place to sit.

I spied my brother Simon at one of the Brainiac tables with a few other senior nerds, all of them doing schoolwork except him. Even though he was only sixteen (going on forty), Simon skipped a few grades because he was super smart. He was reading this super old book *Time and Again* by Jack Finney. The pages had yellowed and the binding was coming apart at the seams, but Simon refused to get another copy since it was his favorite. I barely knew anyone else at the table because Simon and I hadn't been close since we were little. He was a loner who didn't really have friends. He mostly just associated with other Brainiacs to discuss theories about time travel scenarios.

For the past few years, Simon had been working on a Top-Secret invention. He never said it what it was exactly, but I guessed that it had something to do with time travel since he always would say that "time wasn't linear" and that "traveling through eras was scientifically doable with the precise equipment," or some type of smarty-pants speak like that. Of course, I didn't really believe this, but if anyone could find a way to travel through time, my genius brother would probably be the one.

Our parents referred to Simon as the "prodigy" and barely acknowledged me. Though I couldn't blame Mom. She hadn't been feeling too well for years and mostly just zoned out and slept, but Dad made it clear that intelligence was the thing he valued most. He taught math at the local community college, but his dream was to be an inventor. Unfortunately, his inventions only half worked, and our house was cluttered with various remnants of his failures. Simon was the only creation he thought of as his "one true success!"

When I was younger, I idolized Simon since he seemed to know everything. Sometimes he used to wake me up in the middle of the night and we'd go out to our front lawn. He'd tell me about all of the stars and galaxies and that there was more to the world than what I thought was out there.

"Like what?" I'd ask, blinking the crust out of my eyes and staring up at the universe in wonder.

"Someday, you'll know," Simon would say, pushing the thick glasses up his nose. "I promise."

It had been over three years since Simon woke me up in the middle of the night to head out to our front lawn. He was barely at home anymore and always working on his Top-Secret invention in an undisclosed location. Soon I began to feel like I didn't really have a brother at all.

At school, we rarely socialized besides a grumpy "hello" as we'd pass in the hallways, so it would've been weird for me to go and sit with him. Instead, I leaned against the wall and waited for Kevin to show up so I wouldn't have to try to find a seat alone. Kevin had probably fallen asleep in class and no one bothered to wake him.

Just then, someone slammed into my shoulder and practically knocked me over. My backpack fell to the floor, and when I looked up, I saw that one of the members of this asshole trio of bullies had deliberately bumped into me, muttering, "*dick*-tective's gotta small dick" under his breath. This group consisted of three degenerate tormentors who only got pleasure from making everyone's lives miserable. The head of this douche nozzle gang was named Jojo. He had a shaved head and a self-inflicted tattoo across his chest that said *Terrorize* (surprise) in blue pen. His face looked like a bulldog's and girls wanted nothing to do with him, but his two other sidekicks worshipped him like a god. Today it seemed as if they had set their sights on going after the Brainiacs. I always clammed up around Jojo, hating him but also finding myself flushed when he was around.

Simon's so-called friends had already closed their textbooks and scurried away, but Simon was too entrenched in Jack Finney's *Time and Again* to notice. His glasses were askew, his hair uncombed, and he had buttoned his collared shirt up to his neck. He had the slightest grin on his face, which meant that he'd probably reached one of his favorite parts of the novel. Before I could warn him about the approaching trio, Jojo had swatted the book out of his hands and kicked the seat out from under him. Simon let out an embarrassing gasp that caused the rest of the cafeteria to look and laugh at his misfortune.

"Didn't anyone ever tell you that only losers read?" Jojo asked, smirking at his gathering audience.

"Only an illiterate person would say that," Simon

replied as he fixed the framed glasses on his nose and got to his feet. I saw that Simon's hand was shaking ever so slightly, but the rest of his body managed not to show his fear.

"What did you say to me?" Jojo asked, grabbing Simon by his collar and causing one of his shirt buttons to pop off. Jojo's giant fist was inches away from Simon's face. I couldn't help but imagine the baseball-sized shiner that my brother would have as a result.

"I didn't realize that you're not only illiterate but also have abysmal halitosis," Simon replied.

Jojo scrunched up his mug and turned to his cronies, who shrugged in confusion as well.

"Brainiac, you are deader than dead."

Hearing those fatal words caused goose bumps to spring up all over my body. I wanted to save my brother, but I knew I'd probably just get a pounding as well. I'd never been in a fight before, and I hadn't planned on today being my first.

That was when I saw Simon's physics teacher, Mr. Congley passing by the cafeteria. Mr. Congley was Black and pretty old and so skinny it always looked like his pants were falling down. He could usually be seen quietly talking to himself and muttering about some formula he was working on. I pictured him coming home every night and microwaving a TV dinner surrounded by an army of wailing house pets.

I rushed outside and began tugging on Mr. Congley's sleeve.

"A fight…a fight…" was all I could say.

Mr. Congley waved me away.

"It's Simon!"

At the mention of Simon's name, Mr. Congley's

eyes bulged. The guy had some weird mentor relationship with my brother, and Simon always spoke of Congley as if his intellect was on par with Albert Einstein's.

Mr. Congley marched right into the cafeteria, yelling: "Jojo, put down that boy this instant or the principal will have you expelled."

Jojo took a second to register what was going on. His face turned red like he had a bad sunburn and his fist was twitching to come into contact with Simon's face.

"Jojo, yo quit it," one of his sidekicks said, pulling him off of Simon.

"Let's go, Jojo," Mr. Congley said, beckoning him. "I'm taking you to Principal Mynad."

Jojo fixed Simon's collar and then held his hands up in defeat.

"Mr. Big Words is gonna get put in the ground someday soon," he muttered, with an evil glare that rivaled any comic book villain. He and the rest of his followers followed Mr. Congley out of the cafeteria. Once Jojo was gone, I was able to breathe.

Simon picked up his abused copy of *Time and Again* and brushed it off. A few of the pages had ripped, and the binding was broken. He carefully slid it into his backpack as if it was a hidden treasure and then made his way toward the cafeteria doors as everyone stared.

"You…okay?" I asked.

Simon looked up but didn't say a word, his eyes cutting into me as if he blamed me for what had happened. He held his backpack close to his chest and then ran out of the cafeteria. I wished I could've said something more uplifting, but I was never good at making uncomfortable situations better.

Everyone went back to eating the terrible food, forgetting what had just occurred. I couldn't believe they were acting so blasé. I felt a slap against my back and turned around to see Kevin.

"Looks like your dorky brother almost bit it."

"Don't say that," I said, giving Kevin a dirty look.

"Simon may be a dweeb, but he has the kind of balls that will get him in trouble one day."

We both got in line as a lunch lady dumped smelly beef and mushy potatoes onto our plates.

"I wanted to save him," I said softly.

"You did. You went and got that spooky teacher Congley."

"Yeah, but I think that embarrassed him more."

"What's worse, being embarrassed or getting your ass handed to you?"

"Good point, I guess," I said, sniffing a plate that smelled worse than the locker room after gym class.

"I think this school is trying to kill us," Kevin said, poking at his immovable lump of sad potatoes.

"I think I'd rather experience death by Jojo's fist."

"C'mon, let's try to snag a table."

"There're some spots by your…girlfriend," Kevin said, louder than he should have. "I found out that her name is Maisie and that she and her dad just moved here a week ago from out West."

My stomach fell as I followed Kevin's finger over to an empty table off to the side where the cute girl from earlier that day was eating lunch alone. Luckily, she hadn't seen Kevin pointing at her, so I didn't have to make a decision right away about sitting down. She didn't seem uncomfortable to be eating by herself. She had kicked her sneakers up on the table, showing off the intricate clock doodles she had drawn. Like before, she was absorbed in a book, although this time I was close enough to see what it was—*The Complete Sherlock Holmes* by Sir Arthur Conan Doyle!

I did a double-take. Was it possible there was a girl who loved Sherlock Holmes and sleuthing as much as me??? Could this be a sign not to give up on my struggling biz?

While I was thinking of something clever to say, Kevin started making his way over to her table before I could come up with a good opening line.

"No, no, no," I said, tugging Kevin by the back of his shirt.

"Dude, I'm starving," he said, brushing me off.

I could feel the sweat pouring from my forehead. My hands were clammy too.

"Wait, I'm not ready."

"She's not going to bite you. Or maybe that's her thing?" Kevin added with a wink.

"Tomorrow! I promise I'll sit with her then."

"You never know what might happen tomorrow." Kevin shrugged. "By then, you could've already missed your chance. *Carpe diem*, like our Latin teacher Mr. Schwartz says, right?"

"I'm surprised you stayed awake enough to absorb anything from that class."

We found two other seats wedged between a few Glee Club Kids that were practicing for their upcoming competition.

"Ugh, I don't know what's worse," said Kevin. "Having my stomach poisoned by this food, or my ears poisoned by their glee?"

The Glee kids continued their a cappella assault while glaring at Kevin as they sang in pitchy highs and lows.

I chose to stare at Maisie instead. She was still glued to *The Complete Sherlock Holmes*, but tears started forming in her eyes. She hadn't turned the page in a long time, which made me realize that the book was nothing more than a prop, so she'd look busy and not desperately in need of company. Finally, one eye released a tear that zigzagged down her freckled face and plopped into her plate of uneaten food. She closed the book with a sad sigh that broke my heart before tossing it in her backpack and gliding out of the cafeteria on the tips of her toes while leaving behind a trail of discarded tears.

I wondered if Kevin was right by saying that "you never know what might happen tomorrow." I could've blown the best chance I'd ever have to get to know this new girl. I got up from my seat and rushed over to bend down and collect one of her tears off the cafeteria floor as if it was some type of special clue.

I rubbed the tear between my fingers as I caught a final glimpse of her blond ponytail bobbing away before she vanished entirely.

Chapter Three

I didn't have time to think about Maisie too much during the rest of the day since I had to go over my notes for the case of Ms. Kissey's chronically missing cat, Peaches. The last time Ms. Kissey hired us, Peaches had capitalized on his chance to run away from the batty old woman by fleeing all the way to the neighboring town of Collier. Knowing that the fat cat loved to eat, I spent a whole day knocking on every establishment in both towns only to be rewarded by a bar manager who saw Peaches dart out into traffic and then had taken the flighty cat home. The case didn't involve much sleuthing and I worried that the only way to find Peaches again was to go knocking on every restaurant door in a five-mile radius.

As Kevin and I headed to Ms. Kissey's house after school, I wanted to go over some of the notes I jotted down but he was more interested in talking about Maisie.

"Hello, she reads *Sherlock Holmes*," Kevin said. "It's like the two of you are made for each other."

"She was probably reading it for a class. Now can you focus? We need to be prepared for Ms. Kissey."

"Kissey is cuckoo with a capital K, and that dumb porker of a cat is bound to turn up. Anyway, I thought of a good opening line on Maisie."

"I'm not burping in her face."

Kevin ignored this jab. "Tell her that you're Miles Hardy, president of *Mr. Hardy's Detective Agency* and that you're investigating the case of the hot new girl at school."

Kevin mimed a drum roll and flashed a stupid grin as if he was waiting for applause.

"How many times have you fallen on your head? That'll never work. And besides, I'm getting tired of everyone just knowing me as Detective Guy."

"Well, how's avoiding her working out for you? You might as well give my smooth moves a try."

"Shut up, we're here. Now act professional. You have a big glob of gravy on your shirt."

"What do you want me to do about it now?"

I pinched the bridge of my nose and muttered "amateur" under my breath. Even though I didn't want this lame case, I prided myself on maintaining some type of competence.

As we turned the corner onto Ms. Kissey's street, we saw Reed from the neighborhood playing on the side of the road with a couple of mousetraps. Reed was about the same age as us but developmentally disabled and home-schooled instead. Most of the time he hung around the neighboring blocks involved in some type of unsafe activity. Once Reed's lesson was done for the day, his mom Annalee sent him out into the street to play so she could watch her soap operas. Hours later, she'd rise from her couch to call him inside. I had no idea how Reed had survived this long.

"What're you doing, Reed?" I asked.

Reed gave a couple of blinks before he registered who was talking to him.

"Hi, Miles!" he said with a wave. He wore a giant T-shirt that said, "Fun in the Sun," which depicted a sun with a face lounging in a pool and sipping a cocktail.

"You catching your dinner, Reed?" Kevin asked, hiding his laughter.

"None of your business," Reed said, shooing at Kevin. "Now you get outta here before you scare all the mice away."

I inspected the three traps that Reed had laid out with cheese.

"The trick is peanut butter, Reed, not cheese. Does your mom keep peanut butter in the fridge?"

"She does for peanut butter and jelly sandwiches!" Reed said, licking his lips.

"I guarantee that'll bring out the mice."

Reed swayed back and forth considering my suggestion before picking up the traps and rushing back to his house screaming, "Peanut butter, peanut butter, mmmm, mmmm good!"

"You're the Reed whisperer," Kevin said. "Hopefully he'll forget about the mice now before he gets his fingers caught in one of the traps."

We continued down the block up to Ms. Kissey's front steps and rang a doorbell that sounded as loud as a car alarm. No one answered so Kevin kept ringing it again and again until it broke off and fell to the ground.

"Oops," Kevin said, brushing the doorbell under the doormat with his foot.

"What is wrong with you?" I said, punching him in the arm. "I can't take you anywhere."

The door finally opened and Ms. Kissey stood there in a lavender nightgown. She was working some vapor rub into her chest with one hand and holding a long cigarette with the other. Her neck was fraught with veins that bulged as if they were about to burst. She was basically a skeleton brought to life, and I wondered if a big gust of wind might just blow her away.

"Oh boys," she said, her voice hidden under layers of smoked-riddled phlegm. "I'm just beside myself about Peaches. Come in."

She spun around, and we followed her trail of smoke into a dark house that smelled like strawberry pies. She removed a ball of wet tissues from the nightgown's sleeve and blew an endless parade of snot until the tissues crumbled apart in her hands.

"It's been two whole days," she exclaimed to the ceiling. "Peaches has never taken a vacation this long."

"A vacation?" Kevin snickered, poking me in the shin.

"Yes, a vacation!" she snapped. "To say that Peaches is missing is too morbid. A 'vacation' eliminates that sense of finality. Come, come."

She ushered us over to a dusty couch and went to sit in an armchair. Her bones cracked as she sat down. Out of instinct, she reached beside the chair to put Peaches in her lap, but then she realized her mistake and gazed at the empty spot full of cat hair.

"Peaches is turning fifteen tomorrow," she said,

angrily stabbing out her cigarette. "I was planning a surprise party."

"Maybe the cat caught wind of it and doesn't like surprises?" Kevin said, picking at some plated crackers on the coffee table.

"Why don't you tell us the last time you saw Peaches, Ms. Kissey?" I asked.

She glanced out of the window as the tears started spilling.

"I was preparing dinner for my little darling. Peaches is spoiled like his mother and only eats people food. I had opened the door to let him out in the front yard to get some fresh air like I always do."

I'd gotten out my yellow notepad and started writing all of this down.

"Did you see anyone outside when you opened the door?"

Ms. Kissey opened up another button to spread more vapor rub on her chest.

"I apologize, but Peaches' vacation has made me so sick," she said and blew into her disintegrating tissues again. "No, I didn't see anyone outside, but I had on my Big Band music and didn't really look."

Kevin decided to speak up with three crackers in his mouth at the same time.

"Since Peaches ran away before, maybe you shouldn't let him out anymore?"

"Peaches never ran away. Something caught his interest, and he got lost!"

"We'll check the restaurant in Collier where we found him the last time," I said. "Maybe he headed there after he got lost?"

"Such a good boy."

She smiled at me and then frowned at Kevin.

"Is there anything else you could tell us that might help?" I asked.

"I call him Walter when he's being naughty. By now he knows he's in trouble for being on vacation so long so you should call him Walter when he turns up."

"Those pies aren't done yet, are they, Ms. Kissey?" Kevin asked, his nose darting around.

"Pies are a payment upon delivery of Peaches, not any sooner," she said, slopping on more vapor rub until the neckline of her nightgown became soggy. "Now one of my judge shows is coming on so…"

She tossed her eyes at the door, indicating that it was time for us to leave. I stood up while Kevin stuffed the remaining crackers into his pockets.

"Thank you, Ms. Kissey. I promise we'll find Peaches…I mean, Walter."

"Such a good boy," she said, squeezing my hand with her slimy one. "The pies will be cooling."

She held out her cheek for me to kiss. The cheek was riddled with moles and hairs coming out of the moles, but to be respectful, I gave her a quick peck and then scurried out of the door with a wave. Kevin grabbed some candies in a dish as he followed.

"So, should we head over to Collier?" Kevin asked, popping a few of the candies in his mouth. "Gross, these taste like mothballs," he said, spitting them out and swatting at his tongue.

I didn't respond. I was staring into the distance at Reed who had returned to the curb to lay down some mousetraps.

"Earth to Miles, hello?"

"That's it!" I said, snapping my fingers and running down the street.

"Dude, I just ate all those crackers, I can't run,"

Kevin exclaimed and took a few jogs before becoming winded.

I reached Reed who was surprised to see me again.

"Look, Miles, peanut butter! Yummy in the mice's tummy."

"Why are you trying to catch mice, Reed?"

Reed looked away toward his house and shook his head.

"No…reason."

"Are the mice…food for something else?"

"Well…"

Reed locked his hands together and swayed from side to side.

"Food for a…cat?"

Reed shrieked and then kicked at the dirt by his feet.

"Do you have a cat that you're trying to feed?"

Kevin had finally caught with up me, wheezing and panting as if he'd run a marathon.

"C'mon, Miles, let's head to Collier so I can be back in time for dinner. My mom's making a roast."

"Kevin, Reed is laying mice traps."

"I know," Kevin said, rolling his eyes. "We saw him doing it before."

"What likes to eat mice?"

"Uh, I don't know, who cares?"

I pinched the bridge of my nose again.

"Seriously, dude, have you ever felt for giant lumps on your head?"

Reed was quietly gathering up the three mice traps.

"I got to go," Reed said. "See you both later."

Reed ducked his head down and sprinted for his

house, but I was on his tail. He shrieked as he got to the door and fumbled with the doorknob. The door swung open as he almost knocked over Annalee.

"Reed honey, you know not to come home before sundown while momma's watching her stories."

"Momma, move!" Reed said, shoving Annalee aside and dashing into the house.

"Hi, Ms. Redding," I said. "Reed kinda took something of mine."

"He's probably in the basement," she said, pointing around the corner and wandering back over to the couch.

Sure enough, I followed her directions and saw a door slam at the end of the hall. I opened the door and headed down a set of creaky stairs to a dimly lit basement. At the bottom, Reed sat with his legs crossed, sobbing into Peaches. Peaches stared back with a look that said, *This place is even worse than the one I was trying to get away from.*

"Reed, you know that's Ms. Kissey's cat, Peaches."

"She always lets the cat outside and the cat almost gets hit by cars on the road," Reed said, shaking his head.

"Did you save him from getting hit, Reed?"

Reed ran his sleeve across his teary eyes and nodded.

"That was really good that you saved him. I bet Ms. Kissey will give you some of her strawberry pie if you tell her you found him."

"Strawberry?" Reed sniffled.

"I bet she has some ice cream, too."

Reed tapped a finger against his chin considering the deal and then got up and handed Peaches over.

"See you later, cat," he said. "You're fun to play with but you're not strawberry pie with ice cream."

"Good choice, Reed," I said, giving him a high-five.

When we emerged from the basement, Annalee was still enraptured with her stories while Kevin waited at the door. His eyes bugged when he saw Peaches.

"Of course," Kevin said slowly. "Reed was catching the mice to feed to Peaches."

"Yup," I said, patting my slow-witted friend on the back. "Let's all go get our desserts."

Reed clapped his hands and shrieked again, which caused Annalee to look away from the TV for a second. I marched out of the door with Peaches in my arms.

Once we stepped inside Ms. Kissey's house, she immediately gave Peaches the side-eye.

"How was your vacation…Walter?" she coolly said as I placed the heavy cat down. Peaches stared at the door as if he was second-guessing his decision to leave Reed's basement.

"Three giant pieces of strawberry pie with a scoop of vanilla," Ms. Kissey said as we all sat at her dining room table and dove in.

"Remember to tell all your friends about *Mr. Hardy's Detective Agency*," I said, my face stuffed with pie while trying to be enthusiastic. "We guarantee a hundred percent success rate."

"Just precious," she said, patting my hand. "Now you boys finish up. One of my talk shows is coming on so…" she said, tossing her eyes at the door.

I stabbed my fork into my piece of pie. Old Ms. Kissey really had some nerve! Here I had found stupid Peaches/Walter and she couldn't wait to get rid of us so she could watch TV. I gulped down the rest of the pie as I got up to leave, swearing that if something more daring didn't come along that could earn me some overdue respect, I'd hang up my deerstalker cap and snuff out my briar pipe for good.

It was time to stop chasing missing cats.

Chapter Four

My parents had already sat down for dinner when I returned home from Ms. Kissey's. I was lucky that I had some strawberry pie in me since dinner looked about as appetizing as my school's cafeteria food. Ever since my mom started sleeping for most of the day, there was a slim chance for a home-cooked meal that actually tasted good. Much like my dad's inventions, his ability to cook ranked up there with some of the worst of his failures. Today he had attempted some sort of stew that looked like sewage and didn't smell much better.

"Hi, Mom," I said, parting her long black hair to the side so I could kiss her on the cheek. She responded only by blinking. Her skin was pale and delicate, the result of never really going outside. In front of her was a plate with a little bit of stew and about a thousand multicolored pills.

"Mom had a rough day," Dad said, slopping some stew onto his plate and passing it over.

When does she not have a rough day? I wanted to say.

"Ludmila couldn't get her to eat much."

Ludmila was the Czech woman in the neighborhood who watched Mom during the few times a week Dad had classes. She barely smiled but gave Mom the tough love she needed when she'd refuse to eat or drink.

If I really thought about it, I had some good memories of my mom from when I was younger. While she was never an energetic person and had been taking those multicolored pills for as long as I could remember, her "sadness" used to only affect her occasionally. There were many times that Dad warned me "not to bother Mom because she needs her space," but sooner or later she'd emerge from her bedroom ready to play a board game, or whip up a soufflé, or listen to me talk about what I did at school that day. She loved Monopoly and always let me be the dog since Dad never wanted to own any pets. We'd play for hours and if my money ran low, she'd slip a few bills from the bank and pass them my way as a secret. But my favorite times were when she'd read me my *Hardy Boys* and *Sherlock Holmes* books before bed. She had such a soothing voice, a born storyteller, and would come up with different accents for all of the characters. Every time I reread those books, I can still hear her imitating all the characters. Afterward, she'd call me a junebug or some other nickname and turn out the lights. Once she left, I'd kneel down in front of my bed and pray that tomorrow would be a day that I got a happy Mom. For a while, I convinced myself that it worked, but then a few years ago, she started to go away on "trips" for long periods of time when her sadness got worse. I used to think that her sadness came from being physically sick, but as I got older, the trips became longer and Dad said she was sick in the mind. I tried to get him to tell me more, but he said I wasn't old enough to understand. Recently, the trips had stopped because they didn't seem to be helping at all.

Even though Mom was mostly catatonic now, I pretended that she still understood everything I said.

"That boy Reed from down the road had Ms. Kissey's cat all along and I figured it out since he was laying down mice traps."

I took a bite of Dad's terrible stew. I wouldn't make that same mistake twice.

"I've solved every case we've ever gotten," I continued, trying to offer up anything positive to get her to flinch.

Mom managed the tiniest of smiles, but it was enough to make me feel good. I reached over and stroked her hand, which felt cold. Dad had explained a while back that one of the side effects of all of those pills was a lowered body temperature.

"Miles, your mother needs to concentrate on taking her medication," Dad said. "Go on, Patricia, you can do it," he continued, but without much enthusiasm. Her doctor said that she should try to do things on her own, but I knew that it would take her hours to get a few pills down and then Dad would have to force her to swallow the rest.

While Mom's state made it tough for us to have a real relationship, things were even worse with Dad. He was beyond moody and spent most of his time in the basement working on his "inventions." There was the vacuum cleaner that attempted to empty its own bag of dirt, but always made more of a mess. There were the "coffee balls," which were supposed to be added to hot water to make instant coffee but tasted more like sludge. And his *pièce de résistance*, an oven/fridge that tried to combine the two appliances in an attempt to save space but wound up imploding.

Right now, Dad was mixing up some of the pills with the stew for Mom. Probably not the best way to get her to eat them.

"Don't let this detective nonsense get in the way of your schoolwork," Dad said, pointing at me with his fork.

"It's not nonsense," I mumbled.

"Finding old ladies' cats…last year you got a C minus in mathematics."

"What does that have to do with anything?"

"It's about applying yourself, Miles. School is only going to get harder, and you need to put the time and effort into your studies."

"What's the point of math anyway? It's just about a bunch of dumb numbers that can be done on a computer."

"Math is the foundation for everything. It's essential to know."

"If that was the case, how come it hasn't helped you make any of your inventions work?"

The table became silent. Even Mom seemed to lose her smile. Dad pushed his glasses up his nose, a gesture that was very Simon-like, and then ran his hands through what was left of his hair. During Mom's better days, she used to say that Dad had "a face only Picasso could love." She was right. Dad's eyes weren't aligned properly, and he had a long nose that skewed to one side while his mouth tended to veer in the opposite direction. He was a little man in stature, and the phrase Napoleon complex rang true in his case. But Dad didn't shout or yell back like I expected; he laid down his fork and let out a sigh that caused me to feel nauseous.

"Simon is always working on his Top-Secret project and you never complain about what he's doing," I said, pushing the food around on my plate.

Dad picked his fork back up like he was going to stab someone with it. For a second, I pictured him going wild and stabbing me. Since Mom had already gone bonkers, would it be that much longer before he lost it too?

"You and your brother are nothing alike," Dad said, his face getting redder and redder.

"I know. You've spent my whole life telling me how much better he is."

I got up and slammed my chair into the table. Mom winced as the table shook. I was about to storm up to my room when the front door opened and Simon stepped inside. He was sweating all over, which was strange since it was a cool October evening. It was also strange for Simon to be home so early. He never came back for dinner and usually started working on his Top-Secret project right after school, only returning home to go to bed.

"Simon?"

Dad rubbed his eyeglasses as if Simon was long dead and a ghost had returned in his place.

Simon looked up, spooked beyond belief. If I didn't know any better, I would've guessed he was on drugs, but my brother would never be the type to let any mind-altering substances affect his brain. He was gazing around the room as if we weren't even there and then disappeared up the staircase before Dad or I could say anything.

"I'll save you some dinner," Dad called out as we heard Simon slam his bedroom door.

I went to go after him, but Dad grabbed my arm.

"We're not done talking about this detective baloney."

I tried to get out of his grasp, but he was holding on too tightly.

"If I see that any of your grades are suffering, you can say goodbye to your little side business."

"At least my side business paid me in pies today. What did your inventions get you?"

I yanked my arm and was finally able to remove it from his grip. We stared each other down.

"Kip," I heard Mom say. She hadn't altered her expression and was still staring straight ahead. "Kip... hungry."

Dad resumed his place at the table and began spoon-feeding her a few of the multicolored pills.

"I wish some new family would come and take me away," I said and then booked it upstairs.

Around the fifth stair, I started to feel bad about what I said to Dad. I knew how much his inventions meant to him, but it was getting a little pathetic already. Maybe my honesty would finally be the wake-up call he needed to get a new hobby? But I knew that would never happen. He'd be on his deathbed still tooling with some invention that had no shot at working. A part of me wanted to go back down and apologize, but I was still mad about the dig at my detective agency, and I felt that I deserved an apology first.

Simon's bedroom was at the other end of the hallway and the door had a giant DON'T ENTER sign as a warning for the entire family. While Simon often kept to himself even as a kid, he took things a step further by putting up the DON'T ENTER sign when he started working on his Top-Secret project.

As I went to knock, I tried to think of good memories with Simon from long ago, but mostly it was all a blur. All I could remember were those times he woke me up in the middle of the night to look at the stars and discuss the vastness of the universe. That was around the time that Frontier, Iowa began to feel too small and I was getting of sick of the Made-Rite Diner, and the Ice House Museum, and the rows and rows of cornfields, and only having Kevin as a friend, and a grumpy dad that always put me down, and a mom who never stopped sleeping even when she was awake.

I was nervous to knock, afraid that Simon would yell at me for bothering him. But I was desperate to talk to the only other person who understood how Dad gets.

"It's me," I called out. "It's Miles," I added, correcting myself.

No answer.

"C'mon, Simon, let me in. I won't bug you for long. I had a fight with Dad and…"

The door unlocked and swung open.

As I stepped inside, I realized that I hadn't been in Simon's room in a super long time. I recognized the hanging Salvador Dali painting with all of the melting clocks, but other than that, the walls had been stripped bare. Simon used to have posters of his scientific heroes like Albert Einstein, but no more. Besides an impeccably made bed, a desk with a cage for his elderly guinea pig Stinkers, and a few neat stacks of paper and a laptop, there was no evidence of the Simon I once knew in this room. I wondered where that Simon had gone. Now he was pacing back and forth and shoving the stacks of paper and the laptop into his backpack and acting like he drank ten cups of coffee.

"What happened to your room?" I asked.

"I need to go," Simon said, slinging his backpack over his shoulder and heading for the door.

"I'm sorry about what happened today with those asshole bullies," I said, chewing at a fingernail.

Simon stopped at the door, fixed his glasses, and stared at me as if I was some type of alien.

"What?"

"I only went to get Mr. Congley because I didn't want Jojo to beat the crap out of you. And after you ran out, no one was even talking about it or anything, I swear."

Simon took off his glasses to rub his eyes. I couldn't tell if he was crying or if he had made his eyes sore by rubbing. Without his glasses on, I was amazed at how different my brother looked than usual. Sure, his shirt was buttoned up to his chin, and he wore pleated pants and old people walking sneakers, but without the glasses we looked more alike than I'd ever realized.

"Listen, Miles," he said, getting annoyed. "School is infinitesimal to what I'm trying to accomplish."

"And what is that?"

Simon closed the door, his eyes darting around the room as if someone was watching. He stepped over to the window and moved the curtain out of the way to look outside.

"Changing the world."

Simon had always spoken seriously, but something about the way he talked now was eerie.

"And this'll happen because of your time machine…?"

Before I could finish my thought, Simon ran over and clamped his hand over my mouth. He then put his finger to his lips as a warning.

"There are variables out of my control that are preventing me from what I want to accomplish," he said and then carefully took his hand off my mouth.

"Can I help?" I whispered. I didn't know why I was whispering, just that it felt like the right thing to do.

"No one can help me."

Simon fixed his backpack on his shoulders. He headed for the door and then turned around. His lips started to move as if he was about to say something else, but then he shook his head.

"Goodbye, Miles."

His voice was shaky and all I could do was wave goodbye as a response. He pushed his glasses up on his nose to hide his teary eyes. Then the door slammed, and I was left alone in the empty room. Stinkers fussed about in his cage, and I went over to pet him. Above the cage was the poster of the Dali painting with the clocks melting as if they were made of hot cheese. At the bottom of the poster, I saw that Simon had scrawled the words, *Can time be manipulated????*, and then crossed it out with a heavy black pen.

I wondered why Simon had crossed out the question. Was it because he discovered that time couldn't be manipulated? Or had he crossed out that question because he'd succeeded with his time machine and no longer had to ask?

I took the yellow notepad out of my back pocket and jotted down, *Can time be manipulated?????* Then I pet

Stinkers again, stuck the notepad back in my pocket, and shut the door.

Chapter Five

BANG!

The sound interrupted the dreams I'd been having about clocks, each of the hands spinning faster and faster.

BANG!

There was the sound again. Outside, no truck had backfired. It was coming from inside. The air smelled like gunpowder. Mom was still asleep, and Dad already left for work. Ludmila would be coming by soon. Simon's door had been left open a crack, which he never did. I began to shiver, the hairs on my arms standing on end.

As I pushed open the door, it smelled as if someone had gone to the bathroom.

"Simon?"

The first thing I saw was blood on the walls, a crimson splatter that I first thought was paint. Simon lay slumped in his desk chair, barely recognizable. A gun looked as if it had fallen from his fingers and rested in a pool of syrupy blood beside the chair.

I couldn't scream, couldn't even breathe. My throat closed up, and I gasped for air. Everything became hazy as I slumped to the floor.

"Simon?" I said, softer than ever.

Was it a dream? The deathly smells attacking my senses were all too real. I managed to get on one knee and hoist myself up. Next to the gun was a piece of paper. I snatched the paper from the bloody puddle. It was a typed note. The words were blurry at first because I was crying so hard that I choked on my tears. I ran my arm across my eyes and focused with all my might until the words became clear:

I am a failure.
What I've spent years trying to accomplish will never be.
I am sorry for this but I cannot go on living.
Please forgive me.
—Simon

The paper fell from my hands as I threw up on the floor, nothing but spit and bits of toothpaste. I thought I had got everything out, but the foul smells caused me to puke again. I doubled over, my face inches from the pool of Simon's blood. I caught a glimpse of what was left of him. One eye remained staring at me. It was practically hanging out of its socket, but it still gave off the impression of being shocked.

On the desk, I saw Simon's cell. I scooped it up and dialed 911.

"My brother," I shouted to the operator. I could barely hold on to the phone. "Please come, he…he shot himself. He…he's dead."

I gave our address and then dialed Dad's number, unsure what I was going to say. The voicemail picked up.

"D-dad?" I pictured Dad returning home to see Simon in this state and flinging himself upon the disfigured body. "Daddy?" I murmured again, barely more than a peep. "You…you have to come home." I chewed a fingernail off while thinking of what to say next. "Something happened to Simon."

I ended the call and slipped Simon's cell into my pajama pocket, knowing that it might be the last possible link I had to my brother.

Memories began to flood into my brain at an alarming speed. Times when we were kids and Mom and Dad took us to the Okoboji region in Northern Iowa bordering on Minnesota to swim in the Great Iowa Lakes that were crystal clear. I even kept a poster of the Okoboji region on the wall above my bed so I wouldn't forget about those vacations. We always wound up being closer then since we'd be forced to play with one another, and Simon wouldn't have some test, or a scholarship, or an award ceremony that he'd be prepping for. At those lakes, Simon would proclaim he was king of the waters and I was his loyal prince. In this world, the fish were our devoted subjects, everyone was able to breathe underwater, and our parents weren't allowed. We called our empire Okoboji and whenever the world above sea level became too much to deal with, we could dip a toe into the wonders of our realm and never have to resurface again if we so pleased.

I could see Simon so clearly, doggy paddling over to a giant rock that he dubbed his throne. I'd swim over and bring pebbles from the lake that we'd pretend were gold. I must've been about six or seven when this tradition started. We even had a secret code whenever we wanted to write about Okoboji-related things without anyone knowing. The Okoboji language had the same alphabet as English, but in each word, only the first and every third letter after that mattered. That way no one would ever be able to decipher any notes passed about our hidden realm.

I wanted nothing more than to dive back into Okoboji now and have it ease my troubles.

"Why would you do this?" I yelled, unable to look at Simon anymore. I was trying to focus on any part of the bedroom but him. "WHY did you give up?"

Once Simon reached high school and we began to grow apart, I couldn't sleep one night and went into his room to ask how come he never hung out with me anymore. The days of Okoboji were long gone. I questioned why he didn't do normal kid things like watch TV, or play basketball or video games, and why he always disappeared for hours at a time to some hidden laboratory.

"You don't understand," Simon had said.

"Remember Okoboji?" I asked. "What do you think is happening in our kingdom right now?"

"I'm not some child anymore," Simon said, grinding his teeth, his words like needles pricking at my skin.

I hated that Simon was no longer interested in imagination anymore. Science had triumphed and all that mattered to him was his Top-Secret obsession.

"I…miss you," I said.

Trading fart jokes with Kevin all day was usually enough to keep me happy, but sometimes I longed for my big brother.

"You don't know what it's like to be in my mind," Simon sighed. "The responsibility. You don't have a responsibility like that."

"My detective agency!" I stuttered. Kevin and I had founded it that summer and solved our first case of Mr. Clemson's lost car that had been parked and forgotten about on the other side of town.

"You're just a little kid," Simon said. "You're not going to change the world."

Simon brushed me away as if I was nothing more than a speck of dust. I tried to stay strong to show that I wasn't just a little kid, but the gooey snot dripping from my nose begged to differ.

"My mind doesn't work like yours, Miles. Don't you understand that? It's relentless, it's exhausting, it never stops. It's full of formulas beyond your comprehension. It will never let me rest until I've completed what I've been put here to do."

"And what's that?" I asked, angry now. I wanted to punch him in the stomach. I was tired of Simon acting like he was better than everyone else. I was tired of my family treating him like he could do no wrong. I was tired of being invisible.

"I can't tell you," Simon said, shaking his head.

"I'm not just some dumb kid," I said, stamping my foot.

"Goodbye, Miles."

He pushed me out of his room and closed the door in my face. In the morning when I woke up, the DON'T ENTER sign had been displayed as an absolute reminder.

"Well, I hope you die!" I had shouted then, punching the door. "Die, die, die!" I punched the door again and whimpered as my knuckles started to bleed.

Rushing outside to our front lawn, I had plunged my face into the grass to wipe away the tears. I'd come into Simon's room in the middle of the night because it seemed like forever since we looked at the stars and he told me how the universe was far grander than we ever imagined.

Staring at Simon's disfigured face now, I knew that we'd never look at the stars together again.

I cringed. How could I have wished Simon dead? How could I have said such terrible things?

"I'm sorry," I said to him now, wishing I could rewind time and take it back.

I heard sirens blaring down the block and saw police cars and an ambulance outside the window.

"I'm so sorry," I said, as the doorbell rang and rang. I was too frozen to move. Moving meant that my brother would be taken away and that he was truly dead, never to return.

I managed to thrust one foot in front of the other to go let in the police. In the hallway, I spied Mom peering out of her room, her long black hair covering most of her face. She rocked back and forth, groaning under her breath. She looked as if she was trying to say something but couldn't form the words. Her lips were twisting in different directions as she stared into Simon's room. The door had been left wide open and Simon was in clear view. Mom reached out her arm and pointed her finger at the horror that had occurred that morning.

Finally, her lips parted.

"It…happened…again," she said as spittle drooled from her mouth.

I whisked past her to answer the door. Running down the stairs, I took out my yellow pad to write down her ominous words as a reminder, but it didn't matter since her chilling declaration would be seared into my mind for good.

"It…happened… again." Her voice echoed through the halls. "It…happened…again!"

Her cries didn't stop until hours later when Simon was finally taken out of the house in a body bag.

Chapter Six

I had only been to one funeral before when my grandma Lillian died, but I was too young to remember much about it. Grandma Lillian, Mom's mom, was a pretty mean woman who used to poke me with her cane. She was even meaner to Mom and would always curse at her and put her down. This was before Mom completely turned into a zombie. When Grandma Lillian died, no one was at her funeral except for Mom, a minister, and me. No one else wanted to show, not even Dad. The box she'd been put in was so small, as if for a pet. When the minister asked if anyone wanted to say anything, Mom was quiet. After the body had been lowered into the ground, I heard Mom say, "Good."

The days after Simon's death had been loaded with downpours unlike Iowa had seen in a long time. After a summer of drought, a rain like that would've normally been a good thing, but on the day of Simon's funeral, it was the worst. In the car on the way to the cemetery, I watched the rain beating down against the window. It felt like we were driving into a flood.

I hadn't cried since I found Simon's body. I stayed up each night trying, but I couldn't shed one tear. It felt like something bad rumbled inside of me, and I was afraid that once I finally cried, I wouldn't be able to stop. The only thing that distracted me from being sad was to put all my focus on being a detective again. If I ever had any doubts about giving up, this was the sign I needed to pursue my calling, since I refused to believe Simon killed himself. It didn't seem possible, even though there had been a note. For all of Simon's faults, I knew deep down that he would *never* stop working on his time machine. It had been more than his obsession. Simon assumed that he was put on this Earth to create the single most important creation of mankind, and he *never* would've admitted he couldn't do it. That was why he distanced himself from me and everyone else. Nothing would get in his way.

Unless *someone* got in his way.

So far, I didn't have too much to go on. I had Simon's cell, but I didn't know Simon's passcodes for his voice, email, and text messages. One strange thing was that the cell appeared to be brand new without a scratch on it. I thought of Simon's old cell that looked like it had been chewed up by a rat. There'd be no way for Simon to keep a cell looking that brand new for too long. The number was also different than the one I had saved in my phone, meaning that Simon had changed it very recently.

Mom's reaction to Simon's death had been weird as well. The last thing she said had been, "*It… happened…again.*" Oftentimes she made little sense, so it would be easy to chalk it up to one of her fits, but I couldn't get her words out of my brain. During the third sleepless night after Simon's death, I imagined those words spread out across time and the universe, directing me toward some clue that might lead me to the next.

But mostly, I sat around feeling like I couldn't move. Everything in the house reminded me of Simon. Dad didn't want any visitors and even sent Ludmila away, so I got used to dealing with only my thoughts as company. I'd eat but still be hungry, as if nothing could keep me full. I'd make bowls and bowls of nuclear orange mac n' cheese and get into my pajamas like I was five all over again and watch TV until my eyes started to burn, hoping that I'd finally be able to cry again, but still…nothing.

Dad seemed to be handling Simon's death very differently. Throughout the night, I could hear the sound of howling coming from the basement like a stray dog had gotten into our house. Dad had stopped eating and taking care of Mom, which meant that I had to be the one to clean and dress her and make sure she ate some food and took the pills that he had left out.

I had no living grandparents, and my parents were both only children, but luckily some neighbors and the local police helped with setting up the funeral since Dad seemed incapable. In fact, the morning of the funeral was the first time I'd seen Dad wander out from the basement since Simon died. He was staring at himself in the mirror with a tie frozen in his hand. For my sixth-grade graduation, I'd been taught to tie a tie, so I stood behind him and took it out of his hands.

"Oh, it's you, Miles," he finally said, like he was disappointed. He looked as if he had aged ten years in a few days. He hadn't shaved and graying hairs were coiling around his face. Fat black sacks surrounding his eyes made him seem demonic.

"Did you eat breakfast yet, Dad?"

He sneered in response, like eating breakfast meant that he wasn't adequately mourning Simon. He snatched the tie away from me and untied it to start again.

"Get your mother ready so we can go," he said, tying the tie as tight as it could be and then wincing as the knot reached his neck.

I thought I should say something to make him feel better, but I couldn't think of what sounded right so I backed out of the room instead.

In the car on the way to the funeral, I was afraid we'd get into an accident because of the storms. I was relieved when we pulled up to the gravesite, but then I realized how miserable the day would be. The funeral consisted of a small bunch of people waiting under large black umbrellas. As we stepped out, a minister with a giant head and slicked-back hair parted down the middle nodded with sympathetic eyes. Simon's coffin waited to be lowered into the ground. Seeing it made Simon's death all the more real, and I felt like I couldn't stand. A sea of umbrellas parted as we made our way toward the minister. Kevin was there with his parents and his little sister. A few of the Brainiacs stood toward the back. Reed was there with his mom, Annalee. Ludmila held a pot probably filled with goulash in her massive arms. And Mr. Congley was practically hugging a tree in the back and whimpering. I looked for my new crush, Maisie, but I figured it was unlikely she'd show up to a funeral for someone she didn't know. The rest of the procession were neighbors from the block and a couple of other folks from town. I was afraid that if I counted how many people actually showed it would be too depressing.

I wanted to talk to Kevin. I hadn't seen him since Simon died and we rarely went more than a day or so without speaking. Before Dad descended into the basement for good, he'd made it clear that he didn't want anyone else over. Yesterday I heard Kevin ringing the doorbell, but I was afraid that if I let him in, Dad would come up and go ballistic.

Kevin gave me a sad half-wave and looked like he wanted to say something, but there wasn't any time since the minister was already calling us over so the funeral could begin. The minister was a large man whose mouth sparkled with spittle when he talked. Our family never went to church, so it was weird to hear this man we had never met speak about Simon as if he knew him. The minister referred to Simon as a "troubled soul," and that "certain troubled souls aren't meant for this Earth and would finally be free in the afterlife." It bothered me that this minister referred to the "afterlife" without any mention of heaven as if he was trying to be polite since he assumed that Simon would wind up in a place far hotter because of what he'd done.

After the minister finished speaking, he nodded at Dad to give a eulogy. The rain seemed to pick up in speed as Dad shuffled through muddy grass over to the empty grave. He blinked at everyone as if he didn't recognize where he was. The seconds of silence seemed to stretch into minutes as the rain continued its relentless assault and everyone started looking at each other uncomfortably.

"Mr. Hardy," the minister said, his face full of concern.

Dad lowered his umbrella as the rain began to soak him. I could hear people gasping and talking under their breaths. I knew that they all pitied my family. A catatonic mother. A dead brother. And now a father who had lost his mind too. Dad finally broke from his frozen stance and stepped over to Simon's coffin. He raised his umbrella that had a suction cup in place of a handle and suctioned the open umbrella to the coffin before stepping away.

"I wanted to make sure that my son stays dry," was all he said, as if no other explanation was needed. He returned to his place beside Mom.

"Yes…well…thank you, Mr. Hardy," the minister said, and then all of a sudden, the minister was motioning for me to step forward.

I didn't know what to do at first. I hadn't planned on saying anything. Dad never explained that I might have to speak.

"Come, child," the minister whispered and spread one arm out. I found myself being pulled next to Simon's coffin. "What do you want to say to your brother for the last time?"

The minister's ominous words rang in my ears— "*for the last time.*" I'd never see Simon in the school's hallways or in the cafeteria again. I'd never learn any more about what might exist in the universe beyond what we already knew. I'd never see the supposed time machine that had been Simon's driving force and ulti- mately the cause of his death.

Everyone watched and waited for me to say some- thing. The rain tortured them all and even umbrellas became futile since the wind made the downpour hit from all sides. I could've mentioned all the things my brother had been able to achieve in his short life, or I could've spoken about the Okoboji world that we had imagined together and how smart Simon was, I could've even lied about what a great older brother he had been: always caring, always including me, always a role model; but my gut was nagging at me to say something very different.

"My brother Simon is a genius…was a genius," I began, as I heard people sniffling into tissues, expecting a eulogy that would break their hearts. "And while everyone may be trying to figure out why Simon *killed* himself…"

I stopped as I looked out into the rain and saw a few people shuddering at the word '*killed.*' I took a deep breath to begin again.

"*I* don't believe that my brother would do this. Simon was meant to do great things. He NEVER would've given up on life until those great things were accomplished, which only means that this was not a suicide. THIS…was murder."

Everyone stared back at me as if I was speaking another language. Only Mr. Congley stirred. He let go of the tree he was hugging and stumbled away from the funeral site while muttering to himself.

"But I'm gonna solve his murder," I said to my gaping audience. "I'm going to avenge Simon's death if it's the last thing I do. There's no way I'm gonna let his murderer get away with this. Whoever you are!"

I pointed at everyone and then stepped back next to Mom. I didn't care what they would think or say. I wanted to let them all know that no one in Frontier was innocent until the murderer was finally caught. Simon may have been a scientific genius, but I was the genius detective. I'd get to the bottom of what happened, even if this crime took my entire life to solve.

I felt Mom take my hand again. Her touch was soft and warm in the freezing rain as I nestled into her.

"Good," she said so quietly that only I could hear.

Finally, I was able to cry again.

Chapter Seven

After Simon's funeral, Dad refused to have any type of gathering at the house. Originally some of the neighbors had talked about bringing over some home-cooked meals, but after I spoke up about Simon being murdered, it would've been awkward for anyone to show up. I was just as happy not to deal with people. I had said what I needed to say and wanted to be alone while I planned my next move to hunt for clues.

When I got back home, Dad escaped into the basement without acknowledging what had happened, and I was left alone with Mom. Dad had left a week's worth of her multicolored pills, and I boiled some hot dogs and cut them up into small bites like she was a child. She sat staring at the wall with her mouth open waiting to be fed. I'd use this opportunity to grill her about a few questions I had by tempting her with hot dogs.

"Mom, when you saw Simon was dead, you said, 'It…happened…again.' What *happened again*?"

I dangled a fork with a skewer of hot dog just out of her reach. She started to moan.

"You said it over and over. Why did you say it?"

She pounded a fist into the table, her eyes pleading for the hot dog.

"Had you known someone else who killed themselves?"

Her teeth snapped at the hot dog, but I wouldn't give in.

"C'mon, Mom, give me something that I can start with."

Her groans turned to shrugs.

"What about when you said, 'Good' after my eulogy? I know you didn't mean that it was *good* that Simon died. You said *good* in a very different way than I remember you did at Grandma Lillian's funeral. Did you mean that you think Simon was murdered and you thought it was *good* that I'm opening up an investigation?"

Mom gave up reaching for the piece of hot dog with her tongue. She closed her mouth and stared right into my eyes after years of looking off into space.

"Yes," she said.

I dropped the fork with the piece of hot dog, my whole body going cold.

"Wait, did you just say *yes*?"

She turned away and continued focusing on the bite of hot dog.

"Mom, you think Simon was murdered?"

"Yes," she said again, sounding like a robot. "Yes, yes, yes, yes, yes, yes, yes."

"Did you see anything that morning?" I said, getting amped up. My brain was firing in all different directions.

"Yes, yes, yes, yes, yes."

She was still eyeing the piece of hot dog. I grabbed her by the shoulders so she could focus on me again. She let out a scream that made my head hurt. I went to grab her, and she screamed even louder. I tried to calm her down, but it was no use, so I left her screaming at her plate of hot dogs and pills. I'd have to let her cool off and try again once she eventually stopped.

I heard a knock on the door and opened it to find Kevin. He was still dressed in his suit and his shirttail was sticking through his fly by accident.

"Hey, Miles," he said, twisting a toe into the grass.

I stepped outside and shut the door so the rest of my neighbors wouldn't hear Mom's screams.

"Is that your mom? Is she okay?" Kevin asked, trying to peer inside to see what was going on.

"Nope," I replied. I didn't know what to say to him. I didn't know what to say to anyone anymore.

"So, do you really think that Simon was…?" Kevin began to ask, his eyebrows rising to the top of his head.

"You think I'm nuts, don't you?"

"Well…" Kevin scratched his chin. "Just that your brother was an odd guy and sometimes geniuses are wired differently."

"What are you trying to say?"

"Like with superheroes. A superhero can fly or destroy someone by snapping their fingers. But they all have a weakness."

"Simon was not weak!" I said, raising my voice.

"No, no, not weak. I dunno what I mean. Just that a lot of people were talking about you after the funeral. They were saying some pretty messed up things."

"Like what?"

Kevin chewed on his lip and started to back away.

"Well, that your whole family is mental. That your mom obviously has issues and obviously Simon had issues, and now your dad looks like he's losing it, and you seem like you're losing it, too."

I wanted to punch Kevin in his stomach. I was itching to fight someone, anyone, but I knew that hitting Kevin would do no good.

"This is the kind of case that the detective agency has been waiting for, and Simon deserves for me to find out the truth."

"What if you just find out that he…killed himself?"

Kevin said the last part in a whisper as if it was a sin to say.

"Then at least I tried. You always hated Simon and would say things about him behind his back. You'd call him a dork and——"

"You'd call him a dork, too!"

"He was my brother, *is* my brother. I can say whatever I want."

I swiveled around to head back inside. Kevin grabbed my arm.

"Miles, don't be mad at me. I just think you have to let this go——"

"Consider yourself fired from my agency," I said, yanking my arm away.

I opened the door to hear Mom screaming louder than before. I squeezed my eyes shut to brace myself for the assault on my ears and then slammed the door in Kevin's face. I heard him knocking on the door for a while until he finally gave up. I ran up the stairs past Mom's screams and flopped onto my bed. Through the window I could see Kevin walking away with his shoulders slumped forward. I threw my pillow across the room, angry with him for not agreeing with what I said. That was what a best friend was supposed to do, not like lousy Kevin who refused to trust in what I believed was true.

I went online to my detective home page to remove Kevin's name as my assistant. I hadn't checked the site since Simon's death and was surprised to see that I had a new email. I couldn't imagine that someone would want to hire me for a case while I was dealing with such a huge tragedy, but then I saw that the date and time was a few hours before I'd found Simon's body.

To: DetectiveMrHardy@gmail.com
   From: Jack_Finney@gmail.com
   Subject: UKLRBGGRNEIFNWLT

The subject made absolutely no sense and it took me a second to recognize the name Jack Finney. At first, I thought I knew the name because it was someone in town, but then I remembered the *Time and Again* book that Simon always read, which was written by Jack Finney.

My fingers pulsed as I clicked on the email, unsure of what it might say. Unfortunately, it was just as confusing as the subject matter:

Glno tplo tjmhpde agybjnaopnvddrgoiknqlengd boeaayrain odnfrmf Gfeekrnjoewkrnkakttejoier Sjdtejrjeeameent oken tnahkce eendjagwne owof tenoelwlmn. Ujenwndonepmr tanhene byreheljeoejw gjrrjeoisukenisd honaanypmlpmooffant ians ajk tomranafdp dxsoozohnr wmwiontanh apcn elmlheecncvytenrofofgnomianc lunoyhctgk. Tncyzspwse iann tonheve pegajhsybsokwqloenrhnd Obnkenornbrnox-pjlni. Fanuenrhgtfthhjenhr djniikrpoelycrytuhihjotunnfs wrhi-hjlill fasowqlrflrfotgw. Dlkeoplutetetiee tjkhioirds mhgeihshjsklapigrfe aklnkld dejo nbwovst tqaeuilfdl avon-cuydsozznxae. Dlko nbgomht wgfaghsedtrfe abnndfy tfgirfmede.

I stared at the stream of nonsensical words wondering if it was all some kind of joke, but I reasoned that it couldn't be. No one else but Simon would've sent an email from Jack Finney, his favorite author of all time. And the fact it had been sent a few hours before he supposedly killed himself had to mean that Simon was trying to secretly contact me. Right?

While the words in the email were meaningless, the sender had used capital letters and periods in precise places, which meant that it could be some type of code. I grabbed a tennis ball and tossed it against the wall over my bed as I tried to sound out the illegible words to see if they sparked some type of recognition. When that didn't work, I copied and pasted the email into Google to see if it was in a language I didn't recognize. Nothing came up. I minimized the email and took a break by continuing to throw a tennis ball against the wall above my bed. It smacked right into the poster of the Okoboji region I'd kept all these years.

"Okoboji," I said, "That's it!"

I pulled up the email again. When we created our Okoboji world, Simon decreed that with each word only the first and every third letter after it mattered.

That way no one else would be able to decipher our written conversations. I made sure to bold and capitalize those precise letters in the email to see if Simon had left me a message from beyond the grave.

Subject: UklRbgGrnEifNwlT

GlnO TplO TjmHpdE AgyBjnAopNvdDrgOikNqlEngD BoeAayRaiN OdnFrmF GfeEkrNjoEwkRnkAktTejOieR SjdTejRjeEamEenT OkeN TnaHkcE EenDjaGwnE OwoF TenOelWlmN. UjeNwnDonEpmR TanHenE ByrEheLjeOejW GjrRjeOisUkeNisD HonAanYpmLpmOofFanT IanS Ajk TomRanAfdP DxsOozOhnR WmwIonTanH ApcN ElmLheEcnCvyTenRofOfgNomIanC LunOyhCtgK. TncYzsPwsE IanN TonHevE PegAjhSybSokWqlOenRhnD ObnKenOrnBrnOxpJlnl. FanUenRhgTftHhjEnhR DjnlikRpoElyCryTuhlhjOtuNnfS WrhlhjLilL FasOwqLrfLrfOtgW. DlkEopLutEteTieE TjkHiolrdS MhgEihShjSklApiGrfE AklNklD DejO NbwOvsT TqaEuiLfdL AvoNcuYdsOzzNxaE. DlkO NbgOmhT WgfAghSedTrfE AbnNdfY TfglrfMedE.

Once I finally deciphered the code, the email read:

Subject: URGENT

GO TO THE ABANDONED BARN OFF GENERATOR STREET ON THE EDGE OF TOWN. UNDER THE BELOW GROUND HAYLOFT IS A TRAP DOOR WITH AN ELEC-TRONIC LOCK. TYPE IN THE PASSWORD OKOBOJI. FURTHER DIRECTIONS WILL FOLLOW. DELETE THIS MESSAGE AND DO NOT TELL ANYONE. DO NOT WASTE ANY TIME.

When I finished decoding the message, I sat back and had to remember to breathe. Simon must've realized that someone was after him hours before he was murdered and sent this email just in time. Either this trap door under the hayloft led to information about whoever was after Simon, or it possibly led to some lair where Simon had built his time machine!

My first instinct was to call Kevin, but we'd just had a fight, and Simon clearly stated not to tell anyone. I was probably the only one Simon trusted. Even though I'd thought that my brother wanted nothing to do with me anymore, that couldn't have been further from the truth. The Okoboji language that we created as kids would allow us to communicate even after his death, and this message probably wouldn't be the last coded one I'd receive. As far away as Simon was now, I was psyched that we would still manage to be connected.

I deleted the email at once and then cursed myself for not checking the account anytime sooner. What if I'd gotten up really early that morning and saw the email before Simon was murdered? I wondered if I could've stopped it from happening? If I could've saved my brother's life?

But I couldn't worry about that now. Simon was dead and not coming back, but his murder could still be avenged. I grabbed a hoodie off my bed and flew downstairs. Mom had stopped screaming and started chanting, "Yes, yes, yes," over and over, as if cheering me on. All of the pills and the pieces of hot dog had been eaten. She watched as I made my way to the doorway, her "yesses" getting louder and louder. I doubled back and gave her a quick kiss on her cheek that was wet with perspiration.

"Don't worry, Mom. I'm gonna find out what happened to Simon."

She blew a spit bubble that was riddled with hot dog bits.

"Good," she whispered, drawing me close.

When I broke away, my eyes were fuzzy with tears. I wiped them away with my sleeve, then hopped on my bike and took off like a beast to the abandoned barn at the edge of town, ready for whatever waited for me under that trapdoor.

Chapter Eight

I pedaled faster than I had ever pedaled before on the way to the abandoned barn. I kept looking over my shoulder to see whether I was being followed. If Simon had gone to the trouble of sending a coded message, it might mean that some shady person could be scoping out our house as well. As I neared Generator Street, I got a bad feeling in my gut. It was one of those parts past town that I'd always been warned about.

The area surrounding the barn was worse than I'd imagined. Broken bottles, smashed cigarettes, and flies swarming around moldy fruit that had been discarded. Dead rodents slowly decomposed. I'd heard that kids used to go there to smoke pot and get wasted off whatever alcohol they could get their hands on, but now the area had become too sketchy even for that.

The barn itself was as much of a mess as its surroundings. I parked my bike and went inside as bats flew out and collected around the weathervane. The barn smelled like a mixture of dampness and rot. I had to cover my nose as I walked inside. Sure enough, I spied a below-ground hayloft like Simon's message had stated. I dove down into the scratchy hay and began to search for the trapdoor.

Simon obviously didn't want easy access to the trapdoor. It took many frustrating minutes until my hand brushed across something metallic and cold. I brushed off the remaining bits of hay and keyed *Okoboji* into the electronic lock. I heard a click and then was able to pull open the trapdoor.

I had no idea what to expect as I eased my way down. The whole thing could be a trap and the killer could be waiting for me to eliminate any possibility of someone finding out the truth about what happened to Simon. But I was excited at the same time. None of my other cases ever had the added element of danger.

Once my feet reached the ground below the hayloft, I stared into the darkness of what felt like a huge room. I ran my hands along the wall until I found a light switch and turned it on. There was no murderer waiting for me, but my jaw dropped anyway. This was clearly Simon's laboratory and looked as if it had enough machines set up to send a man into space. There were different-sized computers throughout the cramped room, all of them beeping in various monotones and flashing distinctive colored lights. The walls were covered with bookshelves of time-traveling tomes all the way up the ceiling. The tables were covered with stacks of printed papers with formulas that looked written in some alien language. In the center of it all was a large glass tube with a mechanical gloved hand inside. Next to the tube, a remote control had been left with an attached note that said AIM ME AT THE WALL AND PUSH ON in Simon's bad handwriting.

I aimed the remote at the only space of wall that

wasn't covered in bookshelves and pushed ON. A video image of Simon appeared. He looked like he always did: messy hair, thick glasses, and a plaid shirt buttoned up to his chin.

"Miles," the video image said.

"I'm here, Simon," I replied and then felt stupid that I was talking to nothing more than a hologram.

"If you're seeing this, Miles, then something has happened to me, or I am possibly dead."

Simon took a deep breath. This couldn't have been an easy message for him to leave.

"As you know, I've been working on a Top-Secret project for the last few years. Very few people knew what I was doing, and I wasn't sure I could trust those who did. Someone else has caught wind of what I've been doing. I am not sure who they are, or if they are part of a larger threat. Over this last week, I am certain that I've been followed and that someone has been watching our house. Thankfully I've been carrying out my work in a different location recently to throw whoever it is off track, so I don't think my stalker knows about this lab. Make sure you are not being followed when you come to this barn. It is crucial that you are the only one who learns what I have been able to accomplish."

Simon's image coughed into his hand. He had a look in his eyes that I'd never seen him convey before. He was acting confident, even cocky. Usually he blended into the shadows, but this Simon clearly knew that he had his audience (me) hanging on every word.

"The big news is that I've completed my time machine, and it works. While I haven't personally had a chance to test it myself, I've sent Stinkers back in time. He even returned, which means my past self was able to send him back to the present. Take a moment to let this sink in. Your heart rate is probably up right now, so count to ten slowly."

I did as I was told, but my heart felt like it was burning through my chest.

"However, I fear that I am not long for this world," Simon said, his tone changing. His confident swagger had been replaced by a sad sigh. "The possibility of time travel has been sought after for centuries. My legacy is at stake if it falls into the wrong hands; but more than that, it is still an imperfect science and there is much more that needs to be studied. If a rival inventor has killed me, or if my stalker is even part of some division of the government who wants my creation kept mum, you need to figure out who has been after me and make sure they are stopped. This could even be someone at Jeremiah Boonton, so everyone is a suspect. I may have been kidnapped, or brutally maimed, or very likely killed. I know I am putting you in danger, but it is paramount that you find the culprit before it becomes too late. You do know what this means, don't you?"

"You want me to go back in time," I said, as a chill began at the top of my spine and slinked all the way down my back.

"I want you to go back in time," Simon confirmed. "I cannot guarantee that there won't be risks. There will be many that I will try to prepare you for and many more that will be out of my control. A week before I made this video, I began to feel as if I was being watched. You will travel to right around that time. I only sent Stinkers back a few days into the past, and I don't want to risk sending you back much further. How's that heart rate going, Miles?"

"It's o…kay," I said, feeling the crazy thumps.

"Stinkers's heart rate spiked when he was sent back, so make sure that you stay as calm as possible. First, I need to know if you will accept this mission. If not, I implore you to take the time to reconsider. I know I haven't been a good brother to you over the last few years, but my absence has been in the name of science. You were too little. You wouldn't have understood. Back when we were younger, we'd sneak out in the middle of the night to our front lawn and look up at the stars. I'd tell you how vast this universe was, beyond just planets and galaxies. Time's mutability is out there as well, which will completely change everything that modern man thought they knew. But it has to be done right, and I have to be around to make sure of it. If people are already after me then there is no telling what they will do if they get their hands on this machine and the horrors they might be capable of."

I looked over at the mechanical glove in the glass tube. It seemed like some old video game controller, not an object capable of holding the course of humanity in its robotic palm.

"If you haven't switched off this video yet, then I know you're curious. You have a detective's spirit in you and there is no one else I'd trust in completing this mission. Are you ready for a briefing of all the vital things you'll need to know should you take the plunge?"

I nodded.

"The number one thing to remember, Miles, is to hold on to this book I'm about to show you. It is called *The Dos and Don'ts of Time Travel*, and it will be your Bible. It is an amalgamation of various scholars' speculations along with my own. The desk in front of you has a locked drawer. Type in the passcode EMIT, or TIME spelled backward to retrieve the book."

I did as I was told and removed the book from the locked drawer. Simon had printed it on paper the size of a pocketbook and had the manuscript bound. *The Dos and Don'ts of Time Travel* was written on the cover in a nice script that couldn't be Simon's poor handwriting. I figured Simon had to be working with someone else. His lab with all of his computers would've been too expensive to finance on his own, even counting all of the money he'd won with his scientific inventions at State Fairs over the years.

"The book outlines in great detail rules that I implore you to follow. Time travel is a tricky, brand-new world that you'll be entering. A lot of the book also isn't written in layman's terms. Some of the greatest scientific minds might have a hard time following the further along you read. But there are a few rules that I need to make sure you'll understand. Are you ready?"

I turned to the First Rule of the book, which stated: *You May Not Speak of the Time Travel Device to Anyone.*

"Knowing your curiosity, Miles, you have already turned to the first page."

I cringed, as if Simon had actually caught me.

"I applaud that speculative mind, Miles, never lose it!" Simon said, making his hand into a fist and shaking it. "So, the First Rule is to never speak about my time machine to anyone else. Obviously, it is too compli-cated for most people to understand, but I cannot be sure whom I can trust. No one at school can know, not our teachers, not any of your friends. This means that under no condition can you tell Kevin."

I bit my lip nervously. Simon had read my mind. I was thinking about Kevin, who'd crap a brick when he found out about the time machine.

"Kevin's biggest detriment is his big mouth. Your best friend will be completely useless for this mission and will only get in your way. Under no circumstance can you tell our parents either. Mom obviously isn't an issue, but if I've been followed and monitored, then whoever is after me might be watching Dad too. Since Dad's an inventor, they've probably assumed he has a stake in the time machine. But the two most important people you can never tell are in this room right now: you and me. You will be going back to the week that I will have completed the time machine. If I know it will be completed, we run the risk of distracting me and causing me to miss the crucial element I fixed, which allowed Stinkers to go back into the past. The next most important thing to remember is the Second Rule."

I turned to the next chapter of *The Dos and Don'ts of Time Travel*, which stated: *Your Past Self Also Cannot Know About the Time Machine, Nor Can Anyone See the Two of You Together.*

"Like the book states, you cannot, under any circumstance, let your past self know what you are doing. Countless literature has speculated about seeing one's future self and the terrible impact that might have. So, this is where things get tricky. In the drawer where you got *The Dos and Don'ts of Time Travel* is a small baggie with about a dozen white pills. They are nothing more than extreme sleep aids, completely harmless. The first thing you must do when you travel back in time is to go to our home in the middle of the night, feed your past self a couple of pills until you are sure he is unconscious, and then bring him to this lab. Do you see a switch next to where my image is being displayed?"

I saw the switch and went over to it.

"Flick it up and down five times and one of the bookshelves will open to a secret passage. This is my panic room, completely stocked with food and drinks that can last for a week along with a bathroom."

I flicked the switch five times. The bookshelf opened and displayed a room big enough for one person to comfortably fit along with shelves that held various nonperishable food items and a few dozen glass bottles. The walls were metallic, which I assumed made it soundproof. A small fluorescent lamp provided the only light. I flicked the switch five times again until the panic room closed.

"Your past self will be fine there. Since I'd been working on the time machine in a different hidden place so my stalker wouldn't discover this lab, we won't run the risk of me running into you or your past self here. I've racked my brain trying to figure out if there's another option, but you must do this and take your past self's place. You must shadow me at school and exhaust every available suspect that I come into contact with. No one can be assumed innocent except for you and me. Do you hear me—*no one*!"

"No one," I said in agreement.

"Good," Simon continued. "Now before you make a decision, you must know what will be happening to your body should you take this trip into the past. Under no circumstance can I guarantee that the time machine will work. Stinkers could've been a fluke, or your body mass may be too great to propel you through the time vortex. There has been speculation from physicists about the possibility of closed time-like curves, which are world lines that form closed loops in spacetime, allowing someone to return to their own past. The first of these was proposed by Kurt Gödel, an Austrian-American logician, mathematician, and philosopher. If someone were able to move away from the earth at a velocity faster than the speed of light, more time would have passed on Earth than it would for the traveler. So if that person managed to locate one of these closed loops, the loop could be opened and the person could be inserted into some part of their past. The first trick was to create an advanced propulsion system, hence the glove. After many formulas and trials, I found a way to break down matter into its infinitesimal core and then propel it into the far reaches of the universe. The second challenge was locating these time loops. The machine must be able to do what I just stated, but also track these supposed time loops. I tried to send many objects into the unknown over the past few years, but none have ever returned. It only worked when I used Stinkers, which means that only living creatures are capable of penetrating the time-space continuum. Objects by themselves do not have a past; therefore, an object cannot locate its time loop, but I found that whatever the traveler is holding on to becomes a part of them and travels through time as well, since Stinkers came back with his collar. However, the gloved machine will always remain in the present because of its built-in time circuits.

"After Stinkers successfully completed his trip in time, I started working on the possibility of someone attaching themselves to a time loop other than their own. I believe I am close, but not quite there. If I were able to achieve this, the next step would be traveling to the future. My theory is that all universes exist in a never-ending time loop. Past, present and future are meaningless concepts, and we should be able to control where our time begins and ends. The possibility of this is still far away from completion, but I am convinced that in our lifetime it is attainable. The question remains as to whether I will be alive long enough to accomplish such a feat."

Simon stopped speaking to catch his breath. He had worked himself up into a frenzy, his face red and his glasses foggy from sweat. He took them off to rub away the condensation. He looked sad, as if he realized how far-fetched this idea was and that it would be unlikely I'd be able to save him.

"I'm counting on you, Miles. If you are still ready for this mission, I'm ready to give you instructions on how to operate the time machine."

I wanted to give my brother's image a big hug and tell him that I'd do everything I could to prevent his death. I hadn't hugged him since we were little kids. Dad used to force us to hug after we'd gotten into a fight, but he'd given up on that many years ago. I felt myself getting teary-eyed again. I wished that I had woken up early enough that fateful morning of Simon's murder and hugged him tightly. Just to tell him not to be scared and that his time machine would fix all of this in the end.

"First off," Simon began, "you need to place the *Dos and Don'ts* book back in the drawer. There is no need for it to travel into the past with you since it will be there already, and I don't want to take the chance of losing this copy."

I fished for Simon's cell in my pocket and turned it

on. I keyed in EMIT on the off chance that Simon used the same code for two different things. Sure enough, it worked. I wondered if he had changed his cell's code to an easy one right before he died so I'd be able to figure it out. Unfortunately, when I checked for his email and voice messages, none had been saved. The only thing I saw were numerous texts to someone named EL. The texts were all in gibberish like the email I'd gotten from Simon earlier. I tried to decipher it with our Okoboji language, but it still seemed nonsensical. I grabbed a pen from the desk and scribbled EL on my palm. Once I'd go back to the past, I'd try to figure out who Simon had been texting the week before his death.

"Once you travel back, Miles, do not forget to go into the desk drawer and take the *Dos and Don'ts of Time Travel* along with the white pills to knock your past self out. You will also find a specially made eye mask I have created for your past self so he won't be able to identify you. It will lock with the code 03141879, Albert Einstein's birthday. Please go over to the mechanical glove right now."

I did as he said.

"The glove sits in a bulletproof chamber. Nothing can penetrate it without the passcode. This one isn't EMIT. Type in LEDOG, which is Gödel spelled backward."

I keyed the word LEDOG into a tiny keyboard attached to the glass chamber. The chamber opened from the top as the mechanical glove ascended.

"Now pick it up and place it on your hand," Simon continued.

The glove felt as heavy as a bowling ball. It was made out of sleek metallic silver with a keyboard and a screen built into the arm. I made sure each of my fingers comfortably fit and then awaited Simon's next instruction.

"I have already set the machine for a little over a week in the past. Do not alter the time I set. As I've explained, Stinkers only went back a few days, and I do not want to chance you taking a much longer trip and possibly never returning. There is a button with the word SET on it. Push that to bring up the date and time I have planned."

I pushed SET as the tiny computer screen flashed the date I'd be returning to.

"Now push the button MEAS. This will determine your precise measurements."

I pushed it, and my measurements popped up on the screen. Height five foot five inches, weight one hundred twenty pounds.

"Good, now press the button with the word HEART on it. This will locate your heart rate to make sure it is fit for the journey."

I pressed HEART as the glove suctioned against my wrist. It beeped in approval.

"The last button you push will be GO when you are ready. Your body will literally fall to pieces. I don't think this is painful since Stinkers showed no signs of agitation when he returned to the past. After this, you will feel yourself getting snapped back as if connected by a bungee cord. I can't exactly describe the next feeling, but it will probably feel like you are being sucked through a very long straw. You will be entering a tunnel in space. I have no idea what it will look like or how long it will take. If I had to extrapolate, it will be mere seconds. As scary as it might be, I would open your eyes to try to take it all in. You will be the first known human to attempt this amazing feat, and once you return to the present, I would very much like to hear you describe your travels, should I be alive. When you are ready to return to the present, the *Dos and Don'ts of Time Travel* will explain how to key in the date and make the reverse trip. I hope I've been able to answer any questions you might have. I am sorry that I couldn't be present to cheer you on."

Simon pushed his glasses up his nose and grimaced. I knew he probably wanted to be the one to attempt time travel first.

"You're very brave," Simon said, starting to get choked up. I had never seen my brother really get emotional before. "I hope to see you on the flip side, Miles." He held up a card where he had written: Bhgrkjonetjehirenfr flmobar lnjimgfjte, which I deciphered as 'Brother for life' in Okoboji. "And now," Simon continued, his voice strained with tears, "I must sign off. You must destroy this message once I do."

Simon waved goodbye, and the image shut off. The lab was quiet except for my knees knocking together. I picked up the remote, dropped it to the floor, and crushed it under my foot. I looked around at the present for possibly the last time. A stream of worries poured from my brain.

What if the time machine obliterated me to pieces?

How could I leave Mom in her awful state?

How would Dad deal with losing two sons in one week?

How could I attempt this death-defying trip without ever talking to that girl Maisie at least once?

I pictured Maisie at a table by herself in the cafeteria, pretending to read her *Sherlock Holmes* book so it would seem like she chose to sit alone. I hated that I hadn't taken the chance and sat down with her before, just to prove I had guts. Right now, my knees were knocking into one another so bad that I was afraid I'd chicken out on the whole mission.

Simon's words in Okoboji reverberated in my head —"*Brother for life*." His fate was in my hands; the very core of the universe was possibly in my hands as well. My nervous finger hovered over the GO button.

"Push it, push it, push it!" I yelled to myself, but my finger wouldn't budge.

I shut my eyes tightly.

"Push it, Detective Hardy," I whispered ever so softly. "This is what you're meant to do."

As if my brain no longer controlled my movements, some overwhelming impulse intervened and caused my finger to come into contact with the GO button and I shattered into trillions of microscopic pieces. Just like Simon had described, I felt myself being yanked back like I was attached to a bungee cord before the universe sucked me up and propelled me into another dimension.

Chapter Nine

Like a bullet, I shot through a tunnel that looked as if it was made out of red and blue lightning bolts. I tried to scream but realized I didn't even have a mouth. My body didn't exist anymore either, at least not at the moment. Outside of the tunnel, the universe rushed by —stars and planets I didn't recognize as a part of our galaxy; but I could've been wrong since science was never one of my strong suits. The rollercoaster of a tunnel dipped and swerved, did loops through space that would impress any jet fighter pilot. I wondered how far away from Earth I'd traveled and if I'd ever be able to return?

Simon had done the impossible. Even as I put the mechanical glove on my hand, I still had doubts it would work. But this was so real. I saw what scholars had longed to view through high-tech telescopes, what astronauts only dreamed could be a possibility in their lifetime. Over half a century ago man had walked on the moon, and now I had a firsthand view of galaxies unknown. If I had a mouth, I wouldn't have been able to wipe the smile off my face if I tried.

A star to my right shone so brightly that my eyes hurt, or whatever it was that allowed me to see at the moment, since I had no eyes. The star exploded into a ring of sparkling fire that looked like a giant jewel. I wondered how many of the star's connected planets would fall into darkness and freeze. It all happened in seconds, an entire solar system swallowed up and turned to ash. I never thought of the earth being so insignificant, but it was. Just a tiny rock in the midst of galaxies that stretched out from the beginning of time to whenever the end of time occurred. I thought of Frontier, a place that had always felt small but that now seemed completely minuscule and unimportant. Once I solved Simon's murder and saved him, there'd be no way I could stay in Iowa, or even in present time anymore when there was so much more out there to explore.

I'd been flying through the tunnel at an alarming rate, and then, all of a sudden, I stopped and floated in the air. A black hole appeared in the lightning bolt tunnel, and I felt myself getting pushed through. As my body began to take shape again, the lightning burned my face, my arms, and my legs. Now I could finally scream so I let out a super loud yell that echoed through the universe before the black hole consumed my entire body and the universe disappeared.

My eyes shot open. I was shivering on the floor in the fetal position, my heart pounding like mad. It felt like I'd gotten the wind knocked out of me. I managed to rise to my feet, blinking in confusion as I saw Simon's lab. Everything appeared as I remembered. I flicked the light switch on and off five times until the panic room opened. Then I gobbled up some of the food that was stored there and ate about two meals worth in one setting.

"I guess time travel leaves you hungry," I said, belching up an entire big bag of M&M's.

I keyed in the code EMIT for the desk drawer and removed the *Dos and Don'ts of Time Travel* along with the baggie of white pills that I needed to knock my past self out. I threw it all in a backpack. I also grabbed a tiny box that said *Side Effects* on it, which contained a bevy of red pills. Inside was a typed note:

> Si - Remember to take a few of these after any time trip. Heart rates are bound to spike along with dizziness, headaches, nausea, vomiting, nosebleeds, etc.

I gulped down a few red pills and instantly my heart rate returned to normal.

A clock on the desk said that it was five in the morning. I had to go home as soon as possible so I could drug my past self and bring him to this lab before he woke up for school.

I reemerged through the trapdoor, practically choking on the piles of hay. I closed the door and darted out of the barn. It was still dark out, but the sun was rising in the east. I stared at its orange curve and thought of the star I saw exploding. My wild travels felt like a dream, too insane to be real. Had I really just gone through time? Or had I put on the mechanical glove and then somehow fallen asleep? The first test would be if my bike waited for me outside the barn.

As I turned the corner, goose bumps sprouted up on my arms and legs. Seeing my bike would mean I hadn't traveled anywhere and that Simon would stay dead for good. I closed my eyes, not wanting to see the disappointing truth. I stood outside of the barn with my eyes shut, the foul smell of Generator Street wafting into my nostrils, my teeth chattering from the cool autumn morning.

"The bike can't be there," I muttered to myself. *"This had to have worked."*

I took a deep breath and opened my eyes. There was no bike! I let out an excited yell and wished there was someone around that I could high-five. Of course, there was still a small chance that my bike could've been stolen while I was down in the lab. I needed to find a way to know for certain if the time machine had worked.

I took off toward town as fast as my legs could carry me. At just after five in the morning no one was around, all the houses dark and silent. It was about two miles to my house and I raced against the sun. After a mile or so, the sky had turned from black to a purplish blue and I saw an object coming toward me in the distance. As the object got closer, I realized it was a paperboy on his bike flinging newspapers into driveways. The paperboy passed by me in a whirl. I waited until he was out of sight and then crouched down next to a neighbor's driveway.

I picked up the paper, searching for the date to

confirm that I'd gone back in the past. Sure enough, the date was from a week earlier.

"Holy crap," I said out loud as the newspaper fell from my hands.

I felt dizzy, as if on a tilt-a-whirl. Blood dripped from my nose. I puked up a massive amount of the food I'd shoveled down. I took out the little box with the red pills and popped a few more in my mouth. My stomach began to settle, and the dizziness went away.

The sun had now fully risen in the sky. I couldn't waste any more time if I wanted to drug my past self and swap places.

I took off in a sprint and didn't stop until I reached my house a mile later, panting but alive, more alive than I'd ever felt before.

I was the first known human to ever travel through time, and the thought made me giddy.

Now I needed to make sure that the trip would be worth it.

Chapter Ten

As quietly as possible, I opened the door to my house and crept inside. A worst-case scenario would be if my entire family decided to get up early, and I'd come face-to-face with them at the breakfast table. As I entered, I saw that the house was still dark, and I didn't smell any awful cooking coming from the kitchen, so I knew that Dad hadn't woken up yet. I spied a clock on the cable box that said it was six thirty. I had about a half an hour before Dad would get up to go to work, causing my past self to wake up as well.

Nearing the upstairs hallway, I could hear snores coming from my parents' room. Both of them sounded like car horns when they slept. I peered inside. Mom slept on her back with her hands folded over her chest like she was a cadaver. Dad tossed off the blanket and had his nose firmly implanted in the nook of his arm.

As I headed down the hallway and saw Simon's room, I had flashes from days earlier (or actually days from now). Opening the door with the DON'T ENTER sign.... Seeing a pool of dark red blood on the floor.... The gun.... Simon's face half shot off.... The typed note by his foot.

I shook my head back and forth to make those terrible thoughts go away. None of it had to exist if I was successful in stopping Simon's murder. In the future, I hoped it would all become nothing more than a horrific nightmare.

Part of me was curious to check inside Simon's room, just to see my brother in the flesh again, but I didn't have time. I opened the door to my own room instead.

Even though it had only been a few hours since I'd been in my room, it felt like I'd been gone years. I saw my bookshelves filled with *Encyclopedia Brown* mysteries and old *Hardy Boys* classics. A box on my desk held business cards for *Mr. Hardy's Detective Agency*. A huge poster hung on one wall with Sherlock Holmes wearing his trusty deerstalker cap with a pipe in one hand and a magnifying glass in the other. Over my bed was the Okoboji poster.

Below the poster, my past self was sleeping soundly. Dad once remarked that I could "sleep through a war," which was why the volume on my morning alarm was always cranked up to the max. I thought of how odd it was to watch myself sleep. Unlike my parents, my past self didn't make a sound. He was curled up and clutching a blanket to his chest as if it was a stuffed animal. He looked like a little kid with no idea how much he'd be growing up in the coming week.

I took the baggie with the white pills out of my backpack and leaned over my past self. He twitched. Some dust pollen danced around his nose and caused him to let out a giant sneeze. I held up my hands as if I'd been caught and froze in place. My past self rubbed a finger under his nose and went back to sleep instantly.

I placed two white pills in my palm and slowly opened his mouth.

"Gross," I whispered. His breath smelled terrible.

He turned on his back as I held open his mouth and dropped in the two pills. A glass of water had been left on the nightstand, so I picked it up and poured a few drops into his mouth. He let out a cough that sprayed spittle on my face. I thought for sure that he was about to wake up. I raised my hands in the air and didn't move a muscle again. He then let out one more cough and settled back to sleep again.

I climbed off the bed and headed to the door to see if anyone else had woken up yet. All I heard was a chorus of car horn snores. I stepped back over to the bed and tapped my past self on the cheek to see if the white pills had worked. He didn't stir. I raised one of his eyelids and saw an entirely white iris staring back. He was as good as unconscious.

I dragged him out of bed and nearly dropped him on the floor. I'd always thought of myself as pretty skinny, but now I figured I might need to lay off my daily allotment of donuts and Mountain Dews every once in a while. I grabbed my University of Iowa Hawkeye's cap from beside the bed and put it on my past self's head so the brim reached below his eyes. Then I carried him out of the door.

My heart was racing, and I didn't know if it was still due to the recent time travel. I was definitely nervous about being caught by my parents, or even worse, by Simon. Simon had explicitly stated that no one could know about the time travel machine, not Mom and Dad, and especially not him. If something got in the way of him being able to complete the device, there'd be no way to save him.

It's all so complicated, I thought, rubbing my head.

Just as I was figuring out a few of the paradoxes that could occur, Mom emerged from her bedroom and began moaning in the hallway like some monster. I stopped in my tracks with my past self in my arms. She hadn't seen us, or at least she hadn't looked in our direction yet since her eyes usually wound up wandering all over the place.

I took another step to ease past her, but then her arm shot out and blocked my way. She looked right into my eyes as if she knew exactly what was going on. I nearly pissed my pants and almost dropped my past self.

"I gotta go, Mom," I said as I nudged past her outstretched arm.

I looked to see if her moans had woken Dad up, but luckily Dad was still face down in a pillow.

Mom began moaning louder and pointing in our direction as I made my way to the staircase. I turned around to look at her for one last time, and she seemed so lost. Her mind had to have been a mess anyway, and seeing her son dragging his past self down the hall could be the thing to put her over the edge for good.

"I'm sorry," I said to her before backing down the staircase.

When I reached the bottom, I heard Dad's alarm going off upstairs. Dad would be up in seconds since he often liked to head down to the basement to work on some of his inventions before classes started. Even though my arms were starting to strain, I managed to rush to the front door and then closed it behind me.

I let my past self lie in the grass while I grabbed

my bike. Then I propped him up on the bike and hopped on, wrapping my arms around him so he'd stay in place. It was still early enough for the neighborhood to be mostly asleep. No one had picked up their newspapers yet from their front lawns.

I started pedaling and saw Reed sitting on the curb.

"Hey, Reed," I said, whooshing by.

"Miles?" I heard Reed say, but I didn't take the time to look back. "Mi-les, who's that with you?"

I pedaled faster until I was far away from my block and couldn't hear Reed anymore. As I biked the two-mile stretch to the barn, I was anxious as hell. At one point, I swerved to avoid a dead bird, and my past self was almost flung out into the road. About halfway there, I passed by Ludmila, who was watering her front lawn in a housecoat and gaped at us as we rushed by. I'd have to figure out some explanation for when I'd see her next, but I couldn't worry about that now. By the time we reached the barn, I was out of breath as I parked my bike inside. I made sure no one had followed us and shut the barn doors.

I tossed my past self down into the hayloft and jumped in as well. With sweat dripping from my forehead, I moved away the piles of hay and keyed in OKOBOJI into the trapdoor. With all my might, I eased my past self down into Simon's lab and then followed. My limbs ached, I was dehydrated, and I felt like I could puke again. Lugging myself around was definitely a workout.

I flicked the light switch on and off five times until the panic room opened. I found the mechanical eye mask that Simon had created and locked it tightly around my past self's eyes. Positioning some food in his lap along with some glass soda bottles and water, I wished I could tell him not to be afraid, but I couldn't think of any way to do this. I knew that I'd be freaking out if this had happened to me, so I made a promise to head back to the lab as soon as possible after my day of snooping around school.

Hopefully I'd be back in time before my past self would wake up.

"Stay calm," I said to myself, closing the door to the panic room quickly as if my words might linger and echo around the closed chamber as a friendly reminder.

Chapter Eleven

I reached school with over twenty minutes to spare before the bell rang. I still felt bad about leaving my past self locked up in Simon's panic room, but I knew there was no other solution. The goal for today was to find Simon before classes started and make up some story about needing to follow him all day for a class project. I figured I'd try to convince him that I was failing some made-up class and that a fake project detailing a day in the life of a family member would be my only chance to earn a passing grade.

As I parked my bike, other kids were getting dropped off by their parents or had come by bus or on a bike as well. A few old-enough juniors and seniors had their own cars. I was about to head inside when I saw Maisie getting dropped off by her dad. She looked as pretty as ever. She had curled her blond hair and held it in place with wacky-colored neon barrettes. She was wearing a fuzzy sweater, jeans, and the same sneakers I had noticed before with the clock doodles. Her hands were dirty but not in a grimy way. I deduced that she'd probably been working on a drawing before school and hadn't had the time to wash up.

Her dad stepped out of the car to hug her good-bye. He wore thick glasses, but he was a built man with giant forearms. He wore a button-down short-sleeved shirt tucked into his corduroys and had a pocket protector in his front pocket. He hugged his daughter in a considerate way that I could barely remember my own parents doing. If a hug in my house ever happened, it was practically over before it started. Maisie and her dad hugged for about half a minute as if she was saying goodbye to him for a long time. After the hug, she looked really sad and kept pointing toward the school. I figured that she hated to go and her dad was just trying to be as consoling as possible.

As she headed up the front steps, she waved back at her dad. From where I was standing, it seemed like she was waving right at me. My face got hot, and I bent down quickly to tie my shoelace. I knew that I needed to come up with another way of avoiding eye contact with her.

By the time I looked up, Maisie had already gone inside, and her dad was driving away. The plates on his car said Oregon. I remembered that Kevin said she had moved here from out West. I'd think of something cool to say about Oregon if I ever got up the nerve to talk to her.

I glanced at my watch and realized that I only had fifteen minutes before the bell rang, so I rushed inside, viewing all the students I passed by as suspects. If the conspiracy against my brother went all the way up to the government, or some greedy corporation, there was no telling who they might have employed to help get rid of Simon.

When I got to Simon's locker, he wasn't around. Since I didn't know his first class, I took a gamble by waiting. After five or so minutes, I saw him coming down the hallway with a backpack that looked as if it held an entire library of books. Simon hadn't seen me yet, so I took a moment to observe his state. If he deliberately sent me back to this exact date, it could mean that today was the day he suspected he was being followed. Right now, he seemed to be deep in thought. He practically bumped into me as he reached his locker.

"Miles?" he said, scrunching up his face. "What are you doing at my locker?"

I dwarfed him with a strangling hug. The hug was so powerful that it knocked his backpack off his shoulders and almost knocked him over too. Simon was a few inches taller, so I rested my head against his beating heart. I listened to it carefully, since just yesterday I didn't think I'd ever hear it again.

"What's wrong with you?" Simon said, pushing me off.

I wiped my eyes. It was killing me not to tell him the truth. It'd be so much easier if he knew that his time machine had been successful and we could go after his killer together; but I had to trust his *Dos and Don'ts of Time Travel*.

"Nothing, I…uh…smoked a doobie before school started. Just…feeling the love."

"A doobie?" Simon questioned. He opened his locker just wide enough to fit in a textbook from his backpack as if he didn't want me to see what else was inside. "I don't believe people call it that anymore."

"Well…Kevin brought one."

"Why you chose that fart box as your best friend," Simon said, shaking his head. "And don't get in the habit of getting high before school. I heard Dad complaining about your grades the other day."

"That's what I wanted to talk to you about—"

"I don't have the time to tutor you," Simon said, shutting his locker and starting to walk away.

"No, not tutoring. So…I have to do a report about following a family member for the day. Obviously, I can't do Mom, and I've been fighting with Dad, so…"

Simon pinched the bridge of his nose, a gesture that usually meant he was getting annoyed.

"Miles, I need to devote any spare time I have to my…project. And…"

He clammed up, his eyes nervously flicking from side to side. My stomach dropped at the thought of what he was about to say. Was he already being followed? Did he want to tell someone about his suspicions?

"And what? What were you gonna say, Simon?"

"And nothing!" Simon snapped. He'd gotten in my face and then realized he probably looked foolish, so he backed up. "I got physics in five minutes."

"I'm gonna fail, Simon," I shouted. Other students turned around and laughed. Tears welled in my eyes. "Please, I'm… freaking out."

The tears dripped down my cheeks. It wasn't hard to get them to flow. I just had to picture opening up Simon's door that morning….

"Stop crying, Miles," Simon whispered. "You just started here at Jeremiah Boonton and you'll be crucified if people see you cry."

He took a handkerchief out of his pocket and handed it over. I blew a long trail of snot.

"You'll get crucified for being the only sixteen-year-old who carries a handkerchief," I said, managing a small laugh.

Simon took back the handkerchief that was now covered with snotty blood.

"What's this blood from?" he said slowly. I clamped my hand over my nose to stop the bleeding.

"Oh damn, I…started shaving the peach fuzz on the top of my lip and nicked myself bad this morning."

Simon went to fold up the handkerchief in his pocket but then thought twice and chucked it in the trash instead.

"Have you cleared it with all your teachers to follow me for the day?"

I nodded excitedly.

"What class is this even for?"

"It's Drama class!" I blurted out. "I have to write about a family member and then perform a day of theirs in a monologue."

I knew Simon couldn't care less about drama, thinking it a pointless waste of school resources, and therefore wouldn't question the lie.

"All right, hurry up then before I'm late to physics. We have a quiz first thing. And don't distract me. I'm actually in school to learn."

"Cross my heart and hope to di…" I began to say, but I caught myself before I finished those ominous words. It pained me to even mention the word 'death' in front of him.

"I promise," I continued saying.

I sucked the last bit of trickling blood up my nostrils before it could leak anymore and followed Simon into physics class.

Chapter Twelve

Nothing was more boring to me than physics class. I dreaded becoming a senior and inevitably failing. I hoped that Simon would've figured out a way to travel into the future by then so I could fast-forward through that probable low point in my life. Of course, for that to happen, Simon's murderer needed to be stopped so he'd have a chance to keep inventing.

The entire class was engrossed with taking a quiz. I looked at Simon's paper, which seemed like nothing more than squiggles and random numbers. All of the students, including Simon's Brainiacs crew, were frantically scribbling answers and then erasing them in haste while Simon didn't appear like he was stressing at all. His teacher Mr. Congley sat at his desk frantically writing on a stack of papers in front of him as well.

I thought of seeing Mr. Congley at Simon's funeral. The old man's skinny arms had been wrapped around a tree like he'd been holding on for dear life. He'd bugged out and then run away when I declared that Simon was murdered. Had he been spooked because he had something to do with Simon's murder, or had he been unable to deal with the idea of Simon dying? He was definitely one of the top suspects so far.

Simon was the first to finish and handed in the quiz with a righteous air about him. Most of the students didn't seem to care, but his Brainiacs crew seemed like they were pissed. I imagined there had to be competition between them since they were all angling to be the number one student at Jeremiah Boonton.

"I can check your quiz right now," Mr. Congley said. Simon shrugged his shoulders, but I could tell he relished the thought of the entire class watching him ace the quiz.

Mr. Congley got out a red pen and within seconds had checked through Simon's answers and written an A+ at the top of the page.

"He's so Congley's favorite," one of the Brainiacs whispered to another one. I thought I remembered the kid's name being Ellery. I'd heard Simon speaking about Ellery before because he had the second-highest grade point average after Simon. Both of them were eventually trying for MIT and Cal Tech, and it was well known that schools like that rarely accepted two students from the same school.

If someone looked up the word *uncool* in the dictionary, Ellery's face would likely be there. He was riddled with acne scars and had a long thin neck with an Adam's apple the size of a golf ball. He wore T-shirts with various science puns that no one else would get. His hair looked like his mom had combed it for a school picture, and he always had a cowlick sticking up as well.

Ellery was whispering to Linda, who was probably

ranked third at school. Linda headed up most of the intellectual clubs, which was her way of being a stronger candidate for a top school than Simon or Ellery. Her hair usually appeared as if it hadn't been washed, and she was always dressed in a uniform that wouldn't be out of place at a Catholic school.

"What an ass kisser," I heard her say to the third member of the Brainiacs, Quentin.

Quentin was one of those loner types who dyed his hair black and wore eyeliner, but he didn't fit in with the alternative kids since he was too smart. If anyone were to come into school one day with a knapsack full of guns, it would be Quentin. One time when the Brainiacs were over at my house for a study session with Simon, Quentin had brought along a jar of his old scabs. He told me that sometimes he cut himself just to have a fresh scab for his collection later on. Right now, he was staring at Simon and squeezing his fist as if Simon's head was in his palm. Of the three, he was the most obvious suspect, but I knew that the most obvious suspect was rarely the culprit.

"Pens down," Mr. Congley said and clapped his hands a few times. The class groaned and passed their quizzes forward. "Everyone is dismissed. Except for you, Si. Please stay for a moment."

It was weird that Mr. Congley called my brother Si, since I only heard Simon use that nickname when he was referring to himself.

Once the class left, I joined Simon by Mr. Congley's desk.

"Can I help you?" Mr. Congley sneered, looking me up and down with his bloodshot eyes.

"Oh, this is my brother Miles," Simon said. "He's following me all day for a school project."

"Hrrrmpph," was Mr. Congley's only reply.

I was glad that Mr. Congley clearly didn't deem me worth his time. Simon may have bought the drama class lie, but if Mr. Congley asked for that teacher's name, I wouldn't even know.

Peering over Mr. Congley's desk, I tried to see what he'd been writing, but Mr. Congley was hunching too far over the papers and his knobby back blocked everything.

"What did you want to see me for, Mr. Congley?" Simon asked. He leaned against a table to support the heavy backpack on his shoulders.

Mr. Congley rubbed his thin jaw. He had long fingers with curling fingernails that made them appear even longer.

"I...wanted to ask you about the extra credit we had...discussed," Mr. Congley replied, sucking at his teeth. He had an inordinate amount of spit building up in his mouth from an extended lower lip.

"Yes," Simon said, fiddling with his glasses that had sloped down his nose. "I should be able to...give you an update soon."

"Yes, yes, that would be...good."

For a second, I thought that they might be referring to the time machine in code. Simon had always spoken of Mr. Congley as the only other person at Jeremiah Boonton who was on par with his own intellect, but if Mr. Congley knew about the time machine, I doubted he would say anything about it in front of someone else, even if it were in code. Simon had always done extra credit assignments in every class so that was a likelier explanation.

"Yes, why don't you periodically check in with me

this week to go over your…findings?" Mr. Congley asked as he gathered up his papers.

"That should be fine."

"And good work on that quiz. Hopefully, your brother will be following in your footsteps when he reaches my class."

Mr. Congley said this sarcastically; like he knew what a dunce I'd be in physics. I always hated when teachers put me down, or compared me to Simon, as they tended to do.

"Friday it is, Si," Mr. Congley said, heading toward the door.

I looked closely at the papers in Mr. Congley's hands. An image on the front sheet looked like it could be a blueprint for some type of glove. I only saw it for a second before Mr. Congley shifted the papers in his hands and the image was blocked from my view.

I tried to hold on to the picture of it in my mind. Could it be the same mechanical glove that Simon created or some physics-related blueprint? As a detective, I knew there was a danger in wanting a clue to appear so badly that one's mind tended to alter certain things. Maybe what looked like fingers for a glove was really something else? It'd be smart to continue to scope out Mr. Congley and try to get a look at his papers. Congley could've possibly been working on his own failed time machine and killed Simon to get his? Or they could've been working together and the government or some sinister corporation either threatened Congley's life or offered him massive amounts of money to turn on Simon? The possibilities were limitless.

So far, after an hour of following Simon, I had four suspects to keep my eye on between Congley and the

Brainiacs. If the number of suspects continued building up at this pace, I'd have practically the whole school to choose from.

"You look perturbed," Simon said.

"You don't know the half of it," I replied, feeling a headache coming on.

"And you're bleeding again," Simon said.

"Oh shit," I said, clamping my hand over my nose so he'd think it was coming from my upper lip. "Gotta get better at shaving, I guess!"

Simon was looking at me suspiciously as I mopped up the blood with a paper towel. I needed to start taking the *Side Effects* pills more often, or Simon was bound to catch on that his time-traveling machine had worked, and my cover would be blown.

Chapter Thirteen

I followed Simon to two classes that were even more boring than physics: advanced calculus and some type of chemistry where the Brainiacs were the only other students. In each of the classes, Simon raised his hand after every one of the teacher's questions and got all the answers right if he was called on. I got exhausted just watching him.

"How can one person possibly know all that information?" I asked as we both left chemistry class.

"What band does everyone listen to right now?" Simon asked.

"I don't know. *The Young Sheep* are pretty popular."

"*The Young Sheep*," Simon balked. "What an asinine name. A young sheep is a lamb. And what TV show does everyone watch?"

"*Fast Times* is really big. It takes place at a high school and is based on some really old movie."

"Sounds enlightening. See, I don't fill my brain with unimportant things like that. Moronic TV shows, music, who hooked up with whom yesterday, who wore what, how our football team is doing—that's all a waste of my time. And you can put that in your report of me."

"Don't you think you're missing out at all?"

"I don't really have a choice," Simon mumbled, and got real quiet. He was staring at his sneakers.

"When did you realize that you were like this?" I asked. I felt sad for my brother: Simon was so lonely, so fixated on one thing for so long. Since he hadn't fully completed his time machine yet, maybe he was questioning his life's decision, or maybe he wished for a day off from his brain once in a while.

"I always remember being like this," he replied. He didn't seem sad to me anymore. He seemed determined. "It's all for a greater purpose."

"I know," I whispered, but it was so softly that I doubted Simon had heard.

Before I could snoop anymore into my brother's secretive thoughts, Kevin came by with a Butterfinger in his hand.

"What's up, Hardy Farty brothers?" Kevin said, shoving half of the Butterfinger into his mouth.

"Most of us have learned to close our mouths when we chew," Simon said, clearly not happy that Kevin was there.

"Mmmma jummma mooomma bummba," Kevin replied, putting his jaw to work from gulping down the rest of the candy bar.

"Your mother must be so proud," Simon said and started walking away. I scurried to catch up, and Kevin followed with an irritated look on his face.

"Well, we can't all take first prize at the nerd convention, Simon," Kevin said. "I know that's the thing that makes your mom proud…"

Kevin stopped himself. He knew it was wrong to say anything negative about our mom due to her condition.

"Hey, I'm sorry. I didn't mean—"

"It's fine, Kevin," Simon said. "I know you haven't figured out how to properly send information between your brain and mouth yet."

"Why are you hanging out with Señor Dweebnuts today?" Kevin nudged me.

"Miles has to do a report on me so it looks like the two of us are stuck together too," Simon said.

The three of us headed into the cafeteria and got in line for food. Kevin let out a massive fart and then pointed at Simon as a few students turned around.

"Simon, WHAT did you eat today?" Kevin yelled, waving his hand in front of his nose with a smile.

"You are an infantile simpleton," Simon replied.

"And we have a long time till we take the SATs, so save the ten-dollar words for someone who gives a crap."

"Such a waste of air," Simon said as a lunch lady dumped a tiny piece of chicken and clumpy mashed potatoes onto his plate. Simon inspected his food with disdain and took off away from us.

"Leave him alone," I said.

"He called me a simpleton!"

"Stop giving him reasons to."

I followed Simon toward the Brainiac's table, not even bothering to look and see if Kevin was behind us.

"I need to tell you something," I said into Simon's ear, and nodded toward the Brainiacs. "I heard them talking about you behind your back while Mr. Congley was grading your quiz."

Simon turned to me, stone-faced.

"What were they saying?"

"They called you 'ass kisser' and that creepster Quentin kept squeezing his fist like he wanted to crush you."

"Yeah, it's been like that since last year."

"Why are you friends with them?"

"I'm not friends—" Simon snapped and then pinched the bridge of his nose as he calmed back down. "We're not friends, I use them to bounce off theories. I'm sure they're doing the same with me."

"Do you think any of them would want to hurt you?"

I couldn't believe that I flat-out asked such an incriminating question, but the words left my mouth before I could make sure to keep them to myself.

"Hurt me? What do you mean?"

"Nothing…never mind. Just that Quentin seems like he's a trench coat away from going on a killing spree."

"No argument there."

Kevin finally caught up with us while we scanned for a place to sit. The Brainiacs all glared at us with a silent warning, clearly indicating that we weren't welcome at their table, so we had to find other options. The cafeteria was pretty much filled to capacity as always, and I didn't want to eat standing up because Jojo and his asshole crew usually set their sights on anybody vulnerable enough not to secure a seat.

With that freakishly depressing thought, I spied Maisie at a table alone with her trusty *Sherlock Holmes* book propped up in front of her nose. Like the last time I saw her eating by herself, I wondered if she was actually reading as opposed to holding up the book so it looked like she was busy.

"I've seen you staring at her before," Kevin said. "She just moved here a couple of days ago."

"I've never stared at her before," I declared, as my voice shot up three octaves.

Simon and Kevin both rolled their eyes in sync.

"I couldn't care less about paying Cupid," Kevin said. "But there are three empty seats by her."

My hands got all clammy again.

"I don't know what to say," I mumbled, still clueless about what opening line I should use.

"Go on," Simon said. "She's reading *Sherlock Holmes*. You love *Sherlock Holmes*. There's got to be some fact you could impress her with."

"Maybe she's reading it for class?"

"You'll never know if you don't find out."

With that, Simon started walking right over to her table. He was already too far away for me to stop him without causing a ruckus. Once he reached her table, Maisie casually looked up from her book.

"So, my brother is a huge *Sherlock Holmes* fan, too," Simon said, sitting down at her table without even asking. Maisie blinked a few times before Simon motioned toward me hiding behind Kevin. When she saw me, she gave the tiniest smile.

"Oh yeah?" she said, placing a bookmark at the page she was on.

"The biggest," Simon added. "He practically keeps the deerstalker hat industry in business every year."

Maisie covered her mouth and let out a sweet laugh that I found cuter than anything. Since I had no choice now, I headed over to her table on trembling legs and placed my tray down, hoping nothing would spill.

"I'm Miles," I said with a smile, but then I became

self-conscious about my metal braces and closed my mouth.

"Hi, I'm Maisie."

"That's my brother Simon, and this is Kevin."

"M'lady," Kevin said, taking her by the hand and leaving a slobbery kiss. She recoiled, but maintained a smile to be polite.

"So, you're the biggest Holmes fan, huh?" she asked me. "Tell me something I'd never know about his creator, Sir Arthur Conan Doyle?"

"Well…" I began, stroking my chin in thought. "Okay, Doyle was so sick of writing Sherlock Holmes that he killed him off but had to bring him back to life with a convoluted explanation after people got mad."

"Everyone knows that."

"Well…Doyle also believed in the supernatural and that there were things in this world that couldn't be explained logically."

"I knew that, too," she said, crossing her arms.

"Uhhh…okay…years before World War Two happened, Doyle wrote articles about a war with Germany as if he'd been to the future and saw what might happen."

"Wow," she said, her face lighting up. "I didn't know that."

I wiped the sweat from my forehead in relief.

"Miles is such a fan of Holmes that he started his own detective agency," Simon added while poking at the hard lump of potatoes on his plate.

At first, I was embarrassed that Simon even mentioned it, but Maisie seemed interested.

"A detective agency? What kind of cases do you get here in Frontier?"

"Uhh…all kinds."

"Show her your card," Simon said.

I reached into my pocket and then realized that my wallet, along with my business cards had been left in present time.

"Looks like I forgot my wallet today," I said, my face getting redder and redder.

"Voilà!" Kevin said, removing a grubby card from his pocket. He handed it to Maisie. "Miles is the president, and I'm his assistant."

Maisie studied the card. I used to be very proud of how it turned out since I'd spent weeks mowing neighbor's lawns to get enough money to order an entire box. On the card was my agency's name along with the shadow of a man with a deerstalker cap, a magnifying glass, and a briar pipe.

"*Mr. Hardy's Detective Agency*," she said. "Has a nice ring." She passed the card to me. "Here you go, Mr. President, you should probably have one in reserve."

"Thanks, I usually do." I imagined my face was red enough to look like I'd gotten sunburned.

The table was silent as I thought of what to say next to her. I couldn't think of anything. I got lost in her eyes and the smattering of freckles trickling down her nose and across her cheeks. A tent pole started rising in my pants, so I shifted in place to avoid her possibly seeing. Damn you, puberty, I have no control!

"So, you moved here recently?" Simon asked her, and then kicked me under the table.

"Oh yeah, when did you move here?" I asked too.

"Is it that obvious I'm new? Thanks for sitting with me by the way, lunch can be pretty brutal here."

"I know, we usually have to stand up while we eat," Kevin said, spearing his lump of potatoes and shoveling it in his mouth. Now it was my turn to kick Kevin under the table. "Oww!" Kevin exclaimed as the tough potatoes almost fell out of his mouth.

"He's kidding," I said. "We usually have plenty of options to sit."

"It seems like my options here are either being a Cheerleader, a Glee girl, a Brain, or a Druggie. No thanks."

"What do you like to do?" I asked.

"So many things!" she gushed. "Especially back home. I draw a lot. I draw everything really. Like if I see something really cool or really beautiful I feel like it's my duty to draw it. I like to go hiking. I love nature."

"Yeah, nature is really awesome," I said as Kevin looked at me funny.

"Since when are you into nature?" he asked.

"Since always," I replied, kicking him under the table again.

"Oww!" Kevin whined. "Who keeps kicking me?"

"I haven't found Iowa so great for hiking. It's nothing compared to where I'm from. I bet you can't guess where I'm from, Mr. Detective."

Her upper lip curled into a smile. I wondered if this was what flirting was like. I pretended to be studying everything about her and then shrugged my shoulders and said: "Oregon."

"How did you know that?" she asked, grabbing my hand in awe. Even Simon and Kevin were looking at me strange. Her touch was really warm, and I wanted her to hold on forever.

"A detective never reveals his tricks."

"No, you have to tell me."

Now I was uncomfortable because if I said

anything about seeing her dad's license plate, she might think I was stalking her.

"C'mon, the mystery is always revealed in a *Sherlock Holmes* story," she added.

"Yeah, but in real life, we don't always get the answers," I said, looking at Simon. I had to remind myself that I came back to the past for the sole purpose of saving him. As great as Maisie was, I couldn't lose focus too much. I'd have the entire present to try to win her over.

"You sure are a serious guy," Maisie said, scrunching up her face. She leaned back and kicked her feet up on the table. She was wearing the same sneakers with clock doodles as before. "Some jerk already made fun of my sneakers today," she added with a frown.

"Who did that?" I asked, glad that she gave up questioning me about how I knew she was from Oregon.

"I don't know. His name was Bobo, or Jojo, something weird like that."

We all groaned.

"Jojo is a terrorist," Simon said. Kevin and I agreed. "He represents everything wrong with the world—an insecure bully who tramples everyone in his way."

"I'm guessing you've had problems with him before," Maisie said.

Simon went back to eating his nasty potatoes and didn't answer. I remembered the interaction that he had with Jojo in the cafeteria the day before he was murdered. At the time, it seemed as if Jojo was picking on my brother at random, but I wondered if there was a more sinister reason behind Jojo's cruelty that could've been responsible for Simon's death.

"Anyway, I happen to like my sneakers," Maisie said, showing them off. "Who wants to wear the same thing as everyone else?"

"Did you draw those clocks?" I asked.

"Sure did, it's a Maisie Sumpter original. These might be worth a lot one day."

"Why clocks?" I asked.

"I've always loved clocks and watches too," she said, pointing to the one on her wrist that was the shape of a ship. "Like, everyone our age just looks up the time on their phones now. But clocks have history to them. My dad has a grandfather clock that's centuries old."

"That's really cool," I said, glad I'd worn a non-digital watch when I left the present time that I could impress her with. I rolled up my sleeve, but she was looking directly at me instead of my wrist and I got all flustered.

"So…were you sad to move…and stuff?"

"Dad got a job in a factory here and jobs like that had really dried up back in Oregon. He hadn't worked in over a year so we had no choice."

"Yeah, my dad teaches at the community college, doesn't bring in much dough."

"No one likes being new." She fingered a shoelace that was coming apart. "But it was time to move anyway. There were a lot of tough memories there to deal with."

Since she didn't mention a mother, I assumed that either her mom had died or her parents had gotten divorced and Maisie didn't see her anymore.

"Frontier isn't so bad," I said. "Typical small town. Everyone knows everyone…"

Maisie was chewing on her fingernail. Her nail polish had chipped, and it looked like a little girl had applied it. She wasn't paying attention. I figured she was thinking about her mom. Someday I hoped to share with her all that I'd been going through with mine too.

"You have a lot of freckles," Kevin said out of nowhere.

"Yeah? So?" she said, but I could see that she was self-conscious about it, so I kicked Kevin under the table again.

"That time I saw it was you that kicked me, Miles!"

Maisie was off in another world as she spoke. "I was once told that each freckle was an angel's blessing and so many angels wanted to bless me that before long my whole face was covered with them."

Kevin burst out laughing as milk leaked from his nose.

"Seriously, Kevin, were you raised by wolves?" Simon said, wiping the area between them with all of his napkins.

"It does sound kind of stupid," Maisie said as she started to laugh quietly. "I guess when you're little, you'll believe anything."

The bell rang as my heart sank. I wanted to stay at the table eating with Maisie for hours and hours. I was worried that I might not have the chance to do it again in this past timeline, but at least our meeting would've still occurred when I returned to the present, and I could pick up where I left off.

"I have Spanish next," Maisie grumbled. "*No me gusta.*"

"I normally have Spanish too," I said. "But I'm following Simon for the rest of the day to do a report on a family member."

She tossed her *Sherlock Holmes* book into her bag and picked up her empty tray.

"If I don't see you for the rest of the day, don't forget to say '*hola*' tomorrow in class."

"*Sí*," I responded, because that was the only other word I could remember.

"It was nice meeting you, boys," Maisie said with a wave and then fell into the crowd exiting through the cafeteria's front doors.

"Miles and Maisie sitting in a tree," Kevin began singing. "F-U-K-I-N-G."

Kevin snorted with laughter until Simon hit him on the back of his head.

"It's F-U-*C*-K-I-N-G," Simon hissed.

I ignored Simon and Kevin's squabble. I was still staring at the departing crowd and hoping to catch one more glimpse of Maisie. Finally, I spied her neon barrettes flashing against the cafeteria's fluorescent lights. It made me feel all warm and good inside, like my stomach was made up of the most delicious melted chocolate ever.

Chapter Fourteen

The rest of the day proved uneventful as far as getting more leads about Simon's murder. No one in any of my brother's other classes seemed suspicious. I even tried talking to Simon about Mr. Congley a few times, but it was impossible to distract him during classes. I figured I'd spend all day tomorrow snooping around Mr. Congley's classroom to see if I could get another look at any of the formulas he was writing.

Once school ended for the day and we headed out, I was sorry that I wouldn't get to hang out with Simon for longer. We'd spent more time together over the past day than we had in the last few years, and I had the urge to give him a dwarfing hug.

"I guess you need to go work on your Top-Secret project," I said, kicking at a pebble by the front steps.

"Yeah, I'm probably looking at an all-nighter," Simon said. "I feel like I'm so close to it being done, but there's this one thing I can't seem to figure out."

"How about having one of Dad's terrible meals before you start working? You need to eat, right? It's been a long time since we've hung out like this." I didn't want to look Simon in the eye. I was afraid that I might start crying. "Don't think we have since the days of Okoboji."

"Okoboji." Simon nodded, his grin getting wider.

"Yeah, King Simon and Prince Miles."

"And all of our loyal fish subjects." Simon lost his grin. "That was so long ago."

"Sure was," I said, kicking at another pebble. "I'm gonna get my bike and head home."

I started to walk away but Simon called out, "Hey, Prince Miles of Okoboji world?"

I turned around.

"Maybe I could stomach one of Dad's terrible meals really quickly before I delve into my night's work."

"Oh yeah?"

"Sure. C'mon, I biked to school today as well."

If Simon was willing to take a break to have dinner, I figured that he probably hadn't realized he was being followed yet. But very soon something would make him nervous and the killer would be close by, waiting to strike. I shivered at the thought.

As we walked over to our bikes in the alleyway, I spied Simon grinning.

"What?" I asked.

"You like this Maisie?"

"What, I dunno—I—I—"

"I didn't know you liked—"

"What?"

"Girls, or… I've just never heard you talk about it."

"I talk about it with Kevin. And yeah, I mean, I like girls…and guys. I dunno—it's like the person I notice, not their gender."

I waited for his reaction, my stomach doing flips. It was weird to hear me say it out loud to my brother, who I never got personal with, but it seemed right. Like we always should've been talking like this.

"Oh, okay," he said. "Yeah, whatever floats your boat."

I beamed. "Yeah! That's exactly how I see it. It doesn't have to be a big deal. People make everything such a big deal."

"People are morons, most of them. Don't listen to anyone who tells you how to be."

He gave my shoulder a squeeze.

"What about you?" I asked. "Anyone you...like, or love?"

His face dropped. "Love? Science doesn't support love."

We turned down the alleyway at the back of the school where the bikes were kept.

Jojo and the rest of his piece-of-shit gang were there smoking cigarettes. Upon seeing Simon, Jojo flicked his cigarette in our direction and pounded his fist into his palm.

"I'm gonna beat the diarrhea out of you," Jojo said.

At first, I thought Jojo was talking to me, having overheard me saying I liked girls and guys, which wouldn't have flown with a bully like him. Even though Jojo was a terrible person, I found myself noticing him all the time, wishing he would pay attention. I guess I was a masochist. But I wasn't Jojo's target, it was Simon.

Jojo's cronies book ended us. One of them, Rodney, had shaved his head. I couldn't stop staring at his misshapen scalp. The other one, Billy, was always scratching his elbows and sniffing the air.

"Look at the two lovebirds going off for a bike ride together," Rodney said while making kissing sounds.

"We're brothers, ignoramus," Simon said, walking right past them to get his bike.

"Whoa, hold on," Billy said, shoving Simon as he tried to pass. "Who said these bikes were yours?"

"The receipt from my dad's credit card bill says so," Simon said. "C'mon, Miles."

"Yeah, Miles, go and get your bike," Rodney said, pushing me into the wall. My tailbone hit up against the bricks.

"Tell us the combination to your bike locks and we'll think about not beating you up," Jojo said.

"I'm surprised you've been upright long enough to know how to bike," Simon muttered.

Jojo grabbed Simon by the collar and started shaking him.

"What was that, Four Eyes?"

Both of Jojo's cronies started cracking up, but Jojo didn't get the joke. He gummed his lips in confusion and then figured it was easier to throw Simon into the wall.

"Simon!" I yelled. I tried to jump to his rescue, but the cronies each grabbed one of my arms.

"Get up!" Jojo demanded. Simon's glasses had fallen off and he was reaching across the pavement to pick them up. Jojo stepped on his hand instead. "I bet a fookin' geek like you needs both of his hands to do all of your geeky science things." Jojo stepped down harder as Simon let out a cry. "Now give us the combinations so we can take your bikes before I break your wrist."

"Eat…dog piss," Simon struggled to say.

"You're going to *be* dog piss if we don't get these bikes."

I was about to give in and tell Jojo the combination to my lock when I saw a car coming toward us. As it got closer, I noticed the license plates said Oregon. The car parked in front of us and left its motor running. The driver's side window lowered. Jojo craned his neck to see if the car was worth his time. Maisie's dad leaned a heavy forearm out of the window.

"What going on here, fellas?" Maisie's dad said. His voice had a high pitch to it and a little bit of a Southern drawl, not as imposing as I'd hoped. His eyes blinked through his thick glasses like he had some type of tic. Maisie was in the back seat watching the scene play out.

"This doesn't concern you, old man," Jojo said, shooing him away.

"Oh, I believe it does," he carefully said. "My daughter says these are friends of hers."

"Yeah, her friends are about to get their asses kicked and you'll be next if you don't move on along."

"Good one, Jojo," Rodney said as he high-fived Billy.

Maisie's dad put the car in drive and inched it toward Rodney and Billy. When they saw he wasn't stopping, they let go of me and jumped out of the way, screaming. The car was now pointing directly at Jojo who was still stepping on Simon's wrist.

"You don't have the guts," Jojo said.

Maisie's dad revved the ignition. Tires screeched against the pavement. Even Simon looked scared.

"You'll kill him as well," Jojo said, pointing to Simon.

Maisie's dad put his foot on the gas and the car rolled toward Jojo, but Jojo still wasn't backing down. As the car got closer, Jojo's cronies yelled: "Watch out, Jojo!" Jojo took his foot off of Simon's hand and dove out of the way in time. Simon winced as the car stopped inches away from his face.

"You're cracked, old man," Jojo said. His followers helped him up.

"Now I have a gun in the glove compartment if you want to continue this dispute," Maisie's dad said and rested his hand on the glove compartment.

The cronies shook their heads and began to back away. When Jojo saw he had no one on his side anymore, he started backing away too.

"This ain't over," he said, pointing at Simon and then at Maisie's dad before he ran away too. I had to stop liking Jojo in that way, wondering what was wrong with me. Did I only like Jojo because of he was dangerous, drawn to him like a stupid moth?

I shook my head in disbelief over what happened. Maisie's dad won the gnarliest game of chicken I'd ever seen, and if it weren't for him, Simon and I would've been going home with busted lips and two fewer bikes.

"Are you okay?" Maisie asked, getting out of the car.

"Fine," Simon said, brushing himself off as he stood back up.

Maisie's dad stuck his head out of the window.

"You boys were lucky I was driving by. Those bullies come after you a lot?"

"They come after everyone," Maisie said.

"You have to fight fear with fear," her dad replied. "That's what I did right now. Sorry if I scared you."

"Yeah…" Simon said, cleaning his glasses that had become covered with gravel.

"Dad, this is Miles and Simon. They sat with me at lunch today when no one else would."

"Much obliged, Miles and Simon. I'm Smith Sumpter."

Smith extended a hand to me, and we shook. He tipped his head to Simon, who waved back.

"And what're your specialties, boys?"

"What do you mean?" I asked.

"Specialties…what you're good at…what you like to do. Maisie's a gifted artist. She draws better than I ever could."

"Miles is a detective and Simon is…" Maisie began to say and then looked at Simon to finish.

"I'm a scientist," Simon said proudly.

"A scientist?" Smith said, nodding. "You don't say? And a detective?" he continued, turning to me. "Maisie has certainly made very interesting friends."

Smith was smiling so wide that I could see a few of his back molars were made of gold.

"I don't have a gun in my glove compartment, so you know," he added. "Can I give you boys a lift?"

"We've got our bikes," Simon said, unlocking his bike and jumping on.

"To be a teenager again," Smith said, craning his head to look up at the sky. "Riding my bike around and having my whole life ahead of me. I'd love to be able to go back to that time somehow, even if just for a little bit."

"Dad played football at Ole Miss back in the day."

"Yup, until I tore all the cartilage in my knee. Let me tell you, boys, hold onto to these days for as long as you can."

He winked at me and then ducked his head back into the car.

"C'mon, Maisie." He whistled through his teeth.

"Thanks, you really saved us," I said to her.

"Glad we were passing by." She blushed, with her hands deep in her pockets.

Simon had already started pedaling away.

"Sorry my brother's so rude. He's really thankful. He probably just got embarrassed."

"*De nada*," she said and then giggled into her hand when I looked at her funny. "You're not a Spanish scholar, are you?"

"I guess I'm not a scholar at much."

"Maisie!" Her dad whistled again and motioned for her to come.

"I'm being beckoned. Bye, Miles."

We were close enough that I could smell the bubblegum she was chewing. It smelled good. Even though it was far from the perfect moment, I longed to move in for a kiss. Like I'd done at the movies over popcorn with Kaitlyn, like I'd done with Dave in the barn, wine coolers clinking between us, like I'd even thought about with Jojo. I felt my eyes close and my face inching toward hers before I realized what I was doing.

"Sorry," I said. "It's been a long day."

Maisie's dad revved up the engine as a sign that it was time to go. Maisie tucked a strand of blond hair around her ear and got into the car. Her window was foggy and she wrote *Adios* in the fog before the car took off down the alleyway and was gone.

Down the other end, Simon had already pedaled away. I unlocked my bike and took off to try to catch up with Simon. As I headed away from school, I whispered "*Adios*," over and over into the rushing wind.

Chapter Fifteen

By the time I caught up with Simon, we had almost reached our block. I could see our house in the distance as we pedaled side by side. Simon hadn't looked at me or attempted to say anything for the entire ride. I thought of his reaction back in the present time when Jojo bullied him in the cafeteria and that he wasn't too happy when I got Mr. Congley to help. Now he was chewing on his lip with the same pissed-off expression as before.

"Has Jojo and them ever come after you like that before?" I asked, fishing for any info that might prove Jojo or his cronies as the killer.

"Drop it because I don't want to talk about it."

Simon's abrupt response had to mean that there was more to the story. I'd wait till he cooled down and then press further. An important rule to being a detective was to step back when someone was clearly not ready to give any information and to question them again when they were primed to offer up some nuggets.

We turned onto our block filled with modest two-story houses, some with garages and some with cars parked on the street. People kept their front lawns trimmed and most of our neighbors had an American flag. Reed was sitting on the curb in front of his own house, looking up at the clouds. He shielded his eyes from the sun and waved in our direction.

"Hi, Miles!" he said and kept waving. "Hi, Simon," he said without nearly as much enthusiasm.

"What are you doing out here, Reed?" I asked as Simon parked his bike and headed into the house after giving a grumpy nod to Reed.

"N…othing," Reed said, shaking his head back and forth over and over until he got dizzy.

"Stay clear of Ms. Kissey's cat, you hear?"

Reed clamped his hands over his mouth and let out a squeal.

"I-I don't care about no cat," he said to me and then repeated it to himself.

"I know she lets the cat wander out into the street. You can go after it if it's in danger of getting hit by a car, but remember to give it back to Ms. Kissey."

Reed removed his hands from his mouth and gaped.

"How did…you know that?"

"I'm a detective, Reed," I said, proud to say that after a day of Maisie being impressed by my skills. "It's hard to pull a fast one on me."

Reed stood up with a shriek.

"Miles can read minds! Miles can read minds!" he cried and ran back into his house, flailing his arms.

I chuckled and headed into my house. Immediately I smelled something burning when I entered. Sure enough, Dad was in the kitchen with smoke billowing from behind him. It looked as if his oven/fridge invention was the cause.

"The fridge part works fine but the oven…" he said, removing a tray of charred sandwiches. "Probably shouldn't have attempted Monte Cristos. Here, Miles, start scraping."

Dad handed me a knife, and I set to work on salvaging the Monte Cristos.

"I saw your brother is home for dinner. That's a rare occurrence. And he was as rude to me as he ever was. He might be a genius but he's got some lip too. Well, I gave him what for."

I shrugged and kept scraping as a pile of ash started to collect on the countertop.

"Goddammit, Miles, into the garbage," Dad shouted, swiping the knife away.

I stepped back stunned. Dad had certainly yelled at me before, but never over something as trivial as crumbs on the table.

"I'm sorry, Miles. Mom has been a challenge since I got home. Ludmila said that something obviously upset her, but Ludmila's English is so poor I couldn't understand what. The whole upstairs is a mess, and then my FridgeOven is on the fritz again. I tell you when it rains…"

"It's okay, Dad. Do you want me to keep scraping?"

"Oh, I'll just call Pizza Pizzazz. Go get your brother and mom. You know how Pizza Pizzazz swears they can deliver in under ten minutes."

I marched up the stairs and passed by my parents' bedroom. Mom was lying in bed staring up at the ceiling, so I went to get Simon first. Simon's door was shut, and I knocked on the DON'T ENTER sign.

"Go away," he said.

"It's me. Dad is ordering from Pizza Pizzazz, we need to get Mom up."

"I don't have to do anything. I've wasted too much time today anyway."

"You said we were gonna have dinner together."

"Stop whining, Miles. You followed me all day, isn't that enough?"

"But I thought you had a good time—"

"It was distracting! You kept asking me a thousand questions when I should've been utilizing every spare minute for—"

"I didn't mean—"

The door swung open, and Simon stood there finishing up an angry text on his cell. He had a backpack slung over his shoulder, ready to leave. Something looked like it was moving around in the backpack. I saw that Stinkers wasn't in his cage and wondered if tonight Simon would figure out how to send his guinea pig back into the past.

"Where are you going?" I asked as Simon pinched the bridge of his nose in disgust.

"What part of *leave me alone* is too hard for your paltry brain to understand?"

He tried to push past me, but I stood in his way.

"What did I do to make you so angry with me?"

"You don't *do* anything, get it? You're like every other simplistic kid your age. And now I've wasted enough time today not *doing* anything either."

I was about to tell Simon what I was really capable of doing: that *I* was the one who traveled back in time and that *I* was the only person who could possibly save his life, but I bit my tongue to avoid spoiling the entire mission.

"I'm sorry I got in your way," I said. "And I'm sorry I'm such a pain. I…could've done my report on Dad, but I wanted to do it on you. I wanted to spend time with my brother, so sue me!"

"Don't you see? I don't have the time at this moment to be your brother. I don't have the time for anything except for my project. And right now, that time is running out more and more."

He fixed his backpack, so it hung on both of his shoulders and then started walking down the hall.

"Is this 'cause of what happened with Jojo?"

Simon turned around with an accusing finger in my face.

"For such a detective, you really have no clue about anything."

"So, it has nothing to do with Jojo?"

"I'm not entertaining this dialogue anymore. You are inferior intellectually, and talking with you is not going to help me finish my project any sooner. So, screw goddamn Jojo, screw your dumbass friend Kevin, screw your little girlfriend—Maisie, or whatever she is, coming into this town, and screw you!"

I'd never heard Simon yell like that at me before. If the situation was different and he wasn't about to die in less than a week, I would've tackled him to the floor. It took everything in me to restrain myself.

"You see that sign on my door?" Simon continued. "It's says, DON'T ENTER! Leave me alone if you know what's good for you."

Stinkers started carrying on, so Simon held the backpack close to his chest to calm the guinea pig down. He gave me a look that clearly said not to ask any more questions and then swiveled around and took off down the hall. I had no idea what prompted this change in him. The whole day we had gotten along better than we had in years, and I had to admit it was pretty wonderful. When Simon wasn't being such a Brainiac, he was actually a cool guy. Here we'd gone up against bullies and he'd been my wingman to help get a girl just like an older brother should do.

Either the encounter with Jojo and his cronies spooked him, or something happened with Dad while I was talking to Reed, or it had to do with whoever Simon was angrily texting on his cell when he opened the door, possibly this EL. For now, I'd have to let him walk away, rather than endanger the progress I'd made. But there was no way I'd leave him alone for the rest of the week, even if he wound up being sick of my face. The case of his death was starting to unravel as added culprits and motives began to fall into place.

It was only this morning when I woke up in the past. Even though Simon thought I wasn't a good detective, I *had* to believe that I was—otherwise I should give up hope that he'd have any chance of staying alive in the future.

Chapter Sixteen

Pizza Pizzazz delivered the pies like they promised in under ten minutes, but Simon had already left for his other secret lab. As much as I wanted to sneak out and follow him to its undisclosed location, I knew that Simon needed to create his time travel machine without anyone getting in his way, otherwise the whole mission would be for naught.

I got Mom up and led her downstairs, holding her hand carefully as I guided her toward the dining room table. Dad had taken out paper plates and was passing around the slices of pizza.

"Where's Simon?" he asked, pulling out a seat for Mom and making sure she was comfortable.

"He's gone."

"Simon's always working. Nothing stops him," Dad replied, but I couldn't tell if he was angry or proud. He picked up a piece of oily pizza and took a bite as the cheese stretched out. "He ever talk to you about what he's working on?"

"Uhh...I have no idea."

"You'd think having an inventor for a dad would make him want to bounce some ideas off me."

"He hasn't told you anything?"

"You know Simon, always mum."

He took another bite of pizza, the cheese stretching out even more.

"What do you think it might be?" I asked. I had no clue if Dad had any idea about what Simon was working on and what it might mean if he did.

Mom looked at Dad as if she was waiting for him to reveal what he knew as well, but he took another bite of pizza and kept silent.

"I don't want to upset your mother," he said and then wolfed down the rest of his slice.

"It is *TIME*..." Mom yelped, and both Dad and I nearly spit out our food at her response. We waited patiently for her to continue, but she only let out a burp instead. Her lips twisted around, trying to force the rest of the sentence out, but she was unable to say any more. A solitary tear slinked down her cheek.

"Mom, why did you say 'it is time'?" I asked, raising my voice. I didn't think it was possible that she might know something about Simon's time machine, but maybe she had discovered something when no one was looking.

"Miles, don't upset your mother," Dad snapped. He was stroking her hand and shushing her. She trembled from his touch. "She means that it's time for her pills; I had forgotten."

Dad pushed his chair into the table and disappeared out of the room. Mom gave me a terrified glance and under her breath whispered, "Help me."

She reached for my hand and looped our fingers

together. Her touch was colder than ever, like I was touching the dead.

"Help you with what?" I whispered, glancing toward the dining room entrance to make sure that Dad wasn't close by. "Mom, help you with what?"

Her lips parted as she struggled to finish her thought. She clenched my hand and dug her nails into my palm.

"Help me," she said again, this time louder than a whisper. Another tear rushed down her cheek. I had no idea what she meant. She could be referring to her state in general, or it could have to do with the various pills that Dad had been feeding her all these years. I had a scary thought that the pills could be what were keeping her in this state, although I couldn't figure out why Dad would want to do that. I'd have to find her stash and check the prescriptions to see if she was actually being drugged with something dangerous. I felt guilty for even thinking this. Dad was a strange dude but never psychotic. Still, a good detective always must look into any lead they conjure up.

"Help you with what?" I tried asking again, this time whispering in her ear. My face was so close to hers. Her breath smelled foul from years of being unable to brush her teeth on her own. "Please, Mom?" I said, begging her to tell me more, but then Dad walked out with a fistful of pills and sat back down at the table. Mom removed her hand from my grasp and sat rigid in her chair. Dad looked over at Mom, who'd become much more upset since he left the table.

"She's crying, Miles. What did you say to her?"

He blotted her face with a napkin from Pizza Pizzazz.

"Nothing, I just wanted her to talk to me."

Dad pushed his glasses up his nose. He looked tired, like the world had beaten him up and he'd decided to give in. He brushed back Mom's hair since it was clinging to her sweaty face and planted a hesitant kiss next to her dry lips. Then he took a deep breath as he pried open her mouth and began to place each multicolored pill on her tongue.

"Good girl, good girl," he sang, sounding like he was serenading her with a lullaby.

"I love you, Mom," I said, stroking her hand again as Dad tipped back her head and massaged her throat as each pill struggled to go down.

———

It took about half an hour for Dad to get Mom to take all of her pills. Then he led her up the staircase. I stayed at the dining room table, nibbling on what remained of the pizza. When Dad came back down, he went toward the basement like he usually did to work on his inventions until all hours of the night.

"What are you working on now, Dad?"

He looked at me, confused. I rarely asked him about his inventions since all of them had been failures so far. He also barely made an effort to involve himself in my life so I figured that it wasn't worth my time to make an effort either.

"Why do you want to know?" he asked, suspicious.

"Just curious," I replied. I attempted a smile. "Can I see?"

Dad shrugged his shoulders and motioned for me to come downstairs to the basement. I wiped the crumbs off my hands and followed. Of course, I couldn't care less about whatever he was working on, but I wanted to question him more about Simon and Mom's pills as well. For now, Simon was the more pressing matter.

I hadn't been down to the basement in a long time and the sight of it was shocking at first. Piles and piles of frayed and yellowing papers created a lone pathway to his desk. Various half-finished inventions took up the rest of the space: objects that wouldn't have been out of place in some weird modern art exhibit. A toilet bowl with a mechanical seat had been left to rot on one side while something that looked like a mini heli-copter with a bunch of attached utensils had been flung to the other.

"Sorry about the mess," Dad said, scratching his head. "This is my new would-be masterpiece."

He seemed downright giddy. He displayed what looked like a lipstick case with a gleam in his eyes like it was going to change the world.

"What is it?"

He rubbed his hands together as I took off the cap.

"It's a butter stick!"

"Oh. Sure. Cool," I said, even though the butter smelled a little rancid.

"For someone to take with them on the go! Some-times you just want butter for your bread, but there's no butter around, right? I'm going to make ones with ranch dressing, ketchup, mayo, mustard, etc. It's limitless."

"That's really great, Dad."

I had to plaster a smile on my face to pretend I was interested.

"This is gonna be the one that'll make me famous," Dad said. "I can feel it. But keep hush-hush about it. No telling who might be looking to steal my idea."

I handed back the butter stick. "I really thought Simon was going to eat with us tonight," I said as if the thought had just occurred to me.

"What? Oh yeah, well, you know your brother and how he slaves over his project."

"Yeah, I wish I knew what the mystery was. Seems like he's been working on it forever."

"To be a fly on the wall in Simon's lab…"

"Any guesses as to what it might be?"

Dad looked at me carefully.

"What's with the concern about your brother all of a sudden? You two barely say a word to one another."

"Simon's so smart, I think he must be doing something really amazing—"

"He's not the only genius in this family," Dad said, pursing his lips. "I mean, is he making a butter stick?"

"No—"

"I was like him as a kid. A loner. Always tooling on secret projects. Reinventing the wheel. All of his smarts he got from me, you know?"

"I'm sure he did, Dad."

"But does Simon ever acknowledge what I'm working on?" he suddenly shouted, his face becoming flush with sweat. "I've done *everything* for that kid. Drove him to all his science fairs. Worked hard to put food on the table. And do I ever get a 'thanks'?"

"I think that's Simon's way—"

"We should be revolutionizing science together!" he yelled, shaking a fist. "With minds like ours? We'd be a father and son team for the ages!"

"Have you ever talked to him about it?"

"*Don't enter*, that's Simon's motto," he grunted.

"Keeping us in the dark. We'll see if I tell him about my butter stick."

In a fit of rage, he knocked a stack of papers off of the desk.

"Goddammit," he said, exasperated. "I had a system with those papers. Now they're all out of whack."

"I could help more with Mom?" I asked.

He looked at me as if I'd sprouted two heads.

"Your mother…what does your mother have to do with anything?"

"Her pills, for example. I could feed them to her if you tell me where you keep them."

"No need," he replied, brushing me off.

"So you'd have more time to work on your…butter sticks."

"Miles, I said there was no need!"

Dad had bent down to collect all of the scattered papers. I had no idea why he was being so cagey when I was only offering to help.

"What is…wrong with Mom exactly?"

He took off his glasses to rub the bridge of his nose, his eyes brimming with tears.

"Miles, you're too young—"

"To understand? I know, you say that all the time."

"Because it's true!"

He stuck his nose up against one of the papers, scrutinizing what he had written.

"Dammit, I had a system before, this is going to take hours of reorganization."

I opened my mouth to ask about Mom again, but then I figured it'd be smarter to spy on him the next time he went to get Mom's pills. There was definitely something he was keeping from me.

"Why don't you go…do your homework or something," he said, shooing me away.

"I…really like your new invention, Dad," I said as I backed up toward the stairs, but he wasn't listening anymore. He was muttering to himself as he tried to sort all of his fallen papers.

I left the basement, even more suspicious of him than when I first came down.

Chapter Seventeen

After a full day of working on the case, I got the idea to make a list of anyone who might be related to Simon's future murder. Seeing all the names and clues written down might help me figure out who to trail next. In the pit of my stomach, I was more excited than ever as I sat at my desk with a pen and paper in hand. At first, I thought to write it all down in Okoboji language, but then I figured I'd find a secure hiding spot away from any snooping eyes. I'd start with the most likely suspects and continue all the way down to anyone else in Simon's life, even if they didn't seem like a suspect yet.

Detective Hardy's BIG CASE

Suspects/Motives:

1. Mr. Congley – Working on a secret project that looked really similar to Simon's mechanical glove time machine. Possible

motives for killing Simon would be that
Congley wanted to invent the time machine
first to get all of the glory.

2. Brainiacs – Ellery, Linda and Quentin.
Possible motives are moving up in the
rankings to be the Number #1 student at
Jeremiah Boonton with Simon out of the
picture.

3. Jojo and his Asshole Cronies – Hate Simon
and wanted to beat him up. Possible other
motives are uncertain.

4. Dad – An inventor just like Simon and a bit
strange. Possible motives are jealousy since
all of Dad's inventions are failures?

5. Mom – No possible motives but maybe she
knows something and is unable to say
anything due to her condition, (or that she's
being drugged by Dad all these years!!!)

6. Kevin – He and Simon never got along. No
real possible motives except that he doesn't
like Simon.

7. Maisie and her Dad – Her dad saved
Simon and I from Jojo, and they're new in
town. Possible motives are none that I can
think of.

8. Reed and his mom Annalee – Possible
motives none, but Simon didn't
acknowledge Reed when we saw him on
the curb. Unresolved issues between them?

9. Ludmila – Stays with Mom during the day,
but haven't run into her in the past yet so
no motives I could think of. Still, she'd have
close access to Simon's room with no one
else around.

10. EL – When I unlocked the passcode for Simon's cell, he had been texting with someone named EL over and over. Could this be the same person Simon was angrily texting with earlier tonight? And was it a friend or a foe?

11. Anyone else – If Simon's speculations were right, his murder might have been caused by the government or some shady corporation. Possible motives would be that the government wanted to keep the time machine under wraps, or that some shady corporation had been inventing their own time machine and wanted to eliminate the competition.

I tried to think of any other suspects. No one else stood out. The next list I made regarded any details and clues that I'd encountered since the beginning of my investigation.

Detective Hardy's BIG CASE cont'd

Details/Clues/Things to Remember:

1. "It...happened...again." – Mom said this over and over when she saw Simon's body. What could she possibly be referring to?

2. Who was helping Simon build the time machine? Since there was no way Simon could afford all of the equipment in his lab, who else had been funding his invention?

3. Keep taking the side effects pills to avoid nosebleeds and come up with a monologue for my fake Drama class that shows a day in the life of Simon.
4. Keep reading *The Dos and Don'ts of Time Travel* to make sure I didn't fuck anything else up.

I decided to leave the rest of the page blank until more details and clues began to emerge. I opened my desk drawer and got out *The Dos and Don'ts of Time Travel* to see if the book offered up any ideas that might help the case. I flipped through the remaining chapters. The Third Rule stated that *You Can't Change the Past on a Grand Scale Otherwise the Future May be Very Different*. The Fourth Rule specified that *You Can't Use the Time Machine For Your Own Personal Monetary Gain*, while the Fifth Rule instructed that *You May Not Stay in the Past Forever and Must Return to Present Time*. The writing in the chapters had too much scientific jargon to follow so I tossed the book back in my desk since it wasn't offering any help with how to solve Simon's future murder.

I picked up the sheet I'd created with all the suspects and figured I needed to find a good place to hide it. I looked around my room, but assumed it'd be too dangerous to leave in this house. The best bet would be to plant it in Simon's lab, where only I knew the passcode.

"Oh, crap on my shoe!" I said, pounding a fist into my desk. I'd completely forgotten about leaving my past self in Simon's panic room over fifteen hours ago! Even though I made sure that there was enough food and water in reach, my past self must be completely freaking out and hopefully hadn't harmed himself.

I folded up the paper with the suspects and clues and shoved it in my pocket before dashing out of my room and hopping on my bike to head to Simon's lab muttering, "crap, crap, crappity, crap, crap," over and over until the rancid smell of Generator Street wafted into my nostrils. I pedaled over broken bottles and mushed rats toward the barn in the distance, praying that nothing had happened to my past self during the many hours I was gone.

If the unthinkable occurred and my past self wound up dying, I wondered if I would disappear, never to exist again at any point in time.

Chapter Eighteen

I held my breath as I descended the trapdoor in the hayloft, too nervous to breathe. When I reached the lab, I didn't hear any noise coming from the panic room. "Hey," I said, knocking on the heavy door. "Are you okay?"

There was no response. A thousand different scenarios rushed through my head. What if I'd given my past self too big a dosage of white pills? He could be starving and dehydrated after being knocked out for fifteen hours? Or what if he had woken up unable to see anything due to the electronic eye mask and freaked out? Was it possible for a fourteen-year-old to have a heart attack? I tried to think what I would do if I was in that situation. I'd definitely be scared and probably angry, but I didn't know exactly how I'd react since I had never been drugged and kidnapped before.

"I'm coming in," I yelled through the metallic door. "I want to make sure you're okay. I don't want to hurt you."

There was still no answer.

"I promise you there's an explanation for why you're here. I just can't give it now. Do you have enough food? It's all around you. There are bottles with water and soda too. Just tell me you're okay."

After not hearing a peep, I decided to go in. I flicked the switch on and off five times slowly as the bookshelves parted. At first glance, I didn't see my past self in the center of the room where I'd left him.

"AARRGGGGHHHHHH!"

I was knocked to the floor as the yelling continued. My past self had hidden behind the door waiting to attack. Now he was pinning me down with a broken glass bottle pressed into my neck.

"What's going on? Who the hell are you?" he cried. "I'll cut you. I swear I will."

It was obvious that he had been crying for a while. His face was beet red. The broken bottle was shaking in his hands. I tried to think if I'd actually cut someone had I been in his situation. I figured that I probably would.

"I said I don't want to hurt you."

"Then what do you want with me? Where am I? Why can't I see anything?"

The glass bottle sliced at my neck. A drop of blood trickled down my chest.

"Please don't cut me," I begged.

"Take this thing off of my eyes!"

"I-I can't."

"Why is your voice so familiar?" he asked. "Who are you?"

"I'm no one. Just stop asking questions."

My past self started crying again.

"The last thing I remember was going to bed.

Then I woke up thinking I'd gone blind. But this isn't my bedroom. I'm in some basement; it smells damp here. The door wouldn't open. How long have I been here?"

"Since this morning."

"Tell me why you've done this!"

He pressed the broken bottle into my neck.

"Don't cut me, just don't cut me."

"Then take this thing off my eyes! It feels like it's glued on."

I remembered the Second Rule from *The Dos and Don'ts of Time Travel*. Under no circumstance should my past self see me.

"I'll slice you," he blubbered. "I really will. I'll slit your throat. Now take this mask off of me!"

"Okay, okay."

I knew I had no choice, so I entered Einstein's birthday into the tiny keypad on the side of the eye mask.

"Promise me you'll stay calm."

He clutched the broken bottle, ready to attack.

The eye mask de-suctioned and fell to the ground. He blinked a few times, adjusting his eyes before he recognized me and let out a chilling scream. I screamed back in response and our screams echoed throughout the panic room before his eyes rolled up into his skull and he passed out on top of me.

I caught my breath and carefully rolled him off. I reattached the mechanical eye mask to his face and removed all the glass bottles from the room. I had no clue what my next step should be as I left the panic room and closed the door. I'd have to wait till my past self came to. There was a chance he might've forgotten that he was looking directly at himself when the eye mask had been removed. There was a chance that he wouldn't think that it had to do with Simon's secret time machine.

But I knew that was a long shot.

For my past self was as good a detective as me.

Chapter Nineteen

"Are you there? Did you leave me?"

I'd drifted off to sleep when I heard shouting coming from the panic room. I woke up, uncertain where I was and when it was. Simon's lab began to take shape. A string of drool connected me to the cot Simon had set up in the corner. I glanced at the clock and saw it was the middle of the night. A loud knocking came from the panic room, sounding like my past self was hurtling himself into the door.

"Why do you look like me?" he yelled. It was muffled due to the thickness of the bookshelves. "I'll hurt myself," he continued. "I'll run into the wall head-first over and over."

A banging noise came from the panic room. It sounded like he was staying true to his word. I got up off the cot and rushed to the bookshelves.

"No! Don't do that."

He didn't respond.

"What happened?" I asked. "What did you do? Are you hurt?"

Silence.

"I won't fall for the same trick twice," I said. "If I open up the door and you attack me again, I'll tie you up the next time. There's no way of getting out of this place without the passcode. Understand?"

I still didn't hear anything, so I flicked the switch on and off five times as the bookshelves parted. I could see my past self on the floor, holding his head.

"Oh crap. What did you do?"

A small amount of blood was visible on his forehead. I left the panic room and searched around the lab until I found a first-aid kit. I got out some rubbing alcohol and a bandage and went back into the panic room.

"I saw you," he moaned as I applied the bandage. "You were me. You *are* me."

"No, you're hallucinating right now from banging your head."

"You sound so much like I do. Like the way my voice sounds when it's being recorded. Does this all have something to do with my brother…Simon?"

"Stop asking questions."

"I'll do it again. Bang my head. Even harder the next time. Until you give me some answers."

"I know you will," I replied, realizing how stubborn I could be. I finished up with the bandage.

"It's his time machine, isn't it?" my past self murmured. I froze in place as he smirked. I was smarter than I gave myself credit for. "Got nothing to say about that, huh?"

"I don't know what you're talking about," I said, my voice raising a few octaves.

"You're lying. My voice does the same thing when I'm lying. It gets all high and squeaky."

He sat up and felt around until he rested his hands on my shoulders.

"Simon did it, didn't he?"

A huge grin stretched across his face.

"I always knew he was a genius, but I never thought…Wow! So how far in the future are you from? It can't be too far since we look so much alike. You might as well take the eye mask off of me, right? I mean what else is there to hide?"

He was right. There was no point in keeping anything from him now that he figured it all out. Also, the world hadn't exploded when we saw each other so I keyed in Einstein's birthday and removed the electronic eye mask.

"So fucking cool," he said, staring back at me in awe.

"You're not gonna think it's so cool when you find out why I've come back in time."

"Why? What happened?"

It seemed as if I'd walked in Simon's room months ago, even though it was only a few days. I stayed silent, just to give my past self a few more moments of having an older brother. But then I took a deep breath to reveal the terrible truth.

"Simon dies."

———

After confessing what the future held, I watched my past self go through the same stages of grief that I remembered doing. First, he denied it, then he was angry, then he was super depressed and cried, and finally he accepted the news. He wiped away all of his tears and stared at me more determined than ever.

"There's only one thing to do," he said.

"What's that?"

"We team up."

"What do you mean?"

"I'm a detective and you're a detective. What could be better than having two detectives working on the case?"

I had to admit it was a brilliant idea. While I'd made a lot of progress over the last day, it was starting to feel overwhelming due to the alarming number of possible suspects.

"I'll stay in Simon's lab while you follow any leads," he said. "At the end of the day we could go over all of your findings together."

"I was thinking the same thing."

"Of course you were." He laughed, but then he lost his smile again. "Did you see Simon after he…?" He ran a finger under his runny nose.

"You mean once he'd been killed?" A shiver crawled up my spine. My past self nodded. "Do you really want to know what it was like?"

"Only if it could help the case."

I cleared my throat.

"Someone shot half his face off."

"Oh man…Simon. Was it all worth it? I mean… everything he sacrificed all these years, just to wind up dead?"

"I think he'd tell you it was worth it. The time machine was his life and without it he might as well be…"

"Dead?"

"Yeah."

"How could this happen in Frontier of all places? The biggest crime here last week was a missing cat."

"I know, but it has happened. And this is that Big Case you've been waiting for…I've been waiting for…I mean…we've been waiting for. You know what I mean."

"It's bonkers having a conversation with yourself, isn't it? You sure this isn't some wild dream?" He rubbed his palms into his tired eyes. "Who could do this to him? Shoot his face off, make it look like a suicide? We're dealing with some kind of monster."

"Tell me about it. Hold on, I got something to show you."

I left the panic room and brought back the sheet of paper with all of the suspects and possible clues.

"Maisie?" my past self questioned upon seeing her name. "You talked to that girl Maisie?"

I was surprised that her name was the one who stood out to him, but then I remembered how much she'd been on my mind the week of Simon's death.

"We had lunch together, but it's not like I think she's a suspect or anything. I wrote down everyone Simon came into contact with yesterday."

"I'm very impressed, future self," he said. "What's she like?"

I felt the blood rise to my face.

"Great. Real great, smart. And…nice. Real nice."

"Snag a kiss yet? Ha! Who ever heard of being jealous of yourself?"

I let out a laugh under my breath.

"But I can't let her distract me," I said. "I can get to know her better in the future and so can you. But for now, we need to focus on only one thing. Tomorrow I'm going to trail Mr. Congley. Right now, I think he's the biggest suspect."

"You said he was working on papers that had a similar design to Simon's time machine?"

"I only got a quick glimpse, but it looked too similar to be anything else."

"So, what's the plan?"

"Simon is pissed at me right now. Big surprise. He probably won't let me go with him to Congley's Physics class again. I was going to try to snoop around Congley's desk when he wasn't around and even go to his home. Maybe he left a door unlocked or a window partially open?"

"This could be really dangerous. I mean really, really dangerous."

"I have to go through every suspect. We only have until the end of the week before…"

"Oh, it happens that soon?" my past self said, getting teary again. The bandage began to peel off his forehead.

"I'm sorry I drugged and kidnapped you."

I pressed his bandage back down.

"It's cool. Just promise me we'll stop whoever did this to Simon."

"You got it."

"The Hardy Boys," he said.

"What's that?"

"You and me, we really are The Hardy Boys, right? There was never a mystery in those books that those guys weren't able to solve."

He nodded over and over until I began to nod as well. With two minds at work, I figured we should be able to discover Simon's murderer. But now I couldn't stop thinking about all the dangerous possibilities that we'd be up against. If someone shot off half of

Simon's face, there was no telling what awful things they might do to me…or to my *other* me.

I blinked and imagined someone coming toward me with a gun in a dark alley. Missing cats sure never had the added element of death.

Chapter Twenty

I'd stayed up all night talking to my past self about the case. He eventually passed out, but despite how tired I was I had a long day of work ahead of me so I got on my bike to head to school. On the way, I passed by Ludmila's house. From outside, I could hear loud Czech music rocking the foundations so I parked my bike up against a tree and crept toward her window. Ludmila was certainly an odd duck all right. This two-hundred-pound freight train of a woman was dancing in a nightgown in her living room at six in the morning and singing in her native tongue. I'd never been to Ludmila's house before. The décor was old-timey: dusty furniture and she had one of those ancient record players, I think was called a phonograph. The window was open a crack, so I pried it further and leaned closer to get a better look. Sure enough, my uncoordinated ass thunked against the glass causing Ludmila to glare in my direction with her mouth shaped into an umbrella frown.

"My-yells?" I heard her say in her thick accent.

I slumped down and thought about darting away, but Ludmila was quick and already at the front door, motioning for me to come inside. "What you do here?"

"Just passing by and heard your music," I said. "I'll be on my way."

I headed toward my bike, but she motioned for me to come inside with her massive arm. The door stayed open as she stepped back into the shadows and turned off her music. I followed her in and closed the door.

Instantly, I was hit with the overpowering smell of goulash and spied the kitchen where a big pot was boiling with orange bubbles spilling out.

"I make for Mama," she said, proud and thumped her chest. "Maybe she eat it today."

"Oh yeah, Mom definitely has a hard time with food," I said. This was probably the longest conversation I'd ever had with Ludmila, since we were never at my home at the same time. I stared at her face, which had lines and wrinkles all over like a map. Her hair circled around her head, frozen with spray. The nightgown she wore was full of roses.

"Come, I give you breakfast."

We went into her kitchen which had a small table with two chairs. A pot of coffee sat in the center. She poured me a cup. I thought she was gonna offer me the sock-smelling goulash, but she got out a bowl and filled it with Frosted Mini-Wheats and milk instead.

"Cool, thanks, Ludmila."

I was starving and shoveled spoonfuls into my mouth.

"How are you and you brother?" Ludmila asked, lighting a long cigarette. The smoke danced in the morning sunlight.

"My brother?" I asked, almost choking on the Mini-Wheats. "Why do you want to know?"

She shrugged her shoulders, her mouth still an umbrella pattern. "I work for family for two years. I see sadness."

"With Simon?"

She spat out a curl of smoke. "Boy has no friends, no girl he likes either. At least you have red-headed friend."

"Simon is very busy," I said, as if I was his defense lawyer.

"Bah. No good. Teenager should be going out, having fun. Not cooped up where he goes all the time."

One of my eyebrows rose.

"How do you know where he goes?"

"It small town, you know. I see things. He go to bad area."

I didn't know if she was referring to the abandoned barn off Generator Street or Simon's other hidden location that even I didn't know about.

"What area?"

"Place for druggies," she said, taking one last suck and crushing the cigarette in a ballerina ashtray. "I concerned Simon be on drugs. So, I follow."

"What did you see?" I asked, gulping down what felt like a chestnut in my throat.

Ludmila pointed at me and shook her finger.

"Brother has secrets, doesn't he?"

Ludmila got up to turn the oven off. The orange bubbles stopped teeming from the pot. Her thick arm stirred the sauce.

"In my country, boys do not have no secrets. We tell parents everything. Secrets no good."

"Have you talked to my dad about this?"

"Me and you dad only speak about Mama, that's it. So, no. I keep brother's secret."

Beads of sweat built on my forehead. "And do you know what Simon's secret is?"

Ludmila shrugged her shoulders again.

"Long as it is not drugs, it not Ludmila's business."

I let out a long sigh, loud enough for Ludmila to turn toward me. She cocked her head to the side.

"Such, such sadness," she said, wiping her hands off on her dishtowel and sitting next to me. She spread out her arm and I flinched, so spooked by everything that occurred in these last few days, unable to really trust anyone anymore.

"Come, come," she said, directing me into her arms. "I know life is hard. Rest your head."

Her large bosom seemed inviting so I placed my head against it as her strong arms wrapped around. I realized I hadn't been hugged like this in a long time by either of my parents: Dad too preoccupied, Mom too out of it. I felt the tears leaking from my eyes as Ludmila sang to me in Czech. While I couldn't understand the words, they were soothing, and I let myself cry like a baby, wiping my nose against her rose nightgown.

"Mama gonna be all right one day in the future," Ludmila sang, as if it was a lullaby. "Ludmila promise this. Mama gonna be okay one day, and Simon too, and you as well, my My-yells."

She took my face in her hands and wiped away my tears with her thumbs.

"You good boy," she said. "And good boys find happiness in the end."

"Sometimes it's hard to believe that," I sniffled.

"No, no, no, Ludmila knows this. Trust in Ludmila. Let me see smile."

I gave her a dopey smile that actually seemed to uplift my spirits.

"Come now," she said, taking me by the hand and directing me out of the kitchen. "You need school. You have big day ahead."

She opened the door as a gust of cool air blew inside, the sun a red ball rising from the east.

"Look at sun," she said. "Sun comes up, no matter how bad the day may seem. Sun comes up anyway."

Its warmth tickled my face as it continued to rise, blinding me slightly. I shut my eyes. When I opened them, Ludmila had retreated back into her house, a beautiful oracle who'd given me the strength to continue my fight for justice.

I got on my bike and pedaled toward the welcoming sun as if it held all the answers I sought.

Chapter Twenty-One

When I reached school, I'd already forgotten how super groggy I'd been, which was good since I had no time to grab any winks. I knew I had to call the school and pretend to be my dad so I could say I was out sick, probably for the next few days. If a teacher happened to see me, I'd lie and say I felt better, so I decided to come in.

Before the first bell rang, I tried to wait for Simon by my locker but he never showed. I imagined that he had spent all night working on the time machine to send Stinkers back into the past and might've skipped first period for the first time in his life.

After the bell rang, I headed over to Mr. Congley's classroom. Luckily enough it was empty and the lights hadn't been turned on. I got the idea to crawl into one of the lower cabinets and wait for Congley to come in. Hopefully, he'd leave his papers unattended or possibly a spare key that opened his desk.

I wedged myself in between some Bunsen burners

and beakers. A faint whiff of a chemical substance filled up the cramped space, but I covered my nose with my hand. A while later, the bell rang and everyone started rushing through the hallways. I kept the cabinet door open a crack so I could see what was going on.

Mr. Congley walked in looking like he'd escaped from a mental institution. What little hair he had left stood on end. The beginnings of an unruly gray beard prickled around his jawline. He was hunched over and seemed like he was badly in need of a chiropractor. Dark rings had surfaced around his eyes, and he had the shakes pretty bad. He put a briefcase down on his desk that was too far away for me to grab.

The students began to come into class and soon Simon walked in as well. This wasn't the angry, bitter, or stressed-out Simon from yesterday. This Simon moseyed into the classroom as if all eyes should be on him. Since he was the type of guy who rarely smiled, the grin on his face had to mean that he was able to send Stinkers into the past.

Mr. Congley opened his briefcase with some kind of complicated numerical code, but I was too far away to see. He took out a few of his papers and started his lesson. I let my eyes close and drifted off to sleep.

I woke to the sound of the bell ringing. People were rushing past my nose. I noticed the Brainiacs all clumped together making their way to the door. Ellery and Linda were having a debate about some physics equation, but Quentin, the freakiest member of the bunch, looked like he was staring right at me. I had only left the cabinet open the tiniest crack so I couldn't imagine how he noticed me, but then he put a finger to his lips, telling me to remain quiet.

"C'mon, Quentin," Ellery said before he tugged Quentin away.

I wondered why Quentin didn't say anything about seeing me, but I couldn't worry about any of the Brainiacs right now since Mr. Congley was today's target. Tomorrow I'd go after Quentin and the rest of them.

"Stay for a moment, Si," I heard Mr. Congley say, as the rest of the students left the classroom and Simon hung around Mr. Congley's desk. They began talking in hushed tones. Finally, Simon handed Mr. Congley a piece of paper. Mr. Congley said the word "Omni" in response, but that was all I could make out. I had no idea the significance of the word besides that it meant "all." The discussion ended quickly and soon Simon headed for the door.

"Lock it from the inside for me," Mr. Congley said as Simon locked the door and left.

Mr. Congley eased over to the classroom door, peered outside, and shut the blinds. Immediately after doing so, his eyes widened. He rubbed his hands together and scooted back over to the desk, where he opened his briefcase. He got out a pen and started scribbling on a stack of papers at a furious pace. I watched for what felt like hours as he kept writing, only stopping to stroke the hairs on his chin in delight.

Since I couldn't see what he was writing, I shifted to get a better look and caused one of the beakers to fall over and break. The harsh crash caused Congley to shoot up from his papers. His tiny head jerked around like a turtle's, scrutinizing each corner of the room. He ran a tongue across his crooked teeth and then picked up the phone on his desk.

"Uh…yes, Principal Mynad, this is Mr. Congley. I

have an emergency and will need to cancel classes for the rest of the day. No, I'm fine, it is an…aunt that has unfortunately taken a turn for the worse. Thank you for your kind words, sir."

He hung up the phone and angled his ear toward where I was hiding, listening for the tiniest stir. I covered my mouth so my heavy breaths couldn't be heard, but the sound of my heartbeat still echoed throughout the cabinet. Mr. Congley's ear twitched as if he was able to pick up this alien entity that had infiltrated his classroom. He leaped to his feet and took a sniff of the air, his long legs marching up and down the aisles between the science tables.

As he neared my hiding place, I almost lost control of my bladder. I felt dizzy enough to pass out and didn't know if it was still due to the lingering effects of time traveling or if the fear gripping my throat was the cause. Congley stood right in front of the cabinet. I stared at his chicken legs that barely filled out his baggy khakis. He bent down and reached toward the cabinet. I figured it was all over. He'd find and inevitably torture me. He'd use counterterrorist techniques to rip out my teeth until I gave up any information about the time travel machine. But I'd never say a word. If I was to die, my past self would still live on and that would be enough. While I wouldn't be able to explore the far reaches of the universe anymore, my past self would still have the chance. I reasoned that the sacrifice would be worth it.

Congley's knobby fingers gripped the handle on the cabinet as I grabbed a piece of broken glass ready to attack, but instead of opening the cabinet door, he closed it and left me in darkness. I caught my breath as I heard Congley faintly walking away and then the sound of the classroom door shutting. I waited a minute to make sure that he wasn't coming back and then opened the cabinet door. Congley had shut off the lights and had taken his briefcase.

My best bet now would be to follow him to his house and see if there was any evidence I could find there, since I knew that the sick aunt story had to be nothing but lies.

———

I stepped outside of the classroom, sore as hell after being cramped up in a cabinet for over an hour. As I was massaging my twisted neck, I ran right into Simon.

"What were you doing in there?" Simon asked.

"What...nothing," I replied, glancing down the hallway to see if Mr. Congley was anywhere to be seen. "What are *you* doing here, Simon?"

"I forgot to give Mr. Congley something else," he said, narrowing his eyes. "I've been working on an extra credit assignment."

I had no idea if he was telling the truth and if Omni had anything to do with his extra credit assignment. I was about to question him about what Omni might mean when my nose began leaking blood again. I wiped it away, but Simon had already seen.

"Your nose is bleeding this time..." he said, studying me with a scientist's gaze.

"I gotta go," I said, ducking past him.

"What are you up to?" Simon asked under his breath.

I was getting sloppy, and Simon was becoming suspicious. I could feel his gaze boring into my back. It wouldn't be long before he might put two and two together and realize that my bloody noses were due to traveling through time.

I turned around and saw him bend down to the floor to study the drop of my blood between his fingers, like the detective in me would have done.

Chapter Twenty-Two

I ran out of school just as Mr. Congley's beat-up brown car drove away with a cloud of exhaust in its wake. I sprinted to the alleyway where I left my bike, hoping that Jojo and his cronies weren't waiting there to mess with me again. The alleyway was empty, so I jumped on my bike and tried to catch up with Mr. Congley's puttering sedan. As I turned off the main road leading to school, I couldn't see Mr. Congley, but then a stream of exhaust surfaced down an alternate street and I followed its dusty smoke.

Not knowing where he lived, I trailed the guy to the outskirts of town, not too far from Generator Street where Simon had his lab. The area was no better than around the abandoned barn. Dilapidated homes filled up the blocks. An occasional siren wailed in the distance. Mr. Congley parked his car on the street, some of the homes boarded up or looking like they were filled with squatters. He got out of his car, waved away the exhaust smoke, and scurried into his house with the briefcase.

I left my bike around the corner and made my way toward his house. While it wasn't as run-down as some of its neighboring homes, it was strange that a guy like Congley with a steady teacher's salary for over thirty years would choose to live in such squalor. In the house next door, I could hear a domestic fight brewing and the sound of a pot or a pan being thrown at a wall.

I crept up to his front door and slowly tried the doorknob, but it was locked. I went around to the back and saw a half-open window. I tried to look inside, but it was too high, so I grabbed an over-turned bucket and stepped on it to boost myself up. Through the window, I saw that no one was in the room, so I eased myself onto the ledge and slipped inside.

"Gross," I whispered, feeling my sneakers sink into the damp carpet as I stepped down. A black cat gazed at me with its yellow eyes while licking a paw and then took off.

The room looked to be Mr. Congley's study, complete with rows of books about physics and a few posters of Albert Einstein. Now I knew why he and Simon got along so well.

From outside the room, I could hear Mr. Congley muttering to himself. There was a chance that he could be coming inside, so I ducked into a closet that smelled of mothballs. I kept the door ajar just enough.

Mr. Congley walked in holding the black cat in one hand and his briefcase in the other. He placed the briefcase down on his desk and nuzzled with the cat as if it was a lover he hadn't seen in ages. Once their overlong love fest ended, he let the cat leap out of his arms. The cat immediately came up to the closet door with a hiss.

"Ulm," Mr. Congley chided. "What are you hissing at?"

Ulm swiped his paw in the direction of the closet. I swallowed carefully, the saliva struggling to go down.

"There's nothing there," Mr. Congley said. "Come, it's time to eat."

Ulm's yellow eyes remained fixed on me. He let out a long meow that clearly told Mr. Congley he wasn't budging.

"Such a curious creature all the time."

Mr. Congley picked up Ulm but then stood by the closet door as if he had changed his mind about what the cat might've been hissing at. I hid behind a bunch of coats and hoped it was too dark in the closet to be seen. Mr. Congley peered inside and I had no idea what I'd do if he took a chance and looked behind the coats. A million excuses ran through my brain, none of them believable.

Ulm hissed again at me and almost scratched Mr. Congley's arm.

"Ulm!" he said, dropping the cat to the floor. The cat landed and darted out of the room. "What has gotten into you?"

He took a step to leave the room but then looked again toward the closet door. I tried to stay as still as possible. I held my breath, refusing to make any kind of sound. Mr. Congley narrowed his eyes, but then shrugged his shoulders and shuffled out of the room. Finally, I allowed myself to breathe.

The closet door creaked as I opened it an inch. Mr. Congley was heading down the hallway toward the kitchen in pursuit of Ulm. He had left his briefcase on the desk. This was my chance to grab it and run, but it looked like it was one of those expensive titanium briefcases that I had only seen in movies. I knew it'd be pointless to take unless I was able to figure out the code.

I looked at the poster of Albert Einstein. The guy had rumpled hair and a bushy mustache. The date and place of his birth and death was at the bottom. Born–March 14th, 1879, Ulm. Died–April 18th, 1955, Princeton. Since Mr. Congley had named his cat Ulm, he clearly was as obsessed with Einstein as Simon, if not more. The numerical code on the briefcase was eight digits, just enough for Einstein's birthday like Simon had used as one of his passcodes. My fingers trembled as I figured I'd give it a shot, so I keyed in 03141879, praying for once that I could have a bit of luck on my side.

The briefcase snapped open!

"Holy shit," I said, a little too loud. Clamping my hand over my mouth, I opened up the case. Inside, I found a stack of papers. I listened outside of the door and could still hear Mr. Congley banging around the kitchen and muttering to Ulm. I flipped through the papers until I came across the picture of the mechanical glove that I had seen Mr. Congley with yesterday. It was clearly a detailed diagram of Simon's time machine. A million formulas were written under it that made no sense. I flipped through more papers until I came across a sheet with Simon's handwriting.

LE –
LLIW DEEN ENO TSAL DNUOR FO
SLAIRETAM MORF INMO:
OBRUT REGRAHC
ECAPS ELGNAD

RELLEPER YTICOLEV
NOISLUPORP RETACOL
ESAB ROTARELCCA
CIRTCELE SRETNUOM
THGILRATS SREDNILB
-IS

At first glance, the words didn't mean anything until I read them backward like Simon had used for most of his codes. I realized that "LE" had to be the "EL" that Simon was texting, which meant that Mr. Congley must've been working with Simon. I felt like an idiot for not figuring it out before. Mr. Congley's first name was Elton and EL was probably the nick-name Simon used.

I decoded the rest of the message to see what it was about.

El –
Will need one last round of materials from
Omni:
Turbo charger
Space dangle
Velocity repeller
Propulsion locater
Base accelerator
Electric mounters
Galactic MINERAL TRANSPORTER
STARLIGHT BLINDERS
-Si

I instantly felt bad for thinking that Mr. Congley had been the killer. He was probably the only one that Simon had confided in. It made sense now why his house was in such shambles. All of his money was going to the time machine and paying for materials from whoever this "Omni" was. The only thing that didn't make sense was why Simon hadn't told me that he and Mr. Congley were working together in his video message. Simon had said, "not to trust anyone" so maybe he had become suspicious of Congley?

For now, I had at least solved the mystery about EL.

I snapped the briefcase shut, the sound echoing through the room. Ulm dashed back into the room with a hiss.

"Crap," I said, shooing him away. The cat only began to hiss louder.

"Who's there?" Mr. Congley cried as I heard him shuffling back down the hallway.

I hoisted myself up on the window ledge and squeezed my way out.

"Ulm, what made that sound?" I heard Mr. Congley ask.

I fell to the ground outside, skinning my arm. I jumped to my feet and ran away. Halfway down the block, I turned around and saw Mr. Congley at the window holding Ulm in his arms before he pulled down his blinds with an angry snap.

Chapter Twenty-Three

I spent another sleepless night going over the details of the case with my past self. Both of us agreed that Congley was probably not the killer but we couldn't rule him out yet. My past self was very worried about Quentin, since he already fit the profile of a killer and had caught me hiding out in one of Mr. Congley's cabinets. We decided that the best bet would be to sit with the Brainiacs at lunch the next day and try to get them to offer up any clues that might link one of them to Simon's murder.

Bleary-eyed and pedaling in slow motion, I made my way to school in the late morning. I had managed to grab a few winks around sunrise, but my body felt like it had been deflated. I figured I needed to suck it up and would be able to sleep again when I got back to present time.

I arrived at school before lunch, parked my bike, and headed straight for the cafeteria. Usually there was an empty seat or two at the Brainiacs' table since no one but Simon ever wanted to sit with them. I got in line and grabbed some lunch.

As I was about to head over to the tables, someone grabbed my arm. I yanked it back, expecting that whoever grabbed me meant harm, but it was only Kevin.

"Sorry, Miles," he said. He had a tray filled with tater tots swimming in ketchup and had managed to get the ketchup all over his face and hands. "You sure are on edge."

I took a napkin to wipe the ketchup off my elbow.

"Looks like the cafeteria is pretty full today," Kevin said, resting his tray on a windowsill so he could eat more tater tots while he looked for seats.

"Yeah," was all I said. I wasn't in the mood to deal with Kevin right now.

"So, you didn't answer any of my texts," he said.

I was still scanning the cafeteria to see if the Brainiacs were at any of the tables.

"Yoo-hoo, Miles!"

"What?" I snapped. I couldn't hide the venom in my voice. Simon had clearly told me not to waste time dealing with Kevin in the past since he'd just be a liability.

"I was texting you all day yesterday, man. I even called your ass. You weren't in any classes…"

"I was sick."

"But then I thought I saw you leaving school. You got on your bike and took off really fast."

"I didn't feel well and went home…"

Finally, I spied the Brainiacs. The three of them were sitting at a table without Simon, hunched over their trays in deep conversation. I headed straight for them.

"Wait, Miles, wait!"

Kevin swiped his tray and waddled after me. Since it would take more of an effort to tell him to go away, I let him follow.

"Can I sit here?" I asked once I reached the Brainiacs' table. They stopped speaking in hushed tones and looked at me like I'd gone mad.

"Excuse me, what?" Linda said, pressing her hand against her chest as if she was offended. Her unwashed hair seemed extra dandruffy today.

"Aren't you Simon's brother?" Ellery asked. He was wearing a T-shirt that said: "This was supposed to be the future—where is my nuclear-powered levitating house?"

"What does your T-shirt mean?" I asked, zeroing in on the word "future."

Ellery and Linda rolled their eyes at one another.

"So gormless," Ellery snorted, his unwieldy Adam's apple bobbing up and down like he'd swallowed an acorn. Linda pretended to sneeze but was really laughing into her hands. "Well, Simon's brother, it means that modern society is a joke. Technologically speaking we should be way ahead of where we are in terms of what scientists had predicted for the early twenty-first century."

"I bet you think your new phone is the most ingenious invention of our time," Linda added, twisting a split end and getting her fingers caught.

"It can do *so* much!" Kevin said. Everyone at the table turned to him, initially forgetting he was even there.

"You have ketchup all over your face," Linda said as I went ahead and sat down. Kevin stood there, stunned, before lowering his tray onto the table and easing into a chair.

"Why do you want to sit with us?" Quentin said very quietly. He was picking at a scab on his arm with a paperclip and drawing a few droplets of blood.

I speared a tot. "You guys are my brother's friends."

Even Kevin's face seemed perplexed by that remark.

"Fr-iends," Quentin said, spacing out the word and puckering his lips as if he'd taken a sip of fine wine. "Depends on your definition of what a 'friend' is. You've certainly been curious about your brother as of late. Before Monday, we barely knew you existed."

Quentin sucked at his teeth while he flicked the scab off of his arm and brushed it into his pocket.

"I had to follow Simon for my class, so I figured I'd speak to his friends...I mean, the people at school he hangs out with."

Each one of the Brainiacs glanced at one another to see if they were buying my excuse.

"Whatever pedestrian class you need this for, we have far more important things to discuss," Ellery said. He shooed me and Kevin away while Linda nodded.

"Omni," I blurted out and watched carefully to see how each of them would respond. Ellery's ear perked up and turned red.

"What did you say?"

"Omni," I said again, this time with more authority in my voice. "What does that mean to you?"

Quentin smirked as he dipped a finger into the bloody scab on his arm and drew a question mark on the table.

"Are you too insipid to know what that word means?" Ellery asked. "It means 'all' or 'every.'"

"I know what it means, jackass," I replied. "I want to know what it means to you."

Ellery looked at Linda. Linda turned to Quentin. Quentin finished up his bloody question mark by adding the dot. Kevin stuffed four tater tots into his mouth.

"Is this some sort of joke you're playing?" Ellery asked. His Adam's apple bobbed up and down even more slowly. I wondered if it was a telltale admission of guilt.

"I don't have time for jokes," I said. "Who is Omni?"

Linda finally pried her fingers out of her hair.

"We don't have time for these ridiculous questions and games. We have a physics meet that we need to prepare for down in Des Moines."

"Des Moines?"

"Yes, it is the capital and largest city in Iowa," Ellery said as he and Linda shared a smirk.

"When is the physics meet?" I asked.

"Monday through Wednesday of next week," Linda said. "We'll be missing school."

"Crappo," I cursed, under my breath. The Brainiacs would be at the physics meet on the day that Simon was killed, which meant that they weren't suspects anymore. "All of you are going?"

"What a detective you are," Quentin said, filling in the dot on the question mark until it became a dark red.

"What does any of this have to do with your class?" Linda asked.

"This banal kid has taken up enough of our

time," Ellery said, pushing his chair into the table and getting up. "Whatever homework you have to do is meaningless to me. C'mon," he gestured to Linda and Quentin, establishing himself as their leader. Linda scurried to her feet and glowered at me as well, but Quentin set his sights on a new scab.

"Quentin!" Ellery snapped. "We are going."

Quentin curled a string of greasy black hair around his ear and shrugged.

"I'm still working on my tots."

"If you cause us to lose at the meet…" Ellery said with an angry finger in Quentin's face. When Quentin didn't blink, Ellery turned around in a huff and took off with Linda at his side.

"Geez, what a grouch," Kevin said to Quentin. "If you call him a *friend*…"

Quentin glanced at the bloody question mark again before looking back up and silently telling me that there were more questions to ask.

"Kevin, could you leave us alone?" I said.

"Wha…?"

The two fresh tots that Kevin had shoved into his mouth struggled to stay in.

"I want to ask Quentin something."

Kevin swallowed the tots and stuffed his face into his fists.

"There are no other seats around, Miles. I promise I won't get in the way."

"Kevin!" I said, losing my patience. I'd be damned if he was going to screw up my chance at getting more info.

Kevin rose to his feet, his face turning pink.

"I don't know what's been up with you lately," he

said, his eyes brimming with tears. "But I'm not liking this new Miles."

He nearly tripped over his feet as he walked away. Even though I felt terrible, I couldn't worry about him now.

"You didn't leave with the rest of the Brainiacs, Quentin?"

I imagined I was some gritty detective interrogating my suspect under a hot lamp.

"Very observant."

He ran his fingers across the question mark until it became a bloody smear.

"So, the name Omni means something to you?" I asked.

"Why were you hiding in Mr. Congley's cabinet yesterday? I'm guessing that none of this has to do with a report on your brother."

"I'll tell you more if you tell me about Omni," I said, standing firm.

"You run your own detective agency in this town, don't you?"

"So what if I do?"

"Small town like this." Quentin shrugged. "It can't have too many juicy cases, or am I wrong? Does the very nature of a small town mean that some seedy underbelly exists here? Some terrible, terrible form of evil?" He finished his thought with a wicked smile.

"What do you mean by that?"

Quentin tipped his chair back and linked his fingers behind his head. He was wearing a lot of dark eye makeup and strange yellow contacts.

"I have the ability to feel presences that most cannot," he said with his nose in the air. "It makes me more rounded than the other Brainiacs who have nothing but their intellect to boast about. My mother was an Empath."

"So?"

"She was able to sense different energies. She passed that talent down to me before she died. There is a very dark energy in this town. I have felt it for a while, but it has only gotten stronger."

"Like something supernatural?" I asked, cocking my head to the side in mock disbelief.

"No…when I speak of energies and presences, it does not necessarily mean something supernatural. This energy is very much of this world. Someone…or a few people in Frontier are very, very angry, so angry…and frustrated. I can feel their pain. In the last few weeks, I've sensed that pain growing more and more."

I got super chilly, as if a window had been opened, letting in gusts of frigid air.

"You probably think I'm whacked?" Quentin asked with a hint of sadness in his voice. "Most do. Few seem to understand me."

"Not at all," I said, my mouth becoming dry. "I also think something very evil is in our town."

"Well, what are you going to do about it, Detective?"

"I don't know," I said immediately. My words took me by surprise. Walking into Simon's room on the morning his face had been blown off, I knew that something evil had infiltrated Frontier, but to hear it spoken out loud made its terrifying existence much more real. There could be dozens of people behind Simon's death, and I was just one boy trying to prevent it from happening.

"Don't stop asking questions," Quentin whispered

under his breath. "And if you ever need any weapons."
He nodded. "I have enough ammunition to start a war.
All preventative, of course. I may be the poster child
for an alienated teen about to go on a rampage, but I
am an Empath too, meaning I'm a pacifist at heart…"

He gave one last smile that licked at the edge of his
cheek.

"Unless I'm pushed, of course."

He gathered up his tray.

"Don't let anyone push *you* around, Miles. Fire at
them before they fire first." He slipped in among the
crowd that had all gathered to leave the cafeteria.

I saw that he had left his card in the bloody smear.

Q – 319-555-4679. For all of your ammo needs.

Chapter Twenty-Four

I didn't come across any other leads throughout the rest of the day. The next suspects on my list were Jojo and his gang, but they must've all skipped school because I didn't see them around. They certainly represented the kind of evil in this town that Quentin sensed: cruelty for the sake of being cruel. I'd make sure to tail them tomorrow. If I didn't see them in school again, I'd bike around to all the places that kids went when they were playing hooky. Maybe I'd also find a way to finally get over that squishy feeling in my stomach whenever Jojo was around and my dumb flirtation with danger.

I left school feeling like I'd been climbing a giant mountain that kept getting higher and higher, its peak not even in sight. I had less than a week to find Simon's murderer. If Jojo and his idiot followers wound up being innocent, I couldn't think of anyone else at Jeremiah Boonton who really had a motive.

Maisie was sitting on the front steps of the school when I got outside. She was reading her trusty *Sherlock*

Holmes book, oblivious to the world around her. I wanted to ask her for a hug, but I knew how stupid that would sound, so I just took a moment to stare at her instead. She had put her dirty blond hair in braided pigtails and was chewing on a braid. Like she sensed she was being watched, she quickly turned around. When she saw it was me, she smiled.

"Hey, Miles." She patted the step next to her.

"Hey," I replied with a goofy half-wave. I ran my fingers through my hair and made sure not to give too big a smile so she wouldn't see my gross braces.

"You weren't in Spanish today...or yesterday actually."

"Yeah...I..."

"Are you a bad boy?"

She chewed on a fingernail instead of her braids. Her hands were stained with watercolor paint, oranges and reds. She touched my forearm, left a streak of tangerine.

"Yeah...I'm kind of a bad boy..."

She giggled through her nostrils, the sound of a flute. She was still touching my arm.

"You're not really a bad boy," she decided. "You're sweet."

I almost said that I could be whatever she wanted me to be.

"When Señora Hernandez called out your name in Spanish today, I lowered my voice and said '*aqui*.' She actually bought it. I guess that makes me a bad girl."

"No, just sweet as well. This town could use more people like you."

She looped a finger through her shoelace, pulled it tighter.

"So, is there anyone in school you like?"

"Like what do you mean? Like…like *like*? I guess?"

I became aware of her pink tongue lolling in her mouth. The urge to touch it with my own was overwhelming.

"In Oregon, everyone at my school would hook up, even if they didn't really like someone, just at a party or if they were bored. Or they talked about sex like it was no big deal. Something they wanted to do already so they could say that they did."

"That's weird."

"I know! Like even with kissing, if I don't really like…I mean, I've never really liked—"

"Yeah, I wouldn't make out with someone I didn't really like either."

"This girl made fun of my dress today," she said and went back to chewing on her braid. "For it being so long. She called me a nun."

Maisie hugged her blue dress around her knees.

"I think it looks nice," I said. "Like the sky. It's the same color as the sky."

"That's why I wore it!" she gushed. "I have a thick skin, though. I don't let catty people get to me. Thanks for listening."

She looked out toward the road.

"My dad is so late."

"You should get a bike. We could…I dunno… maybe bike home together sometime?"

"Yeah, he's pretty overprotective, so…"

"I was just thinking out loud."

"No, that would be cool, like if my dad would let me. I'd really like that, Miles."

My name in her mouth felt right like she should be saying it a million times over. Miles and Maisie. Our names sounded so good together.

"I see him," she said, slinging her backpack over her shoulder and standing up. Her car with the Oregon license plates pulled up to the front steps. Smith stuck his head out and rested a giant forearm on the windowsill.

"You're late, Daddy," she said, upset.

"Miles, right?" Smith said, fixing his horn-rimmed glasses. "Those bullies try anything with you again?"

"No, sir," I replied. I wanted to act as polite and respectful as possible toward her dad.

"We put the fear in them," Smith said, clenching a fist. His voice had a whistle at the end of each word.

"Bye, Miles," Maisie said. Her lips hovered close to mine. I was certain that if her dad weren't around, those lips would've made contact. But she closed her mouth and hopped into the back seat of the car.

Smith motioned for me to come closer. "So, listen, Miles, Maisie and I haven't had any guests over yet since we moved. How would you and your brother like to come for dinner?"

I saw Maisie sit up straight, nervous to hear my response. Smith licked at one of his gold molars and raised his eyebrows.

"I know Simon's really busy…" I began to say.

"Good Southern cooking. I bet your brother's never had that before?"

"Probably not, but he barely even has time to eat at home."

Smith whistled at the wind. He pressed down a stubborn cowlick into an ooze of gel.

"A boy with a purpose, reminds me of me. And a scientist to boot." He ran a finger along the windowsill and inspected his thumb for grime. "Sometimes I wonder what goes through the mind of a genius."

I let out a laugh that sounded more like a sigh.

"Sometimes I wonder too."

"Well, the dinner invitation will have to be some other time then," Smith said, easing his foot off the brake as the car began to roll away.

"I'm free for dinner," I said, the words independent from my mind. I blurted them out and couldn't take them back. I knew I should only be focusing on solving Simon's case, but watching Maisie's pretty little head bouncing away down the road was like a stab to my gut.

Smith slowed the car to a stop as I caught up.

"What do you think, Maze?" her dad asked through the rearview mirror.

"Sure," she said, trying to hide her wide grin. "I mean...Simon can come some other time, but for now, I could show Miles my drawings."

"I'd love to see your drawings." I said, with my hand on the car's window.

"Okay then, Saturday night, son," her dad said. "Two-two-one Evergreen Street. And if your brother winds up being free, tell him to come too."

"I will."

"Say goodbye, Maze." Her dad whistled with his foot on the gas.

"Bye," she said as the car sped away. She had spun around and gotten on her knees to watch me out of her dusty back window. She blew me a kiss as the car vanished in between rows of cornfields in the distance.

The sound of my heart beating was like the loudest drum ever.

I rushed to the barn, excited to tell my past self about my upcoming date with Maisie. I chucked my bike to the side, but then I figured I should go over the case with my past self first before I dealt with anything personal. He needed to know about my lunch with the Brainiacs and then we had to plan the best way to spy on Jojo and his cronies tomorrow.

"Self, I'm home," I said as I jumped down the trapdoor. He came running out.

"Don't get mad at me," he said.

My stomach instantly dropped.

"I went up into the barn just to get some air…"

"Did somebody see you?" I gasped.

"No, no. I'm pretty sure no one saw me. No, definitely sure. Anyway, so I was in the barn when I heard a car pull up."

"Crap, what kind of car?"

"I didn't see. I jumped down into the hayloft and came right back to the lab. The walls are too thick to hear anything, so I don't know if whoever it was actually came inside or just drove by."

"When was this?"

"I don't know, not that long ago. Do you think this means that someone knows about the lab?"

"That's impossible," I said, feeling like I was in free fall. "I was always careful to make sure no one followed me. Maybe it was Congley?"

"If it was Congley, then why didn't he come down since he knows the passcode?"

"No, Congley wouldn't come here since Simon said in his video message that he started working at a different lab this past week because he sensed someone was onto him. Congley would want to be careful, too."

"Maybe Congley doesn't know about the other lab?"

"That's a possibility. But it doesn't matter. You can't leave this lab again."

My past self kicked at a doohickey on the floor.

"I know, I know. Stay down here, keep quiet until we can go over intel. Do you know how boring that is? You get to have all the excitement."

"Can you imagine how much someone would flip out if they saw the two of us together?"

"I wish I was you…I mean, the me of the future. I feel like I'm worthless down here."

I patted him on the back.

"No, you're crucial to this mission. I need you to bounce ideas of off. C'mon, we'll go over what I learned today."

I told him about the Brainiacs going to the physics meet when Simon's murder would occur. I showed him the card that Quentin had given me if I needed some ammunition. I decided to leave out what had happened with Maisie since it would only make him jealous. I'd confess about the dinner date we had planned some other time.

"And then I was going to follow Jojo and his asshole crew but they weren't in school," I continued.

"I looked up Jojo's address on the computer since I was bored," he said, handing me a piece of paper. "He actually doesn't live too far from Generator Street."

"Really?"

"You should catch him before he leaves for school and follow him wherever he goes in case he skips school again."

"That's a great idea."

"Yeah, I know."

"See how helpful you are?"

"Yeah, yeah. You should go now and take away your bike in case that car decides to come back."

"Good point."

"I'm sorry for complaining earlier. I know you're doing whatever is possible to save Simon."

A pang of guilt pinched my heart. Had I really been doing everything I could? I was starting to feel bad for agreeing to have dinner at Maisie's.

"Thanks," I said, my eyes looking everywhere but at him. If there was anyone who'd figure out I'd been trying to keep a secret, my past self would be able to pick up on every one of my tells. "*Sayonara*," I said, climbing up the trapdoor and back into the hayloft.

I peered through the bushels of hay to see if anyone was in the barn before leaving the hayloft. From now on, I wouldn't take any more chances by leaving my bike at home or at school.

If someone had driven past the barn earlier today looking for Simon's lab, I knew they would certainly be coming back.

Chapter Twenty-Five

I woke up super early the next day to head over to Jojo's house before he could leave for school. Jojo lived on Prime Street in the nicest house on the block, looking like it had a zillion rooms and a front lawn with perfectly cut grass. His dad worked in finance and Jojo always came back from vacations abroad. It made no sense why he was so mad at the world when it seemed like he had everything.

I put on my Hawkeye's hat and crept toward the front door. Just as I was staring through the keyhole, I saw Jojo's dad bounding down the stairs. I rushed behind a rickety porch swing as Jojo's dad stumbled out, tucking in his collared shirt and fixing his tie. Jojo's dad swallowed a final chug of some clear liquor and left the bottle on the front lawn before cursing at his convertible to start and then zooming down the road.

The door had been left ajar, and I was able to see Jojo coming down the stairs next. The faint smell of skunky weed hung in the air. Jojo ambled out of the house without a backpack and picked up the empty bottle of liquor. He stuck his tongue all the way into the bottle to try to get at some last drops and then chucked the bottle at a songbird welcoming the morning in their family's front yard tree.

"Freakin' boozer," Jojo said, and gave the wounded songbird the finger as he walked away. Jojo might be rich, but it seemed like Jojo's family had problems of their own.

I got on my bike to follow, but made sure that I remained at enough of a distance. After a few blocks, Jojo neared Generator Street. I wondered if he was heading to Simon's lab, which would clearly mean he was one of the possible murderers; but Jojo stopped at a grouping of logs. In the distance, the barn was nothing more than a red dot among barren crop fields. Jojo got out a cigarette and a pocketknife and began carving into one of the logs.

A broken-down car rolled down the lone road to the right of the log formation. The car coughed and wheezed and sounded like it had left its muffler behind. It stopped in front of Jojo. When the black exhaust smoke cleared, Rodney and Billy jumped out in a fit of laughter. I watched them from behind a bushel of sagging reeds, but I was too far away to hear what they were saying.

Billy dumped out what looked like a few bottles of cough syrup from a paper bag. Each of them selected a different colored bottle and started chugging. The game seemed to be whoever could finish their bottle first. Just as Rodney was about to finish his, Jojo whapped him in the stomach causing a red river to spew from Rodney's mouth. Jojo then drained his cough syrup and held it up to the sky like a champion.

Billy and Rodney began wrestling until both of them were covered in reeds.

They smoked a few more cigarettes and then got into the broken-down car that weaved down the road. I got back on my bike and trailed them all the way to Jeremiah Boonton. I wondered why they had met by the barn if they hadn't planned on going inside, unless the abandoned area was just a good spot to get high.

At school, they all ditched first period class and roamed the halls with a restless need to destroy whatever was in their path. Lockers were bashed, water fountains were humped, a clock was stripped off the wall and left in pieces, snot rockets flew from their nostrils, Rodney puked up more cough syrup in a back stairwell. I followed their chaos until the bell rang and they turned their abuse toward students passing by. A tiny freshman was given a wedgie, a gaggle of theater girls were mocked, a fight almost erupted between them and some football players, and then they found Simon and descended on him with slithery grins.

Simon had been stuffing some textbooks into his locker. He looked exhausted; his usually pale skin now had a purple sheen like cheese on a pizza left in the sun too long. Simon didn't see them until they formed a semi-circle and blocked him from moving.

"So, what did you decide?" Jojo said with an angry push. "I need to know by today."

Simon stayed quiet and concentrated on putting his textbooks into his locker.

"I'm talking to you!" Jojo yelled with another drunken shove. Billy and Rodney joined in the harassment. They called Simon every degrading name they could think of. I was surprised that Simon was able to keep his cool. Jojo spat a loogie onto Simon's cheek, cough syrup red. The loogie hung in place, refusing to budge. Some students glanced over, but no one stopped to help, and there weren't any teachers in the hall either. Jojo knocked the remaining books out of Simon's hands.

"You better think long and hard about our proposal, Poindexter," Jojo said. "Otherwise, the rest of your year is gonna be pretty miserable."

Each of the piece-of-shit gang shoved him one last time and exchanged high-fives as they sauntered away.

The word *proposal* rang in my ears. An alarm shot through my body since it might have to do with what ultimately got Simon killed. Jojo and his crew had to be responsible, too evil to be innocent.

"What are you looking at?" Jojo said to me as we crossed paths. He held up a fist and then chuckled when I flinched. "Scaredy cat."

I ignored them and went over to Simon to help him pick up his books. He handed me his favorite, *Time and Again* by Jack Finney.

"Did that have to do with why they tried to take our bikes?" I asked, fishing for any kind of information.

Simon grabbed his *Time and Again* book but didn't answer.

"Simon?"

"Leave me alone, Miles."

"Look, you can tell me if there's a reason they're harassing you. We could figure out a way to stop them."

I almost said the word Omni just to get a reaction, but I still wasn't absolutely certain if Simon had completed his time machine yet. I didn't want to say anything that might distract him.

"You don't know what you're talking about," he said, raising his voice.

"You don't have to be afraid of them."

Simon got in my face. I could tell that he had eaten eggs for breakfast.

"Why do you care about my business all of a sudden?"

"I…don't want to see you get hurt."

He was breathing heavily. I wondered if he'd gotten wind of whoever was following him.

"I can take care of myself," he said, although his voice was shaking. I wanted to tell him to run far, far away from Frontier before they got to him. But even if Simon ran, would he die anyway? Was it impossible to pull a fast one on Time?

"Stay away from me," he said with a shove and then took off down the hallway. It was a weird relationship we had. I could love Simon one minute and then feel a boiling hatred for him the next. He was so stubborn, and for once in his life, so clueless. If he only knew how much he needed me, he'd finally treat me with respect.

I saw that Kevin had been watching from his locker. He came over with a powdered donut in his hand.

"Your brother is a weird, weird guy," Kevin said, his lips white from the donut. "He's got issues."

I fixed my shirt, which was askew.

"Why do you always have to say nasty things about Simon?"

Kevin blinked and crammed the rest of the donut into his mouth.

"And can you stop eating for like two seconds?"

Kevin put his hands up. "Whoa, I just came over to see if you were okay."

"What did Simon ever do to you?" I continued, zeroing in on Kevin's thumb-like head and how I wanted to ring his neck, just to take out my anger on someone. "You're always saying bad things about him. You have no reason to hate him, but you do."

"Who said I hated your brother?"

"That's enough motive in my book," I muttered.

"Motive? What are you talking about?"

I poked Kevin in his stomach.

"What do you gain with Simon out of the picture?"

"Simon out of the picture? You've lost me, Miles."

I poked him again in the belly button.

"Oww, dude. Stop doing that!"

I imagined myself as a gritty detective that wasn't afraid to rough someone up.

"What do you have planned for next week, huh?"

"Next week?" Kevin jammed his hands into his pockets. "I dunno. It's my sister Kennedy's birthday. My mom's throwing a party in the backyard."

"And what else? Has someone gotten in your ear?"

Kevin twisted his ear and stared back in confusion. "My ear…?"

"Because I don't have a lot more time to solve this," I babbled. "I'm running out of suspects if Jojo's ass-jerk bunch aren't at fault." My voice dropped to a whisper. "Why were you watching us now…?"

"Who?"

"Me and Simon!"

"I was just at my locker, dude!"

"What do *you* know?" I yelled. It felt good to shout like this, to direct my frustration somewhere.

"Are you on drugs?" Kevin responded with a laugh that sprayed powdered sugar over my face.

"You spit on me," I said, grabbing at Kevin's face and scratching his cheek.

"Ow, Miles, what the hell!"

I mushed something of Kevin's that felt warm—an eyeball possibly?

Kevin yelped and covered his face with his hands as he tried to pry my fingers away.

"Stop it, Miles, stop it!"

Kevin swung his arm, and his fist came into contact with my jaw. I clamped down on my tongue and tasted blood. We started pummeling one another. Fists flying everywhere. Spit and blood on the floor.

"I hate you!" I screamed. I didn't mean it, but kept saying it over and over until my throat became hoarse. Kevin's knuckles dug into my eye socket before two teachers broke us up.

I was still swinging as they hauled us both off to the principal.

Chapter Twenty-Six

In Principal Mynad's office, Kevin wouldn't even look at me. It was actually a blessing to have him stay mad for a few days. At least he'd leave me alone so I could try and save Simon. All I needed was for Kevin to get too involved and somehow put himself in danger. I pictured him being lowered over a cauldron while a masked man cackled at his misfortune.

"Miles…"

I vaguely heard my name being called in the distance.

"Miles…"

"*Miles!*"

Principal Mynad slammed his fist on his desk.

"Son, what is wrong with you? I just asked you five times why you boys fought."

I shrugged in response.

"Can I call my mom?" Kevin mumbled, with a twisted tissue jammed up his bloody nose.

"We've already called your parents," Principal Mynad said. He had a giant bald spot in the back of his head that he'd glued a few hairs over to minimize the fallout. Kevin and I always called him Principal *My bad*.

"Momma's boy," I muttered.

"Hey!" Principal Mynad snapped. "That's enough from you. You both will be suspended for the rest of the week. Do you have anything to say to one another?"

"I don't know why he hit me," Kevin sighed.

"You hit me too."

"I hit you because you hit me."

"Enough!" Principal Mynad said, waving his arms like an orchestra conductor. "Now apologize to one another and get out of my office."

"I'm sorry," Kevin said, crossing his fingers.

"I'm sorry," I said, doing the same.

In the hallway, Kevin pulled the bloody tissue out of his nose and wiped the residue on his shirt.

"I'm through with *Mr. Hardy's Detective Agency* by the way, since you obviously don't appreciate what I do," he said in a huff.

"Great, maybe now I can find an assistant who actually helps me solve crimes."

Kevin held up his fist like he was ready to fight again.

"I've helped you solve every case we've had, ass bandit."

"No, *you've* eaten your way through every case *I've* had."

Kevin crossed his arms and rested them on his stomach.

"And what is that supposed to mean?"

"You eat and you sleep, that's it. I've been the one solving every case the agency's had. You're just along for the ride because you have no one else to hang out with."

"I have other friends!"

"Name one."

Kevin started to speak, but I cut him off.

"Besides your sister…and besides that kid from Taiwan you chat online with about horror films."

"Well, you never want to watch any horror films."

"That's because they're ridiculous—ghosts in TVs, little kids with giant mouths."

"Aren't you gonna at least say you're sorry that you hit me?" Kevin asked.

"Dude, you hit me, too."

"Only after you started hitting me!"

"Look, let's steer clear from each other for like…a week."

"I was thinking the same thing and was about to say that before you did."

"No, you weren't."

"Fine, take a week to figure out why you've become such a dick, Miles. Some new girl says like three words to you, and all of a sudden you're so cool."

"Me and Maisie have a date this weekend."

"Whoop-dee-doo."

"Whatever, no one's ever even liked you before, Kevin. You don't understand."

Kevin simmered in place, unable to respond. I knew I shouldn't have gone there, but I didn't want to waste any more time. I needed to find Jojo and figure out what he meant by *the proposal*. As dangerous as Jojo's posse might be right now, all hopped up on cough syrup and adrenaline, it was time to start getting some answers.

Kevin stayed in the hallway twiddling his thumbs

and mewling like a lost puppy while I left the school. Outside, autumn had arrived in full force, the wind a nuisance that kept blowing off my Hawkeye's cap. I headed to the back alleyway to see if Jojo and his band of titheads were after any other kids' bikes. Sure enough, Rodney and Billy were roughing up a twig-like sophomore for his lunch money. Jojo paced back and forth like a mob boss ordering a hit. When they saw me, they got distracted and the kid wormed away and took off down the alleyway.

"Shit, man," Billy said, punching the brick wall. Rodney went to go after him, but Jojo held up his hand.

"What's this dick for brains doing here?" Jojo asked as the trio all glared at me.

"Looks like he already got a beatin'," Billy said, punching his fist into his palm.

"You were following us earlier," Jojo said. His breath was hot as an oven as he got closer. "I saw you before school watching us like a little snooping bitch."

Jojo picked me up by my collar. My feet dangled in the air as I wiggled from side to side.

"No, I was just on my way to school…"

"That's a bunch of BS," Billy cheered from the sidelines. "Make mincemeat outta him, Jojo."

"You lookin' to tattle on us, pipsqueak? Or blackmail us? We weren't doing nothin' illegal, we all have bad coughs."

Rodney and Billy gave some fake coughs to prove their leader's point.

"But even if we just felt like drinking cough syrup before class for the hell of it then that's our business. We don't answer to no one, ya hear?"

He dropped me onto the ground.

"So, you can admit to why you've been following us before or after your beatin', but either way you're gettin' a beatin'."

Jojo admired his fist as he prepared to swing. This fight was bound to hurt a lot more than the one I'd had with Kevin. There would be no nicks and bruises from a tussle with Jojo, who was enough of a sadist to relish in broken bones.

"I know what will happen to my brother. I'm onto you all," I said, covering my face with my hands.

Jojo lowered his fist and scratched his chin. He looked at his cronies for verification. Both of them stared back even more confused.

Immediately after I revealed this accusation, I wished I could take it back. The First Rule of *The Dos and Don'ts of Time Travel* clearly stated that no one else could know about the time machine. But I was starting to get real desperate and scared. I'd trailed each suspect like a good detective, but it had gotten me nowhere. I needed to know right now if they had anything to do with Simon's murder. If they did, I swore I would kill them before they had the chance to commit the crime.

Jojo's face was hard to read since his expressions usually only alternated between pissed off and even more pissed off.

"You're Poindexter's brother," he said, as if he'd reached some awesome revelation. "Yeah, yeah, the kid whose bike we tried to nab the other day."

"Why are you after my brother?" I spat. I'd take any beating they wanted to give. I was ready for it, almost wanting it to occur.

Jojo gave a wicked laugh. Rodney and Billy joined in until tears were crinkling from their eyes. I brushed off the dirt from my pants and got to my feet.

"I'll hurt you if you hurt him," I said. "I have access to guns."

The three of them laughed even louder. Rodney and Billy were holding their stomachs in pain, too bombed to really process what was going on.

"Calm down, little man. Just tell your brother to take my algebra test later today and we'll leave him alone. Mrs. Candleshine is so old she won't know that it's him takin' the test instead of me."

"What?" I said as my stomach felt all prickly like I'd swallowed a porcupine.

"You hard of hearing?" Jojo sneered. "Your dorky ass brother needs to take my test, or I'll fail the class. Get it?"

"What was the proposal you were talking about to him?"

"Shit for brains, that's *the proposal*. If he doesn't take my test, I'm *proposing* to wail him good."

"Wail him good…" Rodney and Billy echoed.

"And then you'd kill him, right?" I asked, barely above a whisper. Rodney and Billy stopped laughing and stared at me with gaping mouths.

"Kill him?" Jojo said, scratching his head. "Who said anything about killing him?"

"Who do you think we are?" Rodney asked as he lunged at me. Billy held him back.

"I'm not going to jail over a dumb math test," Jojo declared. "You think I'm a moron?"

I shook my head.

"This kid must think I'm a moron," Jojo gesticulated to his cronies.

"Give him your famous knuckle sandwich," Billy shouted.

"I have a reputation to uphold," Jojo continued. "We may be bullies, but we ain't criminals."

His cronies nodded in agreement.

"I am offended, boys," he said to his crew. "And when I get offended, I get punchy."

"Punch him, punch him," they chanted.

"Lights out, Poindexter's brother."

Jojo popped me good in my right eye. The impact of the punch caused me to spill onto the ground, my face throbbing. I saw only half of the world as my right eye closed.

"And you can tell the King of the Geeks that he's getting what's coming to him unless he agrees to our proposal. Billy and Rodney, leave us alone for some more punching."

Billy and Rodney grabbed their bikes and hopped on, zipping away.

I tried to open my right eye, but it felt like it'd been sewn shut.

"A killer?" Jojo questioned. "I should sue for character assassination."

He leaned over me, his lips inches from my own, a buzzing between us, like the conversation could turn into a kiss. He sneered, a hot gust of air coming through his nose.

"You afraid?" he asked, ending the question with a wink.

"No."

"Yeah, you like it."

He touched my chin, gave it a caress, his finger rough. He looked from left to right, checking if the coast was clear. Then he kissed me, slobbering all over like a dog, his tongue darting. When he pulled away, he looked confused, as if something had taken over him.

"You tell anyone that happened, I'll show ya I am a killer."

He licked his lips, masking a smile. I wiped my mouth, his saliva stinging on the back of my hand. I didn't like the kiss at all. Whatever had attracted me to Jojo had vanished, and since he wasn't a suspect anymore, he was no use to me. He was a distraction, and I wouldn't be distracted anymore.

I sat up and brushed the asphalt off my cheek as Jojo took off. I'd just obliterated three more suspects from my list and all it took was a punch to the face (and a pretty awful kiss). In my mind, I mentally drew a line through each of those dickweeds, but then my heart sunk at the realization that I didn't really have any other promising leads.

The morning of my brother's death was only getting closer; time ticking down even faster than I ever imagined it could…

when you who is go back because me of a figure...

Chapter Twenty-Seven

I bought a package of frozen peas at the Zippymart to ease the swelling on my eye and biked home one handed as I held the pack up to my face. Having never been in a fight before, I couldn't believe that I'd been in two in one day. I knew I'd get hell from my dad about being suspended, but at least I'd have an hour or so of peace before he returned home from teaching. My plan was to sneak one of his canned beers and shut my mind off.

Reed was playing with some matchbox cars on the curb when I biked up.

"Miles, your face!" Reed said, pointing. He chewed on his bitten-down nails in fright.

"I'm okay, Reed," I said, removing the peas to show Reed that it wasn't so bad.

"You look like an evil guy on TV," Reed said, wide-eyed. "Can I touch it?"

"Maybe later, it still hurts a lot."

Reed put one of the matchbox cars in his mouth and shook his head.

"I'm on the neighborhood watch to look out for evil guys." The matchbox fell from his mouth, covered in drool. "Whoops."

"I'm the same good guy I've always been. But keep watch out, Reed. I feel a lot safer knowing you're out here."

The door to Reed's house swung open and Annalee stepped out in fuzzy slippers and a fuzzy bathrobe.

"Reed, baby, I made some ants on a log for you."

"Ants on a log! Ants on a log!" Reed clapped and scooped up his matchbox cars to run inside.

"Miles?" she questioned, squinting her eyes as if she wasn't sure who it was, but then one of her slippers fell off, and she forgot about me to concentrate on reinserting her foot into the slipper.

I headed inside my house and went straight for the can of beer in the fridge. Mom wasn't around, probably sleeping upstairs, which meant Ludmila had already left. I cracked open the beer and took a few cold gulps. I could see why grown-ups like Dad were so fond of a drink after a long, weary day. The frozen peas had melted, so I put the half-empty can of beer up to my eye instead. I tried to think about anything besides Simon's murder case just to give my brain a break, but it was impossible. The names of other suspects kept swirling around, refusing to give me a moment of peace.

This is the life of a detective, I thought. *This is what you were born to do.*

I mentally pictured the list I'd created. Now that Jojo and his cronies were eliminated as suspects, Dad was the next one on the list. Either I could sit at the kitchen table drinking the rest of the beer and feeling sorry for myself, or I could use the hour I had till Dad came home to start snooping around the house. Since Mom was asleep, at least she wouldn't be in the way.

I spilled the rest of the beer in the sink and darted upstairs to my parents' room. Mom was there under the covers, snoring like a trombone. I went to their closet and started rummaging through their things, but there was nothing of interest. I opened up every drawer in the room until it looked like they'd been robbed. I'd blame it on Mom. There was one draw with a lock on it so I grabbed a bedside clock and whapped it against the lock until it broke. Opening it, I found a sea of pill bottles, each with Mom's name. I whipped out my phone to check out what Google said about the prescriptions. She was on Zoloft and Lexapro for depression along with Lithium and Ativan along with a few others that seemed holistic—certainly a shitshow of medication but nothing that seemed if my dad was doing her harm. Unless there was another drawer with even more out-there meds.

Heading back downstairs, I figured the basement would be the best bet to find something incriminating. I was glad that Dad would never realize I'd been snooping in the basement since it was in such disarray anyway. Already buzzed from the beer, I began rifling through his failed experiments at random: sneakers that doubled as a radio but only played static when you stepped down, an electric blanket that seared Dad's arm hairs when he tried it out in front of the family last year. After half an hour, the only thing I had discovered was that Dad was even more demented than I thought.

But then I spied a different kind of lock attached to one of Dad's desk drawers. The lock had a minuscule keyhole. I knew how scatterbrained he could be and assumed that he probably kept the key close by. I felt under the desk but there was nothing. My feet slid on an area rug but there was nothing under it either. I looked around the basement at all the wannabe inventions, zeroing in the toilet seat that was supposed to release a good scent after flushing, but smelled worse than whatever someone would leave. Since it was an arm's length away, I removed the toilet tank to find a key taped on the inside. I took off the key and unlocked the lock.

Opening the drawer, I nearly passed out when I saw a Xeroxed copy of the *Dos and Don'ts of Time Travel* with passages highlighted and nonsensical notes written in the margins. What could Dad possibly be doing with the book? He had to have known about it for a while, which either meant that he found Simon's copy long before I traveled to the past, or I hadn't hidden my own copy well enough. This didn't mean that he was necessarily Simon's killer, but there was a big chance now that he could be involved. A zillion scenarios cluttered my mind. I turned the pages about to read the notes scribbled in the margins, but then I heard the front door slam. Dad was muttering "Miles" over and over along with a stream of curses, the curses getting louder and louder until the basement door opened with a bang.

I threw the copy of the *Dos and Don'ts of Time Travel* back into the drawer and locked it just as Dad reached the bottom of the stairs.

"Miles, what the hell are you doing down here?" he yelled, looking angrier than I'd ever seen him before.

I figured he'd seen me with the very book I was trying to hide.

Chapter Twenty-Eight

As Dad reached the bottom of the basement stairs, he went to grab me but tripped over a box of broken butter stick prototypes. I took the chance to leap over him and bolt upstairs.

"Miles!" I heard him yell as I reached the door.

I went to shut it, but he was too fast and grabbed me from behind.

"Let go of me," I said, thrashing around. Dad may have been a little guy, but he was surprisingly strong.

"How could you get suspended!" he squawked.

I had completely forgotten about the suspension.

"And fighting with Kevin, of all people!"

I tried to weasel out of his grasp, but he wasn't easing up.

"If I let go, will you stay put?" he offered.

I caught my breath and nodded. Dad turned me around so we were face-to-face.

"Jeez, what a shiner you got there. And Kevin did this?"

"I saw the book—" I began to say, ready to have it

out with him but Dad already wandered off into the kitchen.

"Have you been drinking beer?" I heard him yell before he returned with the empty can of beer as evidence. "We need to have a serious talk. Park it, bud."

I flopped onto the couch.

"Look, I know things are challenging at home with Mom, but I can't have you acting out, Miles."

"I'm sorry."

"And what were you doing downstairs in my basement?"

"I…uhh…thought I'd help clean some of it up for you."

He made a sour face.

"I had to leave classes early because I got a call from your principal."

He jammed his hands into his pockets. I could tell he was thinking of what to say next.

"I got a lot on my plate right now, Miles. On my mind. Things have not been going well lately in terms of…"

He waved off that thought.

"And I can't be worrying about you getting into trouble like this. You need to apply yourself."

I inched forward on the couch.

"What do you mean that things haven't been going well lately?"

"Nothing. Forget what I said. You're…grounded."

"Has something gotten worse with Mom? Or… does this have to do with Simon?"

Time slowed down while I waited for his response. I studied his face to see if it offered up any telltale signs. All of a sudden, he started choking on something and nursed a coughing attack that purpled his face.

"Why did you ask about Simon?" he said once he got his coughing attack under control.

"I found—"

He glanced at his watch nervously and then his eyes bugged out.

"Oh no! I have to go."

He reached for his jacket that was hanging over the couch.

"What? Where are you going, Dad?"

"Nowhere, Miles. It's nothing!" He put his face in his hands. When he emerged, he looked like a lost child. "My whole day is messed up because of your suspension."

"I'm sorry."

"You're going to stay put here and you can clean this house as a punishment, but stay out of my basement. Understand?"

He made his way toward the door.

"And stop asking me so many questions. It's... giving me a headache."

The door slammed as he waddled across the driveway to his car. I wasn't going to let him get away without giving me some answers. I waited until he got into his car and then hopped on my bike to follow.

Staying a block behind, I pursued him out of our neighborhood. I wondered if he was going over to the barn on Generator Street. I rehearsed what I'd say if I had to confront him. I decided I'd admit that Simon had given me the time travel book, but I wouldn't say anything about actually traveling back in time. Then I'd figure out what to do next depending on how he responded.

We were closing in on Generator Street and I felt a nervous whoosh sloshing around in my stomach. As kooky as Dad was, there was no way he could be responsible for murder, but I wondered if someone had offered to buy his inventions as a trade for info about Simon? Dad might be pathetic enough to give up his son for a little bit of personal glory.

I saw the red barn in the distance as I followed him down the road. As we got closer, I held my breath in anticipation, but he drove right past the red barn. Did he know that I was on his tail? Was he trying to throw me off? I made sure to stay far enough behind so I would appear as nothing more than a dot in his rearview mirror.

The road forked, and we passed by rows and rows of soy fields or cornstalks until we reached the neighboring town of Gatson. Gatson was way smaller than Frontier with a population under ten thousand of mostly farmers. We came upon a main street where no one was outside. At the end of the street, Dad stopped in front of a two-story walk-up. He jumped out of the car and entered through a blue door like he'd done it a thousand times before.

I propped my bike against a wall and walked toward the blue door. It seemed as if the first floor used to be a storefront that sold wigs but was now all boarded up. I opened the blue door and went up a skinny staircase. On the second floor was a hallway with a few doors off to the left and the right. I peered through the glass windows in each door and only saw empty rooms filled with about a dozen chairs set up in a circle. I could hear murmuring coming from the door at the end of the hall. I crept closer and pressed my ear up against it. I was still only able to hear faint mumbling. Looking through the window, I saw Dad sitting in the circle with about a dozen other people. There was a man in a tweed coat with patches on his sleeves who was talking to everyone else. The man seemed very upset. His face was turning red, and a giant vein on his temple throbbed.

Soon he stopped speaking, and Dad stood up. He appeared as upset as the other man did. Everyone in the circle nodded in agreement at what he was saying. Some of them were even crying. After an impassioned few minutes, Dad finished and the person next to him stood instead. I almost burst into the room to confront them all. They had to be talking about Simon. Maybe Dad was telling them about the time travel book, or maybe he was warning them that his other son had a copy of it as well? This could be some type of cult that for whatever reason wanted to extinguish Simon or wanted to steal his success.

I decided that I had no other choice but to wait outside for him to finish and then get the answers I was due, no matter what might happen next.

Chapter Twenty-Nine

After a long wait, I stopped hearing murmurs from the room that Dad had gone into and the door opened. I'd been sitting down with my back up against the wall and leaped up immediately. The man with the tweed jacket stepped out first wiping his eyes with a handkerchief. Others followed, each consoling one another before saying goodbye. They all glared at me as they passed, the sight of me unwelcomed. Finally, Dad left the room with a short woman at his side. The two were engaged in whispers and he was rubbing the short woman's back until he saw me.

He froze in place. The short woman clearly recognized the tension in the hallway and bid goodbye to Dad before heading downstairs.

"What are you doing here?" he asked. He seemed so tired, like the words were a struggle to form.

"I should ask you the same thing," I said, standing firm and highlighting the anger in my voice.

Dad ran his fingers through the little amount of hair he had left and clenched his teeth.

"You shouldn't be here—"

"Well, I am," I said, crossing my arms. "And I want some answers."

"Come," Dad said, grabbing me by my sleeve and pulling me toward the stairs.

"Let go of me!"

"Jeez, Miles," Dad said, stamping his foot. "I can't seem to do anything right with you anymore. Let's go to the car."

"Why should I go anywhere with you?"

"You asked me why I was here. I'll explain in the car."

"You have a LOT of explaining to do," I said and then ran past him. I bolted down the skinny staircase back out to the deserted Main Street. All the other people from the room had already driven away and became tiny colored blurs in the distance. I grabbed my bike, feeling a lot safer with it next to me in case I'd have to take off.

Dad came out of the blue door, huffing and puffing.

"Miles, what has gotten into you?"

"Why do you have Simon's book?" I yelled, my voice echoing down Main Street.

"Get in the car," he said, losing patience.

"Answer my question."

Dad swiped the bike out of my hands and wedged it in the back seat. He got in the driver's side and then opened the passenger's side.

"I promise I'll explain everything," he said, looking at the road ahead. He seemed lobotomized, his will to fight vanished, just like Mom.

I got in the car and closed the door, my curiosity outweighing any fear. Dad put the car in drive, and we rolled down Main Street and out of Gatson. Instead of taking the highway, he swerved onto the back roads instead.

"I don't think you understood what you just saw. Why I've been coming to Gatson."

"I know it has to do with the book," I said, trying to remain as calm as possible.

"The book? What—"

"Simon's book—"

"Simon? What about Simon?"

"I told you I saw his book in your desk drawer. I won't let you get away with whatever you're planning."

"Whatever I'm planning...?" Dad let out a solitary bark of a laugh that soon turned to tears. "It was just a thought," he continued, wiping his eyes. "That's the way my brain works. I get some wild idea and then I can't get rid of it. So, I thought, what if... what if..."

He flicked on the air-conditioning and cool air filled up the car.

"She's sick, Miles. She's so sick," he blubbered. "Not physically sick, but sick all the same. But I love her. I'd do anything for her."

"Are you talking about Mom?"

"Who else? She's always been the love of my life, even in the state she's in now. I thought, what if we could go back and fix her, rewrite her past?"

"So, you took Simon's book?"

"I know it's foolish. Your brother is a genius, no doubt, but time travel...?" He gave another laugh. "Ludicrous, right? But there are things that our rational minds can't explain in this world, and who's to say that the impossible is truly impossible?"

"It's not impossible," I admitted and then warned

myself not to say anything more. "I mean... we don't know for sure."

"I found the book in your room and made a copy. I haven't confronted Simon about it yet. Due to the findings, he chronicled in his book, I don't know, it seemed feasible. I wondered about going back in time to fix your mom, not changing any big events, not trying to win the lottery, but fixing your mom because she never had a real chance at a happy life but deserves one."

"When did Mom start acting that way?"

"You must have memories of when she was more lucid. When you were a child, she was even present at times and loving."

A tear snaked down my cheek.

"But she was always abusing," Dad sighed.

"Abusing what?"

"Drugs, Miles."

I pictured Mom in bed surrounded by syringes filled with the worst kind of drugs. I imagined her sneaking into back alleyways for her next score.

"Pills. Whatever she could get her hands on. Whatever would take the pain away."

"What pain?"

"Do you remember your Grandma Lillian?"

I thought back to Grandma Lillian's funeral, one of my earliest memories. When her coffin descended into the ground, Mom had said, "Good."

"Not really." I shrugged.

"Well, we tried to keep you away from her as much as possible. She was a pretty bad woman: cruel, spiteful, greedy and vengeful. Mom was always her biggest target."

"Why?"

"Mom was the only one in Grandma Lillian's life.

Sometimes we hurt the ones we love the most, or however the saying goes. Lillian used to beat her. She'd always hit her in places no one could see, so the school never checked up about it."

"How long did Grandma Lillian do this?"

"Up until she died. She was a shriveled-up old thing, barely over a hundred pounds, but she would hit your mom with a cane and your mom took it."

"Why?"

"It was all Mom was used to. She felt like she deserved it. She felt like it would only be worse if she didn't let Lillian torture her."

"But why was Lillian so mean?"

"Lillian's husband did the same thing to her and so Lillian continued the cycle of abuse."

"Did my grandfather get abused too?"

"No, no. Your grandfather had amassed a fortune and owned his own financial business. He threw lavish parties, truly lived a charmed life. But then, he lost it all. Something shady, but I never found out what. He became a bitter alcoholic and took it out on Grandma Lillian. He became a feeble, angry man who hated everyone and everything around him. When she was a teen, he left, just disappeared. Somehow Lillian blamed Mom. I don't know why. That was around the time we met as seniors in 2000, right before Y2K. And that's the sad history of your family."

"So, you wanted to travel back in time to change Mom's past?"

"Well…yes. In some fantasy world, I imagined what it would've been like if Grandma Lillian never abused your mom because she blamed her. And if Mom had never gotten addicted to pills and was there for you and your brother all these years. How could I not wonder?"

After hearing this, I almost confessed that there was a possibility to fix Mom. That Simon had created his time machine. That he'd been able to send me into the past, and that if I could keep Simon alive, he could probably figure out a way to send someone far enough back to stop our grandfather from causing our grandmother to hurt Mom. But revealing the truth now could still jeopardize my mission so I forced myself to remain silent.

"So that's part of why I come to Gatson," Dad continued. "There's a support group for relatives of addicts. I've been going here for as long as I can remember. The people that come here are like family."

"What about all the pills she takes now?" I asked. "Isn't it just as bad?"

"Believe me, if there was any other way to keep her functioning I would, but the dosages she gets are from countless doctors figuring out the right mix. Without them, she'd go psychotic."

"Oh," I said, my voice sounding like it was stuck in a puddle.

I hated myself for even thinking that Dad had anything to do with Simon's murder. I thought of the week following Simon's death when he wouldn't leave the basement and wasn't even able to tie his own tie on the day of Simon's funeral. I reached over and gave him a big hug.

"What's that for?"

"I'm sorry about getting suspended, and I'm sorry about Mom, and I'm sorry if I ever talked back to you, and I'm sorry—"

"Miles, Miles," he said, patting my head with the

hand that wasn't steering. "It's all right, it's all right, calm down. I'm sorry too. I've been frustrated and taken it out on you because you're the only one there. That's wrong of me. And I'll promise to be better. I never told you any of this before because I thought you might be too young to handle it."

"I feel so bad for Mom."

"Just be there for her. That's all we can do," he said as he turned back toward the road.

For the rest of the trip, we sat in silence since there was nothing left to say.

———

When I got home, I immediately went upstairs to my parents' room. Mom was still in bed snoring like a foghorn. I shook her awake. She opened her crusty eyes, unsure where she was, but then her face softened when she saw it was me. She drew me close to her. I brushed back her long, disheveled hair and put my lips to her ear.

"Someday," I whispered. "I promise to save you too."

Then I crawled into bed and closed my eyes, rocking her in my arms.

Chapter Thirty

The next day was Saturday, which meant that I couldn't go to school to do any more snooping. My date with Maisie was later that night, so I spent the day going over to Simon's lab and updating my past self about everything I'd learned so far. He was astonished to find out what happened to Mom. He also liked the idea of traveling to just before the year 2000 someday and changing the entire course of her life.

"I'm seeing Maisie tonight," I told him once we finished talking about Mom.

"Like a date?"

"It's at her dad's place. Her dad's gonna cook some Southern food. So, kind of a date, I guess."

"Don't mess it up. You guys hit it off. That means I have a chance with her in my future too."

"Oh yeah, I hadn't thought of it that way."

"On Tuesday, you'll have to go back to the present whether or not we're able to stop Simon's killer."

When I had first traveled back to the past, it seemed as if I had plenty of time, but now the

215

prospects looked grim. Simon had already disappeared when I woke up that morning so there was no way I could even follow him. I'd have to wake up super early Sunday morning and try to tail him for one last time to see if he'd lead me to any other clues.

"Maybe I should confess to Simon about what's been going on?" I suggested. "He could run away and stay safe, or I don't know."

"I don't think that will matter," my past self said. "I think the killer will keep going after him no matter what unless we stop him…or her."

"You're probably right."

"You still have all of Monday at school to follow people."

"But who else is there?"

"We'll brainstorm tomorrow. There's got to be someone that we've missed."

"Maybe I shouldn't go to Maisie's house."

"There's nothing we can do about the case tonight. She might even be able to help."

"I can't tell her about the time machine!"

"No…I mean…she loves Sherlock Holmes, right? So maybe she's good at solving cases? You could talk about Simon's case hypothetically. Or maybe you can just let on that Simon feels like he's being followed, and you're keeping your eyes open as to who it might be?"

"That's actually a good idea."

"Of course it is. You are a smart guy, Miles." My past self laughed, and I joined along. "Okay, now go get ready for your date. That cowlick isn't going to comb down all by itself."

I pressed my hair down, but my cowlick shot back up.

"And I want a full report," he said. "Aim for second base, but settle for first."

"You sure are ballsy when you're not the one actually making moves."

"You're the older and wiser Miles. You should have a lot more moves."

"Bye," I said, rolling my eyes as I grabbed the ladder.

"Did I ever tell you you're my hero?" I heard him say as I climbed up out of the lab.

When I reached the hayloft, I heard the sound of a car rumbling away. I crouched down low so the driver wouldn't see me, but once the car had gone, I cursed myself at not having the balls to see who the driver was since it might've been Simon's killer.

Who knew if I'd ever get an opportunity like that again?

Chapter Thirty-One

Back at home, I was at the bathroom mirror working on pressing down my cowlick for my date when Simon marched past. I threw the comb in the sink and sped out to the hallway, calling his name. When Simon turned around, it wasn't the confident and assured face of the brother I'd known my whole life. This Simon wasn't scared either, more like he'd realized his fate in this timeline and accepted the awful outcome.

"What is it, Miles?" he asked, each word spoken between a sigh.

I couldn't think of anything to say, so I blurted out the first thought that came to mind.

"I...uhh...finished my project on you."

He let his heavy backpack thud to the floor.

"You've actually worked on this?"

"I have!" I said, way too excited. It was rare for him to pay any attention and I didn't want to lose him. According to the timeline, he'd probably already figured out the missing piece his time machine needed, which meant he was in serious danger. The scientist in him was likely doing cartwheels, but it had to suck to know he might not live to see the success of his work.

"You said it's a monologue, right...for a drama class?"

"Yeah," I said, my brain spinning for ideas and landing on one. "Really it's just a story about you that was inspired by the day I followed you around school."

"Okay then," he replied, pushing his glasses up his nose. "Wow me."

I took a moment to collect myself. I locked my fingers together so my hands wouldn't gesture all over the place like they normally did.

"This week, I remembered a time my brother Simon and I spent together. I thought of it because we really hadn't spent any time together in a while, and I'd forgotten how much he was someone I looked up to."

My eyes started to water, but I clenched my fists and squeezed those tears back.

"Simon was seven and I was about to be five and starting kindergarten. I'd never been to school before, and I was really scared. I was okay on the bus because he sat next to me and let me drink my juice box. But then we got to school, and the building was so big, and there were so many other kids that I freaked out. I was crying and crying, and it got worse when we had to be separated, and I went to my classroom. I guess over the next hour, they couldn't calm me down and I was screaming for my brother, so the teacher went to get Simon. When he came inside, the teacher already had it up to here with me, and so Simon suggested that I come with him to his classroom. I remember feeling so relieved. The teacher said this could only happen this one time and then I had to promise to come to my own classroom tomorrow. In Simon's class, they were supposed to bring in a science project they worked on over the summer. Some kids made solar systems out of cut-up paper and scotch tape, or another kid showed how a compass worked, but my brother Simon, at seven made a robot named Charley! And not just any robot, Charley the robot could say my name and tell dorky jokes. Then after Simon's presentation, he sent the robot back with me to my class. And every time I'd feel sad, the robot would say a joke and make me laugh, and all the kids loved Charley the robot so much that I instantly had a ton of friends. I know that Simon didn't make Charley so I would feel better about going to school, but it was as if he knew I'd need Charley because that's the kind of brother he is. He just... knows things beyond what anyone else has the ability to figure out. And if that's what he could do at seven, I can't wait to see what he'll do at seventeen, and twenty-seven, and..."

I stopped because the tears became overwhelming. I wiped my eyes with my sleeve.

"Charley the robot," Simon said, shaking his head. "He had such bad jokes."

It was hard to tell, but it seemed like Simon was tearing up too.

"What do you call someone else's cheese?" Simon asked.

"Nacho cheese," I said.

"Nacho cheese." He chuckled, picking up his backpack. He went to leave, but something about me caught his eye. I wondered if he'd figured out I was Miles from the present, but then he'd be pissed to know I hadn't come any closer to finding his killer. He may have put all his faith in the wrong hero.

"You're looking pretty spiffy tonight, Miles. Going somewhere?"

"Oh yeah," I said, not expecting that. "I'm having dinner at Maisie's house. From lunch the other day."

Simon walked over and patted down my cowlick until he was satisfied.

"There, that's better," he said, and then turned and walked toward his room.

"Yeah, it is," I whispered.

He closed his door, and I let myself stand out in the hallway for a few more moments to hold on to the memory.

One of the few very best ones from this past timeline.

Chapter Thirty-Two

I showed up at Maisie's house more nervous than I ever remembered being. It was one thing to talk with her during a lunch that lasted no more than an hour and another to have a whole night ahead of us with the possibility of having nothing to say. The doorbell gave a squeak when I rang it. Maisie opened the door wearing a long flowing skirt and colored socks. She had gotten her hair cut and put on the slightest bit of makeup, a dab of pink on her lips.

"Hey, Miles." She smiled and nervously flipped her hair to one side. Was she fishing for a compliment about her new haircut? I figured that you could never give a girl too many compliments.

"Your hair looks really nice," I said, wishing there was a way to stop oneself from blushing.

"Thank you. I got it cut today at that place on Kipling Street. The lady said she wanted to bottle my hair color. I thought that was weird."

"That is kind of weird, but she probably said it 'cause she's going gray."

Maisie twitched her nose in response. I couldn't tell if she found what I said amusing or annoying. She pointed at a bag in my hands.

"What's in that?"

"I brought a fancy soda. Kind of tastes like lemonade."

"I love lemonade. Come on inside."

I didn't know what I expected her house to look like, but it certainly wasn't close to anything I could have imagined. There were literally hundreds of clocks everywhere, all ticking away. Grandfather clocks, antique clocks above the fireplace, long and skinny wall clocks, rows of elaborate watches on the mantel, and a giant painting of a melting clock in a similar style to Salvador Dali.

"God, you must think it's so bizarre," Maisie said, smacking her palm against her forehead. "I guess having a zillion clocks around is like my dad's thing. It all started with that grandfather one, an heirloom that's like a hundred years old."

She pointed at a six-foot-tall grandfather clock ticking away. The face of it showed the cycle of a day: a sun eventually turning into a moon.

"No, it's cool," I said. "My house is so uninteresting. We just have some furniture and maybe one crappy clock on the wall."

Maisie pointed to a pile of boxes. "We haven't even completely unpacked yet, but Dad made sure to get all of his clocks out of their boxes. He says 'their ticking sound' is like his religion…or something."

I smelled a wonderful aroma coming from the kitchen and heard her dad rattling around.

"He's making his gumbo," Maisie said. "It's a family recipe passed down from Sumpter to Sumpter."

"I'm definitely hungry," I replied, and then couldn't think of what to say next. A terrible silence passed between us that I longed to break, but every thought of mine sounded dumb. I focused on the line of sweat above her upper lip and decided that I'd die for one salty kiss.

Smith stuck his head out of the kitchen at just the right time.

"Miles!" he said with a salute. He was wearing an apron splattered with gumbo stains. "Is it just you joining us tonight?"

"Yes, Mr. Sumpter, my brother's too busy today."

"You call me Smith, you hear? I hear the name Mr. Sumpter, and I turn around expecting my father to be here."

"Okay, Smith," I said, but calling an adult by their first name felt kinda weird.

"This gumbo'll be one for the ages," Smith said, catching some dripping sauce on his finger and licking it up. He ducked his head back into the kitchen.

Maisie and I shot each other glances while we both thought of what to say next.

"Your brother seems like a busy guy," she said.

"Yeah, he's working on a project right now."

"Like a science project?"

"Actually…" I motioned for her to come closer. She took a step toward me and I smiled because she smelled like a field of sunflowers on a hot summer day. "The project he's working on is top secret but probably has the potential to be something really important."

"I won't tell anyone," she gushed.

"I don't know what it is exactly, but Simon said that he feels like he's being followed."

Maisie lost her smile and started picking at her chipped nail polish.

"Followed…?"

"Yeah, by someone who's interested in what he's working on."

"That's crazy," Maisie said. She looked like she wanted to say more but then just fiddled with the tablecloth. "Is he freaked out?"

"Simon doesn't get *freaked out* like most people do, but I imagine he is."

The clocks all started chiming because it hit six o'clock. It caused us both to jump a little in our seats, but then we started laughing.

"Our house in Oregon was bigger, so they weren't as loud," Maisie said.

"Yeah, that's kind of intense."

Smith popped his head back out of the kitchen. Sweat was pouring down his face.

"Maze, go set the table for me," he said with his Southern twang in full force.

"Okay, Daddy," she said and shyly looped a strand of hair around her ear.

We headed to the dining room, which also had more clocks on the walls than one would ever need. Maisie began setting the table with the precision of a Miss Manners instructor.

"Dad's a stickler for presentation," she said, lining up the utensils. "My mom liked it that way."

She clenched her jaw as if she had said more than she wanted.

"Where's your mom now?"

"Gone," she chirped and wouldn't say anymore. I was about to ask her if *gone* meant her mom had died or took off, but Smith bounded into the dining room with a steaming pot of gumbo and planted it in the center of the table.

"That smells lovely, Daddy," Maisie said, but the excitement had vanished from her voice.

"Let me wash up and I'll join y'all in a moment."

After her dad left the room, Maisie asked: "So does your latest case have to do with figuring out whoever's following your brother?"

"How'd you guess?"

"I'm sure that's the kind of case a detective like you would be dying to solve."

"I've been following Simon at school, seeing if anyone was hanging around him that seemed odd."

"Any luck?"

I shook my head. "I think I'm running out of suspects."

"W.W.S.H.D., right?"

"What's that mean?"

She tapped a freckle on her chin in deep thought. "What Would Sherlock Holmes Do? The eternal question."

Smith returned, rubbing his meaty hands together. He motioned for us to sit.

"Miles brought some fancy soda," Maisie said.

"That's mighty nice of you, Miles," he said, studying the bottle. "Now let's dig in."

Since Dad's cooking was a small step up from eating roadkill, Smith's gumbo was the best thing I'd eaten in a long time. The gumbo was filled with shell-fish and sausages, the sauce spicy enough for me to have to drink three glasses of lemonade soda.

"You have a really nice house," I said, because I knew that was the kind of thing you had to say to a grown-up about their home.

"Go on," Smith said, "you know you want to ask me about something else…"

I looked over at Maisie.

"The clocks!" he said, clapping his hands. "Bit of an obsession, I know, but you can't help the things you love, right?"

He reached over and pinched Maisie's ear.

"Clocks and my little girl, that's what gets me out of bed in the morning. And I assume being a detective is what does it for you?"

No adult had ever really taken the time to ask me about being a detective before.

"Yeah, it's like, what I'm born to do."

"We're alike, Miles. Kindred spirits." He poured the last swill of fancy soda into his glass and took a final gulp. "Keep your eye on this one, Maze, he's going places."

He winked at me and took the napkin from his lap to dab his mouth. Everyone's plate looked as if it had been licked clean.

"Well, I've got some cleaning up to do. Maze, will you entertain our guest?"

"I could help you clean, Daddy," she said, and I offered to do the dishes too. Smith shook his head and held up his hand in response before walking away from the table.

"C'mon, Miles, I'll show you our backyard," Maisie said.

She led me past hallways filled with more clocks and through a back door that opened to their yard. In the distance, the sun was a setting ball of yellow fire and filled the fields of corn with a haloed glow. The air was crisp and buggy as we fell into a porch swing and watched the sun sink.

"It looks so nuclear," Maisie said.

Her shoulder rubbed up against mine as we began to rock. She still had a fine line of sweat dotting her upper lip. She still smelled the way that girls did and boys never could, like she'd been bathing all day in preparation for our date.

The cornfields swallowed up the last sliver of sun and Maisie clapped.

"People clap when a play ends or their plane lands safely, but why not when the sun sets?" she asked. "Every day there's a chance that the world could end."

"Why would you say that?"

"You asked about my mom before," Maisie said, her eyes directed toward the extinguishing sun.

"Did she die?"

Maisie shrugged her shoulders and let out a sigh that sounded like a whistle.

"Just vanished…like she never existed…about two years ago. Told me she was getting groceries, and then…poof. That was the day my world ended."

"Do you think somebody took her or…"

"I stopped coming up with guesses after she'd been gone for a year." Maisie's lip quivered as she focused on her colored socks that had picked up dirt and crumbling leaves from the porch. "What's worse, to think that your mom didn't want to be around you anymore, or that she was just in the wrong place at the wrong time?"

"Both are pretty bad."

"It's not only that I miss her, I feel like I lost a part of my identity too. My mom's Jewish and without her I'm starting to forget my culture. My grandparents live all the way in Chicago, and my dad likes to avoid anything about her. She pickled everything and she taught me how to do it, but without her…it doesn't taste the same. Or the horseradish she'd always keep that she put on everything. She used to call it foods that last through winter seasons until spring came anew. Like, she had this poetic way of speaking."

"I'm so sorry. My mom kind of vanished too," I said. "She's at home, but she doesn't really speak anymore. She's basically a zombie."

Maisie shifted in her seat and seemed surprised.

"What do you mean?"

"A few years ago, she kind of checked out. She'd taken too many drugs because she was badly abused when she was younger. I just found that out from my dad."

"I'm sorry, Miles," Maisie said, with her hand on my back. Her hand was the only warm thing in the chill of the evening. I wished she could stay touching me like that forever. Then she rested her head on my shoulder. Her hair smelled even more like sunflowers than the rest of her. I took a big whiff.

"Maybe they'll find your mom one day?" I said and took a major chance by stroking her hair. It was soft like a bunny rabbit's. She didn't stir. After a minute, I thought she had gone to sleep. "Maisie?"

"Hmmm?" She angled her head until she was looking at me. Our lips were only an inch apart from one another, close enough to kiss on a whim. I licked my lips, and she licked hers, both teasing each other to make the first move. I didn't want to take advantage of her when she was thinking about her mom, but maybe that was the very reason she needed a kiss, to feel good about something.

"I really like your haircut," I said again.

229

She laughed through her nostrils. "I know, you said that."

"That means I'm not just saying it—"

"I—I need to tell you something, Miles."

"Okay, you can tell me anything."

"I'm not sure if you know. Maybe you do. I can't tell if—"

"I am a detective, so it's hard to pull one over on me."

"I'm...I'm bi, I mean, I like boys and girls, I mean, I don't know yet, which I like more, or..."

She looked at me so hopeful like she was scared I'd break her heart. And maybe I did know, deep down, because we were so similar.

"I'm...I mean, I'm bi too."

Her eyes got wide. "Really?"

"Yeah, I don't know which I like more either. But I also don't like to make a big deal about it. It's just one of the million things that make me *me*. Like I kissed this guy recently, I didn't feel anything, but with another guy a while back, I did. I do know that..." I started twiddling my thumbs. "I know, I...uh...like you."

I kissed her, only a peck at first, the kind of kiss you'd give your grandmother, well not my awful grandmother, but then we both parted our lips and tongues slipped through, hesitant at first, tiny pokes and jabs, before we eased into the kiss, and breathed each other's breath, and forgot about the pain we were separately going through. At that moment, we were the only two people who existed and we wouldn't have had it any other way.

When we pulled apart, Maisie seemed stunned and

giggled into her hands. She then tossed back her hair and crinkled her nose.

"I like you too, Miles."

I wanted to freeze this moment. Since I'd already traveled through time, I wondered what it'd be like for time to come to a standstill, just for long enough to allow my heart to stop beating a zillion beats a minute so I could truly appreciate Maisie's stellar kiss and the fact that she said she liked me as much as I liked her.

"My last school was..." She looked down, tearing. "I was bullied a lot. No one understood me. Even my dad—he tries, but he doesn't really understand. He only doesn't want to upset me after my mom left. But she got me."

I rubbed her knuckle. She was so beautiful inside and out. I was lucky to be here with her in this moment, in my past, and hopefully she'd be my future.

But then the back door swung open, and Smith stood in the doorframe with a toothpick stuck in the side of his mouth. He probably saw our whole make-out session. His whole energy changed, a frown hanging low. Even Maisie seemed out-of-sorts, unlacing her fingers with mine, chewing the hell out of her bottom lip.

Now I wished for time to go by fast enough so I could be far away from Smith's scrutinizing stare.

Chapter Thirty-Three

Smith offered to take me home, so I sat in the back seat with Maisie. We drove down dark roads until we reached a highway lit up only by the occasional passing car. Maisie and I held hands in secret. My hand was sweaty but so was hers so I didn't feel embarrassed. Smith was silent up front with one hand on the steering wheel while he rested his left arm out of the window. I wished that someone would say something.

"Thanks for having me over, Mr. Sumpter... Smith," I finally said.

Smith seemed to wake up. I saw his squinty eyes in the rearview mirror.

"Tell your brother about the gumbo." Smith blinked. "I won't take no for an answer the next time."

"I will," I gulped, thinking that Simon could be dead when the next time came around.

The car reached my street, all the homes with lights on. It was a sleepy Saturday night in Frontier, the smell of backyard grilling in the air. I saw Reed hanging out on the curb by his house, playing with a few headless dolls.

"Who's that?" Maisie asked, with her face against the window.

"That's Reed. He lives on the block. He likes to keep watch over the neighborhood."

"Looks like," Smith said, fixing his thick glasses as he looked at Reed long and hard. He stopped the car as Reed's head perked up.

"Oregon!" Reed shrieked, pointing at the license plate.

"Every town's got their own slow kid," Smith said under his breath.

I pretended I didn't hear what Maisie's dad said. I liked her father so far and didn't want to get into a fight about calling Reed slow, since that wasn't the proper term and was very rude. I let go of Maisie's hand and opened the door.

"Thanks again, Mr....Smith," I said, correcting myself. I still couldn't get used to calling him by his first name. Smith had stuck his head out of the side window and seemed preoccupied.

"Got a real nice house there, Miles," Smith said. "Who's home right now, your parents, your brother?"

"Probably just my mom and dad. Simon's barely home."

"The elusive child," Smith said, turning his body to shake my hand.

When I shook his hand, Smith tightened his grip, a silent warning to treat his daughter right or there would be consequences.

"Bye, Maisie," I said, wanting to kiss her again but knowing that would be impossible with Smith inches away.

"I'll see you in school," Maisie said, and I nodded, even though I knew I'd been suspended and this might be the last time I'd see her in the past. As I got out of the car, I couldn't help but wonder what it would be like between us when I finally returned to the present.

The car sped into the darkness of the street.

"Who was that?" Reed asked, bashing his headless dolls together.

"A girl from my school. We kissed tonight."

"Ooooooooohhhh," Reed said and pushed the dolls together as if they were humping. "That car has been here before."

"What's that?" I asked, not really paying attention. The explosion of Maisie's lips against mine was all my mind could handle at the moment.

"Oregon!" Reed shrieked. "I've seen that car before."

"Oh yeah?" I said, starting to walk inside. I wasn't in the mood to deal with Reed after the awesome night I just had.

"Yup, yup. I seen that car on this very block before," Reed said to his headless dolls. "I seen that car many, many times."

I stopped in my tracks as I reached the front door.

"What do you mean, you've seen that car many times?"

"It's here all the time, usually very late at night when no one is around, when the whole block is quiet and I'm hiding." He shushed his dolls as I felt a twisty sensation in my stomach, a burp of gumbo creeping up my throat.

"Miles, that car comes right up to your house and sits by the curb. No one knows that I am watching, but

I watch this neighborhood all of the time. Sometimes a man steps out."

"What does the man look like?" I asked, the blood rushing to my ears.

Reed scrunched up his face and shrugged his shoulders.

"He has thick glasses."

"And what does the man do when he gets out of the car?" I asked, aware of the rankness of my breath, aware of the nervous throb of my heartbeat.

"He stares at your house, usually looking at a window."

"Which window, Reed?"

Slowly, I followed Reed's finger toward Simon's window. I felt my legs give out as I collapsed to the floor while Reed let out a shriek that haunted our entire block.

I gulped at the air to catch my breath as Reed waved his hands in front of my face.

Had I just shared a bowl of gumbo with Simon's killer?

And now...had I let him get away?

Chapter Thirty-Four

I hopped on my bike and headed to the abandoned barn immediately to discuss with my past self about what I had discovered. It made sense that Maisie's dad could be the killer. Simon hadn't noticed someone following him until recently and Maisie and her dad had just moved to town. Now that I thought about it more, Smith had kept asking about Simon and insisted he come to dinner. Also, Smith was obsessed with clocks, which could give him a possible motive for wanting the time machine. And finally, the car that I'd heard sneaking around the barn must have belonged to Smith as well. The question that remained was whether or not Smith had been working alone and whether Maisie was involved too.

Just my luck, I thought. *I get my first kiss with Maisie and her dad turns out to be a psychopath.*

When I reached Simon's lab, my past self was just as shocked to find out about Maisie's dad.

"What do you think we should do?" he asked.

"That's what I came here to ask you."

"You need to follow him tomorrow, see where he goes, who he interacts with. You said that Simon warned you in his video messages that the killer could be connected to some huge corporation or even the government."

"I think he was just speculating."

"Even if Maisie's dad was arrested or something, someone else could be sent to get rid of Simon."

"I'm scared," I said. I hated to admit that and come off as weak, but I was trembling. I'd spent a whole dinner at a killer's house. Who knew if behind Smith's hospitable gumbo and his aw-shucks y'alls, he'd been plotting to murder me as well?

"I'm just as scared, Miles, we feel the same things."

"I kissed Maisie tonight," I said, rubbing my temples.

"Do you think she's involved?"

I didn't answer. How could I know? She could've been messing with me the whole time: both her and Smith bent on stealing Simon's time machine and getting rid of whoever stood in their way.

"You've talked to her, I haven't," my past self added. "I don't know if she's trustworthy."

"I trust her," I snapped, shutting him up. I didn't even have time to get into with him about her being bi too. My brain was clogged, theories and speculations spilling out of my ears.

"I'm sorry," my past self said, because he saw how stressed I was. "But we have to be smart now. I say that we stake out Smith's house starting tonight and then trail him the next time he leaves."

"We?"

I saw a cocky glint in his eye.

"Two Detective Hardys on the scene are bound to be better than one."

Chapter Thirty-Five

I found two big hoodies so our faces would be covered, and my past self and I got on my bike. When we reached Smith's house, no lights were on. His car with the Oregon plates had been left in the driveway, which meant he and Maisie had probably gone to sleep. We hid my bike behind an unwieldy bush and waited with the binoculars we'd taken from Simon's lab.

All of a sudden, a light turned on.

I swiped the binoculars from my past self and zoomed in on the lighted room. Maisie was wearing pajamas, her hair in pigtails. How could someone so sweet possibly be related to such a monster? Besides, I had been the one who approached her first. If she was aligned with her father, she would've tried to get to me or Simon way earlier. I hoped I wasn't making excuses, since I still liked her so damn much.

Maisie sat on her bed criss-cross-applesauce with a sketchbook in her lap. She was a drawing a face that was a perfect replication of mine since she was such a good artist, but instead of a body she penciled in a giant heart with arms and legs. She closed the sketch-book and shut off the light.

"I don't think she's plotting something with her dad," I whispered.

"Is that your brain talking or has your wiener taken over?"

I punched him in the shoulder.

The house remained still for the rest of the night, no other lights turning on. We each took one-hour sleeping shifts. When the sun finally rose in the morning, I thought of last night when I was watching it set with Maisie and the kiss we shared.

"Miles!" my past self said with a nudge.

Crouching low in the fields across from the house, we were able to watch Smith step out of the front door dressed in a button-down white shirt and a black tie. He adjusted his thick glasses as he observed the morning before getting into his car and taking off.

"C'mon," I said, after he'd gone far enough down the road. We got on my bike and followed him. There weren't many other people on the road so I had to hang far back and almost lost him a couple of times, but I was an expert bicyclist and had developed a strong knack for tailing suspects.

Since it was too early in the morning for Smith to go grocery shopping, or to church if he was a religious man, I had a strong feeling that wherever we were being led would answer a lot of my questions about who else might be involved with Simon's murder. Soon we left Frontier and didn't turn toward Gatson but headed to the next town over, which was Collier.

Collier was the sister town to Frontier, but was made up with a lot of businesses where Frontier was more families and homes. The main street had bars and restaurants just like Frontier did, but off in the distance behind a slew of soybean farms were a few factories that always looked like steel monstrosities.

"Do you think Smith is headed to work?" my past self asked. "On a Sunday?"

We passed by the soybean farms and the smell of cow farts from the one animal farm as we headed closer toward the factories. Most of those factories were grain-related—Collier was big on oats; but Smith's car passed by all of the oats factories and stopped in front of a steel building isolated from the rest. He stepped out of his car munching on a bear claw. By the time that we pulled up, we could barely see the other factories in the distance or the town of Collier at all. The ideal place for something sketchy to go down.

"ChronOmniclast," my past self said, peering through the binoculars and reading the name on the face of the building written in robotic-looking block letters.

"Omni!" I said. "That's who Simon and Mr. Congley were getting the parts for their time machine from!"

"Do you think that could mean that Smith might've been working with them as well?"

"But then why would Smith stare at Simon's window like a creepster every night?"

"Maybe he was watching over him, protecting him as well?"

"You think? Shit, then who killed him?"

"I'm trying to explore all theories." My past self looked through the binoculars again. "Look, Smith is entering some kind of code to get inside."

"Can you see what it is?"

"It's an alphabetical keypad, no numbers. H-O-R-A-T-I-O. Horatio."

The front door opened as Smith slipped inside.

"Quickly, so we don't lose him," I said as we hurried up to the front entrance. My past self keyed in H-O-R-A-T-I-O and the thick door to the steel building opened.

We stared down a long metallic hallway with computers built into the walls. The sound of a video camera zooming in and out could faintly be heard. The place was kept cold like a refrigerator, and I was glad that I brought a hoodie. At the end of the long hall, a door quietly shut.

We headed toward the door and saw another keypad, this time numerical.

"Crap," my past self said. "We just missed him."

"Wait, look at the keypad," I said. "Smith had been eating a bear claw, his fingerprints are all over it."

"How do we know the order?"

"Only the numbers three, six, eight, and nine have been pushed. We'll key in as many different possibilities as we can."

"Did you see a video camera monitoring us?"

"We can't worry about that," I said as I started entering the different numerical options.

After the first ten tries, we started to get frustrated. I was about to key in another numerical sequence when we heard a beeping noise coming from down the hallway. We turned around and saw the front door open with someone standing in the doorframe; but we were too far away for the person to appear as more than a blur.

"Quickly," my past self whispered as I keyed in 8-

9-3-6, and the second door opened with a suction sound.

We entered a vast room with an endless ceiling and a pathway that circled around what looked like a pit. The pathway had high metallic walls that reached up to our noses. The ceiling formed into a dome-like shape at the top. The pathway seemed to spiral all the way down to the dark pit below. We headed down, following the sound of heels clicking against the metallic floors.

At one point, we almost caught up to Smith. He'd put on a white lab coat and we saw the tail of his coat disappearing around a corner so we slowed down. When we reached the bottom of the pathway, the ceiling looked like it was a million miles up in the sky. Smith popped the last piece of bear claw in his mouth and entered through a smoky glass door that snapped shut behind him.

The keypad to this door didn't have numbers or letters but about two-dozen symbols that we'd never seen before. Some of the symbols looked like they could be Arabic or even Asian, almost as if the alphabets from many languages had been combined into one super alphabet. Smith had touched about six of the symbols with his sticky fingerprints so there was no chance that we'd be able to crack the code.

Suddenly, a shadow of a figure passed behind the glass door. We dashed around the corner and saw a woman with a white lab coat step out onto the pathway. She was old but not elderly, her silver hair cut into spikes that looked sharp enough to draw blood. She had a severe mouth, which seemed unable to produce a smile. Her eyes clicked from left to right down the pathway before she turned back into the room and said something over her shoulder in a language that I didn't recognize. Her high heels clomped up the pathway as the smoky glass door was still closing.

"I'm going in!" I declared before my past self could say anything. I ducked inside as the door closed and hid behind a computer bank before anyone in the room saw me.

In the center of the room was a mechanical glove on a platform that looked a lot like Simon's time machine. At first, I was afraid that it had been stolen from Simon's lab, but there were slight differences between ChronOmniclast's glove and the one I had used to travel back in time. This glove was more of a navy-blue color as opposed to black and there were raised dots on the inside of the palm that were likely used for gripping something. A machine with robotic arms was using a laser pointer on the glove, as if making slight adjustments.

Smith was situated at one end of the room in front of a computer frame while another man in a white lab coat was manning the other side. The other man had short white hair and a fish-like face with big eyes and big lips and wore a red bow tie. The buttons they were both pushing seemed to control the robotic arms. They were speaking to each other in a language similar to what the older woman with the spiky hair had used, but then thankfully switched back to English.

"Something is off from the diagram I studied," Smith said with no trace of a Southern accent. His real voice had an almost robotic tone.

"Maybe the kid has discovered whatever the missing element is since you copied the diagram that his physics teacher had?" red bow tie said.

"Possibly. The last time I spied on him, I could see

in his eyes that something has changed, like he'd figured out the mystery. Look how close we've been," Smith said, shaking his fist. "We're on the brink. We sent them into the past before…into the future…I know we have."

"But none of them have ever come back," red bow tie added.

Smith lowered his head. "Yes, that is true. But they are out there and they will."

"*He*…is growing impatient," red bow tie said, as both he and Smith looked up toward the domed ceiling.

"Yes, I know."

"He…wants to take action," red bow tie continued.

"And what does he suggest?"

Red bow tie ran a finger from one side of his neck to the other.

"Why not torture the information out of the kid?" Smith suggested.

My blood ran cold as I heard this.

"Do you really think that would work?"

"No," Smith said sadly. "I don't."

"*He* has been clear that no one else but Omni's people may travel through time."

"Does he really think that he will be able to control that? If we are successful with penetrating the time-space continuum, there are bound to be copycats."

"Just like us?" red bow tie said with a smug look.

"We are not copycats," Smith insisted, his neck getting red. "Two years ago, I sent Talia, long before that kid was able to complete his glove."

"And it has been two years and Talia is still gone."

"Gone from the present time, but not gone forever."

"That is debatable," red bow tie said. "He… believes that she is gone."

"Oh, what does *he* know?" Smith said, jamming the buttons on the computer mainframe with his index finger and taking out his obvious aggression.

I remembered when Maisie said that her mom had disappeared two years ago. I wondered if the Talia that Smith spoke of could be her?

Smith's face had gone pale, tears crinkling at his eyes, but he sniffed them away.

"I didn't appreciate what you just said about… him," red bow tie said. "Questioning that *he* doesn't know what he's talking about." Red bow tie shook a skinny finger at Smith. "That is a no-no."

"I've been a student of his the longest," Smith sighed. "There is no one who believes in him more."

"Horatio," red bow tie said, with a cheer and a salute toward the domed ceiling.

"Horatio," Smith said, mimicking red bow tie's motions.

An alarm sounded through the vast room, loud enough to rattle the floors. My heart leaped out of my throat.

"An intruder," Smith said as both he and red bow tie pushed a ton of buttons on the computer mainframe until a glass cylinder descended over the mechanical glove.

Once they were distracted, I took the opportunity to make a break for the smoky glass door. When I got outside, the older woman with spiky silver hair had her arms around my past self who was trying to wriggle free. She saw me and let out a shrill cry. I charged at her, knocking her to the ground as she wailed in pain.

"There's two of them!" she yelled, looking back and forth at both of us. "And they look alike!"

"C'mon," I said, grabbing my past self as we made our way up the circling pathway. The woman was still screaming, "Two!" but neither of us turned to look back.

Two men in white lab coats rounded the corner, blocking our way.

"Go for their nuts," I said, punching one in the balls. My past self was already doing the same thing. We left our pursuers writhing around on the floor and clutching at their balls.

The alarm got louder as we reached the top of the pathway. We bolted through the door that led to the long hallway. We started to run and saw that behind us a wall of lasers had been deployed as a type of blockade. We had just missed being trapped. Making sure that our hoodies still covered our faces, we made a dash for the front door as an overhead video camera tracked us.

When we reached the end of the hallway, the other door opened and we could see Smith standing behind the laser wall with a bunch of other white lab coats. We keyed H-O-R-A-T-I-O into the alphabetic keypad as the thick door swung open and we ran outside into the welcoming morning sun.

Both of us jumped on the bicycle and I pedaled away. My past self kept saying, "Don't look back, don't look back," but I couldn't help myself. Wandering out of the ChronOmniclast building, Smith had bent down and picked up the pair of binoculars that we'd left behind. He put them up to his eyes as we made our getaway.

I turned back around as we biked past the steel factories on the way to the safe arms of Collier. I had no idea whether Smith and the rest of the white lab coats knew who had infiltrated their corporation. The only thing I could be certain of was that I had to stop them now for reasons beyond just saving Simon.

The future couldn't afford to be at the whim of whatever their evil plans might be.

Chapter Thirty-Six

"This is Q," the voice on the other line said.

My past self and I had returned to Simon's lab to brainstorm about what to do next. I decided that we needed to be armed no matter what so I called the number on the card that Quentin the Brainiac had given.

"Hey, this is Miles Hardy—"

"You're lucky I'm around," Quentin said. "I decided not to go to physics meet this week just to mess with Ellery and Linda."

"You left me your card. I need…well, it's for…"

"What kind of weapons do you want?" Quentin asked. He sounded bored, or possibly wanted to convey an aloof kind of persona.

"I don't know." I looked at my past self who shrugged.

"What are you looking to do to someone?"

"This is for protection. A gun I guess, but not too big a gun. I've never shot a gun before."

"You're in ninth grade, right, about five foot six? I

could get you a Ruger LCR Revolver, 38 SPL. Good for small hands."

"How much does that cost?"

"Four hundred dollars but I'd do it for three hundred."

"What if I wanted to rent it for a day?"

"That's a new one," Quentin whistled. "I'm usually not in the business of rentals."

"This could be a life or death situation."

"That won't change the price."

"Please…" I added, not knowing what else to say. I was getting choked up. "These bad people are after Simon and…"

The line went silent and I wondered if Quentin had hung up. I needed to come up with another strategy since I had no shot at getting that kind of cash.

"You're angling to be the number one student here, right?" I asked, chewing on my lip.

"Keep talking."

"Okay, when you apply to colleges, whatever school is your first choice, I can promise you that Simon wouldn't apply there so you'd have a better shot."

Quentin breathed heavily through his nostrils. I hoped that meant he was mulling it over.

"Tell your brother he can have the East Coast if he leaves me Cal Tech. My pale skin is long overdue for year-round sun."

"It's a deal."

"All right, the gun is yours, Wyatt Earp. Meet me in front of the school's utility room at lunchtime tomorrow."

The line went dead.

The next day my past self stayed behind in Simon's lab for the last time while I went to school. I'd get the gun from Quentin first, and then at night, my past self would come over to my house. I figured that Smith would either kill Simon in the middle of the night or first thing in the morning so it was safer if my past self came over once my parents went to sleep. After that, the plan could only be loosely formed. If we had to shoot Smith, we'd aim for his leg. Once the police arrived, I would take them over to ChronOmniclast to shut the whole operation down. That would be the only way to ensure Simon's safety in the long run.

Since I'd been suspended the week prior, I wore my Hawkeye's cap low over my eyes so I wouldn't be recognized by any teachers or Principal Mynad while I headed to the utility room. I got there a little early to ensure that I wouldn't miss Quentin, which meant I had to wait in the hallway in plain sight since you needed a key to get into the utility room. Usually only the janitors had a key, but I assumed that Quentin must've made some type of deal so he had a key as well.

The bell rang and the hallway became crowded with students rushing off to lunch. I lowered my cap even more so no one would bother me and pretended to be reading the announcements for the casting of a *Guys and Dolls* production later that fall. After reading the list about twenty-five times, I looked away as Kevin was coming down the hallway with a half-eaten ice cream sandwich dripping from one hand and a bunch of sticky homework pages in his other. Even though he'd been suspended too, his nagging mom probably made him come to school to pick up his work.

As Kevin got closer, we made eye contact. He raised his hand to say hi but then he lowered it and scowled back instead, as if he'd just remembered that he was still mad at me. I felt horrible. I wanted to apologize to him for treating him like crap, but I had to hold out for one more day. Once I'd get back to the present and Simon was safe, I could truly apologize. It was one thing to have my past self around to help solve Simon's murder, but back in the present I'd be solo again and would need Kevin reinstated into *Mr. Hardy's Detective Agency*.

As Kevin passed by, I chose not to acknowledge him. He looked so hurt, like his world had fallen apart; but I couldn't worry about that. At the other end of the hallway, Quentin was walking toward me carrying a paper bag, which I assumed held the revolver. Soon Kevin had already turned the corner and was gone.

The students in the hallway started to disperse as the bell stopped ringing. Quentin played it cool by pretending to look at the listing for the *Guys and Dolls* cast as well. When all the students had gone, Quentin slid toward the utility closet, whipped out a ring of keys, and opened the door. I followed him into the dark room.

Quentin turned on the sole light, which consisted of a naked bulb swinging from the ceiling.

"Janitor Kersey owes me big time, I get him hunting rifles for the use of his key ring."

Quentin put the paper bag on a stool and took out the gun. He tucked his greasy black hair around his ears.

"This revolver is as lightweight as it gets. It's very

accurate and doesn't have much kickback. It's small enough for you to conceal it completely. I'm including some regular .38 rounds, otherwise you'll have an uncomfortable recoil and you're a little guy."

I nodded even though nothing Quentin said made any sense.

"This is the safety," Quentin added, clicking it on and off. "Keep it off until you're ready to shoot. Then just aim and fire. If you don't want to kill, aim for a limb, kneecaps are always good."

"Okay," I said, as I went to take the gun but Quentin held it out of reach.

"But if I find out that Simon ever applies to Cal Tech, I will come to your house and put a bullet in both of you."

"Yeah, I swear, it's a done deal."

Quentin stuffed the gun into the paper bag and handed it back.

"And don't do anything stupid. You'd be surprised how many people don't know how to handle a gun and wind up shooting themselves or someone they weren't aiming at."

"I've used BB guns before," I said.

"Yeah, this is like a BB that produces real blood. So, if you're firing it, you're better be certain you're shooting it right."

"Sure, I got it," I said. My palms were sweating like mad. I imagined the revolver slipping out of my hands and going off at random.

"I'll allow you to keep the gun for good," Quentin said. "But we never had this conversation. Understand?"

"What conversation?" I nervously grinned.

Quentin managed the biggest smile I'd ever seen

him give, which amounted to a little more than a tiny smirk.

"Wait two minutes before you leave," he said, and backed out of the door to the utility room.

My stomach got all knotty as I counted down one hundred and twenty seconds. I was scared to actually fire a real gun, but I knew that I might have to shoot Smith if it came to that.

After counting down for two minutes, I turned off the light and left the utility room. In the hallway, Maisie was sitting slumped against the lockers nibbling on a PBJ sandwich with her *Sherlock Holmes* book propped in her lap. She was the last person I wanted to see. How could I even talk to her after what I knew about her dad? I tried to make a getaway, but wound up knocking over a garbage can.

"Miles?" she said, waving at me with half her PBJ. "What were you doing in the utility room?"

I slapped my forehead.

"Utility room! I...uh...thought it was the exit door."

"But it's lunchtime right now, we can't leave the building."

"I know!" I made a circle with my big toe while I thought of an excuse. "But I just got suspended...for missing all those Spanish classes so they're making me go home."

She took tiny bites of the PBJ, observing me closely.

"Wanna join me for lunch before you leave?" she asked, the look in her eyes changing from judgmental to unsure. "I didn't see you...or Kevin in the lunchroom and I didn't want to eat alone again so..."

Just yesterday there was nothing I'd rather do than

sit next to Maisie and share her PBJ, but how could that be possible now? There was no way we could have a relationship. Even if she found out what an evil man her dad was, there was no chance she'd turn on him since he was all she had and she'd only known me for a few days.

"Uhh…Principal Mynad really wants me to leave school right away," I said as I started to back away.

"But no one's around, I promise not to tell."

She patted the floor next to her, but I kept backing up.

"I can't. An expulsion could be next if they catch me."

I started picking up my pace.

"Okay," she said, looking even sadder than Kevin did when I'd decided to ignore him.

I wanted to tell her that our kiss the other night was one of the most awesome moments of my life. Seeing her so sad made me feel like someone had carved a hole in my stomach and left my guts spilled on the floor.

"I really had fun last night," Maisie said. Her chin was quivering as if she already knew she was being rejected. I couldn't bear to see her cry. "Like when we were out on the porch…before my dad came out…just watching the sunset."

"Yeah…it was cool, really cool," I hiccuped as I broke into a full-out sprint. "I'll…talk to you later… some… time."

"I hope nothing freaked you out, or you felt like you had to say you were—"

"No, no! I mean, not about that. I'm happy for you, that you've found yourself. Like, I can relate. Really. I just have to go, I'm sorry—"

I turned a corner and headed out of the front doors before she had a chance to respond. As tough as it was treat her this way, I knew I had no other choice.

Hopefully she'd get the hint and be able to move on, even though I knew it would take me a very long time to get over her.

Chapter Thirty-Seven

Just before midnight, I checked to make sure my parents were asleep. My past self had shown up and was pacing nervously outside. The door to my parents' room was partially open, and I could see them enveloped in the covers snoring away. I shut their door and went down to get him. I let him in, and we headed upstairs to strategize some more.

"Is Simon home?" he asked.

I shook my head.

"Is his room locked?"

"I didn't check."

I held the paper bag with the revolver close to my chest as we tiptoed down the hallway. We tried Simon's door, but it was locked as usual.

"Let's jimmy the lock," my past self suggested. "I could hide in Simon's closet and jump out if you need back-up when we take on Smith."

"All of a sudden I have a really bad feeling about this."

He jogged down the hallway and disappeared

down the stairs. When he returned, he had a screw-driver in his hand.

"Do you think it'll work?" I asked as he jammed the screwdriver into the groove and tooled around until the lock clicked open.

Entering Simon's room brought me right back to the horrible moment when I found my brother dead. The blood that had splattered everywhere...the smell of gunpowder in the air...Simon's shocked expression...

Imagining it all again was like someone had thrown a medicine ball into my chest.

"We don't know how time really works," I said, passing my socked feet across the area where Simon's blood had pooled that fateful morning.

"What do you mean?"

"If someone is supposed to die, maybe there's no way to stop it, no matter how much you try."

Stinkers started squeaking from his cage. The noise sent shivers up and down my arms.

"In a few hours, half of Simon's face is supposed to be shot off."

"But that's in the future," my past self said. "It hasn't definitely happened yet."

"But it has happened to me. I saw it all."

A bubble had lodged in my throat from holding back tears.

"But it hasn't happened to *me* yet," my past self said. "So, it doesn't have to be the future."

"Who says?"

"I say. You say."

"I guess we'll have to see," I replied, barely more than a whisper. I was about to say more, but then I saw the doorknob turning and the door slowly open. I opened my mouth to tell my past self to hide just as Simon stepped inside with a folder full of papers under his arm and his mouth wide open in shock.

Like he was watching a tennis match, Simon's eyes batted back and forth from me to my past self. I was afraid that my brother's head would explode from the sheer bafflement of seeing two Miles in front of him. The folder full of papers fell from his hands, scattering diagrams of the gloved time machine all over the floor.

"I just came from making the video I sent you," Simon managed to say, pointing at both of us. His shocked expression soon morphed into extreme elation. He leaped at us, shouting "Eureka!" and strangled us with a hug. "I've done it! I've…done it!"

Tears dripped from Simon's eyes, and he sank to the floor. My past self and I couldn't help ourselves from crying either, except that we were crying for very different reasons.

"I knew sending Stinkers back wasn't a fluke," Simon said, gathering up his papers with a nervous energy that made him look insane. Once he got all of his papers back into the folder and placed it on his desk, the expression on his face changed dramatically.

"Wait…what happens to me in the future?" he asked as the room became silent. A few crickets chirped from the outside the window; Stinkers clawed at his cage. My past self and I looked at each other, neither wanting to be the one to reveal the horrifying truth.

"Your silence tells me all I need to know," Simon said, lowering his head. Surprisingly his tears had stopped, like he could only cry from being happy.

"I knew someone had been following me," he continued, making his hand into a fist and cursing at his pursuer. "This past week, I felt it. A car in the distance, someone in the dark outside my window."

"It's this guy named Smith Sumpter," I blurted out. "He works for ChronOmniclast, or you probably know them as Omni."

"Omni?" Simon asked, furrowing his brow. "That's who I get the parts for my time machine from. But... I've never met them and they didn't know what the parts were for. I came up with a fake project to avoid any suspicions."

"Omni is making their own similar time machine, except they can't figure out the last detail to make it work. They don't want anyone else to be able to travel through time. They want to control time. So they kil—"

I stopped myself. I couldn't tell him what was about to occur.

"They kill you, Simon," my past self said, jumping in. "It happens later tonight or early this morning. But we won't let them. We have a gun to stop Smith, and once we do, we'll tell the police where Omni's facility is. We can't call them until Smith tries to kill you, otherwise he wouldn't have committed enough of a crime to get arrested."

Simon was taking in all of this, and I could see that for once my genius brother had been overwhelmed. Silence filled the room again. The crickets continued chirping. Stinkers scurried back and forth in his cage. I had the nagging fear of Smith creeping up the stairs.

"Thank you," Simon said, finally able to speak again. "I...I couldn't think of anyone else who'd be able to help me. I couldn't trust..." He leaped to his feet. "What about El...Mr. Congley, did he have something to do with my death?"

"We thought he was a suspect," my past self said. "But then we found out he was working with you. The killers are Smith and everyone at Omni."

"I was going to tell you that Mr. Congley and I were working together," Simon said. "I believed he was trustworthy, but I couldn't entirely be sure. The only person I could trust is you. Which is the Miles who went back in time?"

I raised my hand.

"I have many more adventures planned, even beyond your imagination. And I will take you with me. To faraway places in the past and even to the future. I'm so close to discovering how to get there."

Simon had his hands on my shoulders. He was excited now that he was talking about all of the possibilities his brilliant mind could make happen.

"I'm…sorry," Simon said. It was spoken to the wall. He fixed his glasses that had slipped down his nose.

"Sorry for what?"

"For ignoring you, for not letting you be a part of my work these last few years, for ever shutting my door in your face and making you feel like you weren't important in my life." He turned to my past self as well. "I'm sorry to both of you."

"It's okay," we said at the same time.

"Brother for life," Simon said, and both my past self and I nodded.

"Brother for life," we responded in sync.

The three of us stayed up the entire night. Simon told us of his wild plans for the time machine. He wanted to become a Time Fixer who corrected moments in the past to make for a better future, but nothing too outlandish. Since he already stated in *The*

Dos and Don'ts of Time Travel that "You Can't Change the Past on a Grand Scale Otherwise the Future May be Very Different," he insisted that only small alterations could be made: saving a newborn baby before it fell in a well and died, stopping a school bus from getting into a fatal crash, warning some teenager about to rob a liquor store that it could negatively change the trajectory of his life.

When he started speaking of being able to travel to the future, I got really pumped. To witness what would become of the world thrilled me. The past was dangerous to play with on a grand scale, but the future could be ours to change for the better.

Simon warned us both that no one could ever know about what we had accomplished and about the time machine's existence. Even if we stopped Smith and the rest of Omni, there were bound to be others who'd want a time machine for their own selfish gain. All of us agreed that this was a secret only we could share.

A sliver of sun was nipping at the cornfields beyond our street when I realized that the night had already passed and Smith still hadn't shown up yet. Since I had found Simon early in the morning, it meant that Smith should be arriving very soon. We all kept quiet as I expected to hear Smith's car puttering down the street, and the sound of his car door quietly closing, and him entering the house.

The cornfields became scorched with a brilliant purplish light as the sun climbed higher and the clock on Simon's desk said six a.m. I heard the sound of a stone being thrown at the house. A few seconds passed, and I heard the sound again. I rushed to the window and saw Kevin downstairs, all sweaty and hurtling stones at the window while gobbling up an egg sandwich covered in ketchup.

"It's Kevin," I whispered to Simon and my past self.

"You don't think he's involved?" Simon asked.

"No, we had a fight the other day. He probably wants to make up."

"Ignore him, and he'll go away," Simon said.

We heard an even bigger stone thump against the house.

"Get rid of him," Simon ordered as I rushed out of the room. Passing my parents' room, I noticed that Dad had already left to go to work while Mom was still under the covers.

I headed downstairs as Kevin was about to ring the doorbell. I flung open the door causing Kevin to fall inside on his face. I was about to push him back outside and make up some excuse to get him to go away, but then out of the corner of my eye I saw Smith's car with the Oregon license plate turning down my street.

I quickly shut the door and yanked on Kevin's arm to bring him upstairs, causing him to stumble to the ground.

Chapter Thirty-Eight

"Ow, Miles. I think I broke my nose when I fell," Kevin cried as I attempted to tug him up the stairs. I had wrapped my arms around him but was having a hard time getting enough leverage to make any progress.

"My sciatica," Kevin said, rubbing his stomach.

"That's not where your sciatica is."

"My mom complains about hers all the time and I'm sure it's hereditary."

I gave another tug. Kevin went slack in my arms and tumbled down the stairs.

"Listen," I said, wiping the sweat from my forehead. "Shut your dumb mouth and get up the stairs."

Kevin crossed his arms, pouting.

"I'm tired of the way you've been treating me," he wailed.

"Fine, I'm a terrible person and I'll be sorry forever, but I'm in the middle of a case right now and the culprit is about to break into my house."

"You mean there's a cat on the porch trying to get in?"

"No, there's a man with a gun and if you don't get upstairs, the bullet could have your name on it."

We both heard steps coming toward the door. Kevin gulped. I held my hand out to help him up and finally Kevin took it. We ran up the stairs as the front door creaked open.

"Oh my god, oh my god, oh my god," Kevin squealed as he followed me toward Simon's room. We both went inside and shut the door.

"I've never been in Simon's room before," Kevin said, taking it all in. Then he saw my past self. His face turned white.

"What the…?"

"Why did you bring him up here?" Simon asked, pinching the bridge of his nose.

"Smith is at the door. I had no choice."

"But there's…but there's two of you…" Kevin babbled, pointing at both my past self and me.

Simon put his hands on Kevin's shoulders and looked him in the eye.

"Listen, this is present Miles and future Miles. I have created a time machine. There is a man downstairs that wants to kill me for it. We have to stop him."

Kevin screamed in Simon's face as a response.

"Shut up, you dumbass," Simon said, with his hand over Kevin's mouth. "Now if I let go, will you calm down?"

Kevin nodded, so Simon removed his hand. Kevin started screaming again.

"What is wrong with you?" Simon asked and then slapped Kevin across the face. Kevin stood there stunned until he started blubbering nonsensically.

Simon raised his hand as a threat. "Do you want another slap?"

Kevin finally lowered his head and quieted down.

"What's the plan?" my past self asked.

"All of you hide in the closet," Simon said. "I need to get some answers from Smith before we take him down."

I ran over to the window and saw the front door close.

"He's inside!"

"Get in the closet, keep the door ajar, and the gun on him at all times. You need to shoot him if he looks like he's going to shoot me."

"Okay," I said. I got the gun out of the paper bag and undid the safety.

"Is that a real gun?" Kevin asked.

"Lower your voice," Simon whispered.

From the hallway, we could all hear steps coming toward us. Kevin peed himself.

"You are a foul human being," Simon sneered.

"I'm sorry," Kevin said. He was crying now as well.

"C'mon," my past self said, tugging Kevin into the closet. I followed with the gun and we kept the door open just enough for the gun to fit through the groove.

Simon jumped under the covers of his bed and pretended to be asleep. His bedroom door slowly opened as Stinkers started squeaking again in his cage. Smith's shadow could be seen passing along the wall as he entered with a gun in hand. He crept over to Simon's bed and nudged him with the gun.

"Get up," Smith whispered in his robotic monotone.

Simon pretended to be startled and raised his hands in the air.

"Who are you? What are you doing in my house?"

"Who I am is irrelevant," Smith said, directing Simon to stand over by the wall. "But I will give you a chance to spare your life."

"You've been following me, haven't you?"

Smith didn't alter his expression. He looked like a completely different man than the one I had met before. The Smith I'd known had been nothing more than an actor's creation. This Smith was the stone-cold assassin he'd always been.

"I know you've created your time machine," Smith said. "Let's just say you've been followed for some time, longer than you think."

"Time machine? I don't know what you mean."

"Let's not waste each other's time, Simon. You've been building a time machine with a man named Elton Congley for the past four years. While Mr. Congley is a brilliant man in some respects, he spilled the beans to a colleague of mine a few years back when you were beginning experimentation. It seems as if a few vodka cranberries on his tongue will ultimately be the downfall of your entire project."

"What did you do to him?"

"We have his cat Ulm, and we've sent him one bloody paw as a warning last night. He will keep quiet in regard to anything he knows about us and about you, otherwise we will keep mailing him pieces of Ulm until there is nothing left."

"And what do I have to do so you won't kill me?" Simon asked. He looked toward the closet for a second, signaling to me that I may have to fire the gun soon.

"I want the full diagrams for your time machine. We've managed to steal a copy of yours from Mr.

Congley, but it's about a week old. Our scientists are very close to completing our own time machine based on it, however, there is still one element missing."

"What do you want a time machine for?" Simon asked.

"I'll tell you once the diagrams are in my hands."

"No deal."

Smith squeezed at the handle of his gun in frustration.

"My boss wants me to put a bullet through your head and make it look like a suicide. Your family will think of you as a weakling who was never able to fulfill his dreams. Or you can give us what we want and move on to some other scientific breakthrough that I'm sure you'll be able to accomplish."

"Buttering me up won't produce those diagrams."

"You are so young, Simon. So full of promise. What is so important about Time? Go cure cancer. Produce some other energy source that doesn't suck the planet dry. You know that you have the kind of mind capable of doing that. Don't throw it all away for Time."

"I will never hand over those diagrams…" Simon said, noticing that he'd left the diagrams in a folder on his desk after he'd picked them up off the floor.

Smith must have seen him looking because he was staring at the diagrams now. He reached over with the gun still trained on Simon and grabbed the folder. He smiled wide enough to show his gold molars.

"Guess I showed up at the right time," he said, flipping through the diagrams. "Well, this changes everything, Genius Boy. You're nothing but a liability now if I keep you alive."

He aimed the gun at Simon. I felt my bowels shift

as time slowed. I was aware of the gun in my hand and what I had the power to do. I just had to aim for Smith's kneecaps and pull the trigger.

"Do it," I heard my past self whisper.

I took a deep breath and fired.

The bullet shot into the wall. Smith stared at the hole and then turned his gaze toward the smoke coming from the opening in the closet. He lumbered over, thrust open the door, and began pulling all of us out.

"I'm too young to die," Kevin squealed and covered his face.

But Smith wasn't concerned with Kevin. His focus was on the two Miles standing before him, which clearly meant that Simon's time machine had already been used.

"Hand over your gun," he said to me.

I aimed the gun right back at him.

"Hand me the gun, or he gets it."

Smith turned the gun on Kevin.

"Me?" Kevin sobbed, pointing at himself in astonishment. "Miles, hand him the gun!"

"Kevin, he'll just kill all of us if I do."

"But I've never even gotten the chance to touch a boob," Kevin whined.

"Of course you have," Simon said. "You've got your own, which I'm sure you touch all the time."

"Shut up, Simon!" Kevin whimpered.

"All of you shut up," Smith demanded, stamping his foot. "Now I will shoot this ginger kid in two seconds if that gun isn't in my hand."

Smith closed one eye, zeroing in on Kevin as his target. As he pulled the trigger, Simon tackled him from the side. The gun went off as Kevin collapsed to the floor, holding on to his side.

"Kevin!" my past self and I screamed.

Smith and Simon were wrestling on the ground for Smith's gun.

"Shoot him in the kneecaps, Miles!" Simon ordered.

I tried to aim the gun, but Smith and Simon were rolling around too much for me to have a good shot. Simon landed a punch to Smith's face. The impact caused Smith to lose the grip on his gun as it spun across the room.

"Now!" Simon yelled.

I pulled the trigger and watched the bullet hit Smith right in the leg.

"AAARRGGGGHHHH!" Smith yelled.

"I'm calling the cops right now," my past self said, getting Simon's cell from off the table and dialing.

Smith writhed around on the floor, trying to suture the blood spewing from his leg. Simon went over to grab the gun and then pointed it at Smith in case he tried to get up.

"The police are on their way."

"Miles…" Kevin gulped.

I saw Kevin raise a shaking hand into the air. There was clumpy-looking blood coming from his side.

"Kevin's been hit!"

My past self and I rushed over to my best friend, whose eyes were rolling to the back of his skull. Kevin took hold of both of our hands, his teeth chattering.

"Tell my mom and dad and my sister that I love them," Kevin managed to say through coughs and tears.

"We promise," we said.

"And I want my funeral at the McDonalds on Elgin Drive. You know, the one with the server who always sneaks in some extra Chicken Nuggets for me in the twelve pack?"

My past self and I looked at one another and then nodded. "Of course."

My past self sniffed at the blood that had gotten on his hands.

"It's ketchup," he said.

"And I would like a street in town named after me, so start working on that with Mayor Biggins. Actually, if he could change Elgin Drive to Kevin Drive, that would be great. Then my spirit could always be close to the McDonald's there."

"Kevin, you're not bleeding, it's ketchup," I said, turning him on his side and exposing the three packets of ketchup that had burst in his pockets.

"Ketchup?" Kevin said and scooped up a blob of ketchup on his finger.

"You're gonna be okay," I said, helping him to his feet.

"I'm alive!" Kevin gushed. "I swear I saw my life flashing before my eyes. I saw myself being born and—"

"Do I have to slap you again?" Simon asked.

"AAARGGGHHHHH!" Smith yelled as he started reaching into his pocket.

"He's got something in his pocket!" I said, turning my gun on Smith too.

"Take your hand out of your pocket," Simon ordered, but Smith kept fishing around. "Take your hand out of your pocket!"

Smith pulled out an object that he kept concealed in his fist.

"The police are on their way, but I will shoot you again," Simon said. "You broke into our house. We could do whatever we want to you."

Smith opened his fist and revealed what looked like a tiny red button.

"What's that?" I asked, peering closer.

Smith pushed the tiny red button. For a second, I expected some kind of bomb to go off that would kill us all. We waited for a blast, or for some trick up Smith's sleeve, but nothing happened. Smith let out a cackle through strained tears, popped the tiny red button into his mouth, and crunched down.

The sound of sirens echoed down our street. Smith held out his hands as if the handcuffs had already been put on.

"Let them take me away," he said, strangely at peace.

But I didn't feel at peace. Even though we defeated Smith and saved Simon, I couldn't shake the feeling that all of this was far from over.

"What did that button do?" I asked myself and then said it again out loud. "What did that button do?"

━━━

Before the police came, my past self went out the back door and headed to Simon's lab to avoid any awkward explanations. The cops arrived and took all of our statements while Smith refused to say a word. I insisted on showing them Omni's headquarters. I made up a lie that illegal experiments were being conducted there, which Simon had found out about, so Smith came to silence him. The cops seemed to buy it and took the three of us to the outskirts of Collier. We passed by the oats factories as I led them to ChronOmniclast's steel building, but when we pulled up to where it was, my jaw dropped.

The area looked like an apocalyptic wasteland. Hunks of steel and bits of computer lay scattered across the landscape. A giant pit was all that was left of the Omni building. The button that Smith pushed had obviously set off explosives as a safeguard. The police immediately started searching for bodies, but none were found since it was probably too early in the morning for any of the scientists to have shown up for work.

"That's why Smith was cackling when he pushed the button," I said.

Most of the police squadron remained by the destroyed site while a car took us back to the station for more questioning. We were given blankets for the ride since the morning was cold. Autumn had settled in, and winter would soon be arriving. I shivered. Kevin rested his head against the window and had gone to sleep.

"Hey," Simon whispered to me and took out a notepad and a pen from his pocket. He jotted a few words down and passed it over.

Yjkogeu sheabhvihemfd mhdy lfginefhee, the note read in Okoboji, which translated as, *You saved my life.*

Djeo yndoehu tmfhgeioonvdk thehjkendyke'lkdl cndopemane aleffpetoeeldr yjaoenu akegehauiwcn?" I wrote back, which translated as, *Do you think they'll come after you again?*

Simon nodded sadly.

"In some ways," he replied. "I think they always will."

I stared at the road ahead that seemed to stretch for an eternity until it reached the center of Collier.

With the threat of Simon's time machine in existence, I knew I'd always be protecting my brother. I imagined that I would even until I was old and feeble. Who knew how big Omni was and how far their influence spanned across the world? Simon and I would always have to be looking over our shoulders.

"But at least for now, the immediate threat is gone," Simon said as he lay his head back against the seat.

I did the same and managed to close my eyes.

The ride back to the police station was probably the longest amount of uninterrupted sleep I'd gotten all week.

Chapter Thirty-Nine

After an exhausting day being interviewed by the police, it was time for me to head back to the present. Kevin wanted to see the time machine in action so Simon promised he could as long he didn't say a word about it to anyone, or Simon would be forced to use his Mind-Erasing Device. Of course, there was no such thing as a Mind-Erasing Device, but Kevin didn't need to know that. The three of us made our way to the abandoned barn and went down through the trapdoor in the hayloft. When we got to Simon's lab, we made sure to tell my past self everything that had happened.

"Son of a bitch," my past self said, once he learned about Smith covertly blowing up Omni's building.

"They're bound to resurface somewhere," Simon said. "But it'll take them a long time to rebuild everything. There's nothing I can do now."

"Are you worried?" my past self asked.

Simon smirked. "If something happens, I'll just make sure to send Miles back to save me again."

275

I laughed but my laughs died down quickly at the thought of doing this all over again.

"I guess it's time for me to go back to the present," I said and headed over to the glass chamber that encased the gloved time machine. "Let's hope all this worked."

"How will we know for sure?" Kevin asked.

"In the future Simon is dead, so as long as he's alive, it worked."

"And what about *Mr. Hardy's Detective Agency*?" Kevin asked.

"We'll pick up where we left off with you and I running it, the way it should be. You were really brave this morning, Kevin."

"Miles, I peed myself."

"Trust me, there were moments that I wanted to as well."

I held out my hand and Kevin and I did our elaborate handshake that involved snaps, claps, and a fake punch to the gut.

Simon keyed LEDOG into the glass cylinder and removed the mechanical glove. He handed it to me, and I slipped it on.

"Does the glove travel through time with him?" Kevin asked.

"No, the glove doesn't move through the time-space continuum," Simon said. "Miles should vanish, and the glove stays behind."

"I guess this is goodbye," my past self said.

"I couldn't have done this without you," I said. I stared at my duplicate and knew this was the last time we'd ever be face-to-face.

"I never thought I'd like myself as much as I did," my past self said as both of us gave an identical smile.

"I couldn't have said it any better."

We went to shake, but then decided at the same time to hug instead.

After our hug, I turned to Simon. "So how does this work when I return to the present in terms of the other Miles?"

"You should fuse into one body. Two of you can exist in the past, but once you go back to the moment of your departure, you'll become one again."

"That's freaking insane," both of us said.

Simon keyed the coordinates on the mechanical glove.

"All right, are you ready?" he asked me.

A nervous energy filled the room, but I wasn't nervous at all. I'd done the impossible; I saved my brother. The rest should be cake.

I took a deep breath, closed my eyes, and nodded.

Simon pushed the GO button, and I felt the sensation of being yanked by a bungee cord. I was back in the lightning tunnel with stars and galaxies twinkling around me. It was a much more peaceful journey this time since I already knew what to expect. The tunnel whipped me around like an amusement park ride. I flew faster and faster until my surroundings became a blur. Then time stopped and left me dangling in the air over a black hole before it plunged me inside.

I opened my eyes to find myself in the lab. The glove was on the floor where it had fallen when I went into the past. I picked it up and returned it to the glass chamber.

After I secured the lab, I left the barn, got my bike that had been propped against the side of the barn, and took off toward my house. It was the middle of the night, and there was no one on the streets. *What if it was all a dream*? I wondered. I could be returning to a house where Simon had recently died, and both of my parents were still unraveling more and more. I might've never actually seen the sun from a trillion miles up in space or talked to Maisie, or even spent a final week with Simon, not as passing strangers in the hallways at home or in school, but as Okoboji brothers for life.

My house was silent when I got home. I headed upstairs and stared at Simon's closed door. The DON'T ENTER sign was still there. I felt a pang in my heart because I was certain that the new Simon would've taken down the sign after all he had been through. The new Simon would've wanted to allow me to come into his bedroom whenever I wanted. He wouldn't close himself off anymore. The fact that the DON'T ENTER sign was up had to mean that Simon was still dead.

I rushed to the door and knocked it open, expecting to find an empty room, a shrine kept for the deceased. I could hear Stinkers scurrying around in his cage. The room was dark, and I couldn't see anything. I went to find the light, but then a light turned on before I had the chance. Simon sat up in his bed, wrapped up in his comforter. He reached over to the bedside table and put on his glasses.

"Miles?" he said, squinting his eyes.

I tackled my big brother with a hug and refused to let go.

Chapter Forty

The return trip to the present had knocked me out a lot more than my trip to the past. I spent the next few days under the covers, nursing bloody noses and drinking ginger ale to ease my nausea. While part of me had the urge to get new cases for *Mr. Hardy's Detective Agency*, recuperating was a lot more important. The last two weeks of my life would've been trying for anyone, and a week of bed rest sounded like pure bliss.

Sometimes Reed came over once his mom, Annalee had finished home-schooling him for the day. Since I never would've figured out that Smith was the killer if not for Reed, I let him come and play whenever he wanted. Usually, it consisted of us watching *Wheel of Fortune* reruns while Reed guessed all of the answers with a scary accuracy.

Each day, Kevin would also bring over some comics and fast food after school and we played video games like normal. Kevin never brought up time traveling for fear that Simon would use his Mind-Erasing Device on him, nor did he ever bring up peeing himself out of embarrassment. The ridiculous fight that had happened between us stayed in the past for good. The one big change in Kevin was how proactive he became about finding more clients for *Mr. Hardy's Detective Agency* once I felt ready. So far, he hadn't come across any of interest yet, but I was glad to see that he was trying. I was looking forward to solving more cases with my best friend again.

Dad became more doting than I ever remembered him being. After I caught him in Garson at the support group for relatives of addicts, our relationship became stronger than ever. I shared about my feelings toward girls, and guys, and, well, even my kiss with Maisie, even though I avoided saying her name because of what happened with her dad. He was surprisingly cool about it all, more mystified by how I was growing up so fast. And I actually listened as he showed me some of his new inventions (apparently the Butter Stick wasn't going over with any investors), but he was excited that his new motorized unicycle could be the next Segway.

Mom, unfortunately, was the same as ever. Dad started allowing me to administer her pills, and during my week in bed, she occasionally sat with me—though she stared at the wall the entire time. I'd talk to her about the adventures I had to get some type of reaction. She didn't blink when I spoke of Simon dying. She didn't move when I told her of traveling through time. After I fed her her pills, she would get up and go back into her bedroom to slip under the covers.

"We'll fix this somehow," I said to her every time.

Simon would come into my room early in the morning and make me go over in specific detail what it had been like when I put on the mechanical glove. He longed to hear about the lightning tunnel, the stars and galaxies, the flaming sun below, and the feeling of losing one's body entirely and becoming just a mind floating through space. After school let out, he'd been going right back to his lab to work on advancing his time machine. He needed to find a way to allow someone to go back even further. This would require the device to be able to bring someone back to the present on its own. As of now, if someone traveled back to a time before the time machine had been created, how could they be able to return without having the glove there? Once Simon figured this out, the only question that remained was which era in time we should travel to.

After a full week in bed, I was starting to feel better. The nosebleeds had stopped and the nausea was only happening first thing in the morning. It was a blustery Saturday when Dad came upstairs and asked if I was ready for visitors.

"Who's there?"

"A girl," was all Dad said, raising his eyebrows.

It had to be Maisie since I couldn't think of any other girl that I really knew. I changed out of my pajamas into a more presentable outfit that didn't reek of a week spent in bed and headed downstairs. I hadn't talked to her since I'd been back from the past. I didn't know if she'd be mad that Smith had gotten arrested because of me. I opened the front door with no clue how the conversation would go.

She stood there in a powder-blue sweater and long tangled skirt, shivering slightly from the cold. Her face was puffy. She wasn't crying right now, but it looked as if she'd done a lot of crying since I'd seen her last. She was wearing sneakers, but not the ones with the clock doodles. A few feet behind her was an SUV filled with luggage and two older people in the front seats.

"Hey," I said to her with a sloppy wave.

"Hey," she said. She had tucked her hands into her sleeves, one of which she'd been sucking on.

"I've been sick," I said. I stood at a distance away from her, like I was afraid of being too close.

"I know, I heard that at school. Anyway, I'm leaving town."

She motioned toward the SUV idling on the block.

"Where are you going?"

"Chicago. Those are my grandparents."

I gave them a sloppy wave as well, which they hesitantly returned.

"They're my *mom's* parents," she added as if she needed to make it clear that they weren't related to Smith.

"What was your mom's name, by the way?"

She looked at me funny but seemed too tired to really question why I asked.

"Talia."

I wanted to tell her what I'd heard about her mom. That Smith had sent her back into the past and that she never returned. That her mom had never walked out on her and still existed somewhere in time. But I had no idea how to put that into words without confessing about the time machine, so I remained silent.

"They don't think I should be around my dad anymore," Maisie said. "Like, no matter what happens."

I knew that Smith had been charged with breaking and entering and attempted murder. His bail had been set at an astronomical number.

"I'm sorry," I said, because I didn't know what else to say.

"I don't really understand what happened," she sighed and started to well up. "And I don't really know what to think. The dad I thought I knew would've never done something like that."

"I think it's more complicated than we know."

She shrugged her shoulders and left them hanging up by her ears.

"I'm sorry for what he tried to do to your brother," she said, shaking her head.

"I wanted to check in on you," I said, kicking at a stone by my foot. "I was worried, but I didn't know what to say."

Her grandparents honked from their SUV.

"They wanna get started so we can make good time," she said.

"Oh, okay."

We both fidgeted. I kicked at some more stones. Maisie tucked her hands farther down into her sleeves.

"I didn't know what to say either," she finally said. "Like, I thought you'd be mad at me, but I had no idea why my dad—"

She stopped and let herself really cry.

"Hey, hey," I said, making a move to be closer to her. "I never blamed you. Look, my mom is a zombie. You're not your dad, and I'm not her."

"I really liked living in Frontier," she said, sniffling back her tears. "I mean…I did once I met you."

I stepped closer until my lips were inches away from hers.

"Me too. I've always lived in Frontier, but I didn't start really liking it until I met you."

Her grandmother honked the horn again and threw up her hands, exasperated.

"One second, *Safta!*" Maisie snapped and then turned back to me with the sweetest smile ever.

"Chicago's not too far I guess," I said.

"Would you visit me?"

"Yeah…I understand that you probably wouldn't want to come back to Frontier and all with your dad and everything. That it'd be awkward."

She looked down at her sneakers.

"I didn't mean it'd be awkward to have you back… just that you might be uncomfortable…I mean… maybe it'd be better if I came to Chicago to…see you sometime."

She ran a finger under her nose and looked up.

"Maybe I can run a side practice for *Mr. Hardy's Detective Agency* down there?" she said. "It's a big city with a lot of crimes. Maybe you could help me with some of my cases and I could help you with some of yours?" She crinkled her nose.

"That sounds great."

Her grandma honked the horn again.

"Okay, she's about to wet herself," Maisie said. "Goodbye, Miles."

"Goodbye, Maisie."

The two of us lingered, neither wanting to be the one to initiate the kiss. But then, we plunged into each other without caring. Our second kiss lasted for just a second because her grandma pounded on the horn and wouldn't let up, but when our lips parted, we stared into each other's eyes and knew that this wasn't goodbye forever.

She left me stunned as she ran over to the SUV and got inside. She blew against the window until it became fogged up and then drew a dripping heart with her index finger before the SUV took off and disappeared around the corner.

The smell of sunflowers lingered in the air for a while, even after she'd departed.

I remained standing there frozen until her scent vanished completely.

Epilogue

About six months later, I was at home administering pills to Mom while Dad was off meeting with an investor for his new Unizoom™, the motorized unicycle set to take the Segway world by storm. The school year was winding down, I had just turned fifteen, and I planned on spending the summer taking on as many cases as I could for *Mr. Hardy's Detective Agency.* Business had slowed down. Mostly it was back to finding lost cats again until someone at Jeremiah Boonton had been stealing chemistry equipment to start up a barebones meth lab off Generator Street, and I nabbed them in the act. It actually wound up being Jojo and his ass clown cronies who were then kicked out and sent to reform school. Kevin and I got our pictures in the *Frontier Gazette*, and Principal Mynad gave us an honorary medal. But we still hadn't been paid in cash for solving any cases yet.

As part of a trade for watching Mom, Dad agreed to take me to Chicago for the day so I could see Maisie. She'd been waiting for the news of her dad's trial while he stayed locked up, but when we talked and texted we rarely spoke of Smith. Maisie had started at a new school, which focused primarily on art, and she'd gotten very into Life Drawing. She was having a show for young teens in a gallery in Lincoln Park and had invited me to come along. I was nervous about seeing her but very excited as well, our two stellar kisses still branded in my mind.

As I fed Mom her array of colorful pills, I thought that she seemed to be getting worse. She had started doing this thing where she kept her eyes from blinking for as long as possible until they turned red and raw and shed tears. I hadn't heard her speak more than a mumble in months and she was sleeping about twenty hours a day. Dad had begun to talk of hospitalization. Part of me thought it would be best, and the other part secretly worried that once she went into a hospital like that, she'd probably never return. Dad decided to hold out for a little longer before he made a definite decision.

While pretending the final pill was an airplane and making zooming noises so she'd stick out her tongue, I thought of how unfair it was that Mom wound up this way. Why did her mom, Lillian, have to be so cruel? Why did her grandfather have to lose his business and take his own life at the end of the century? I pictured the era of Y2K that I'd been learning about in my US History class. Everyone was afraid the world was gonna end because all the computers would go haywire. Kids watched videos of Britney Spears and the Backstreet Boys on MTV because I guess it was a music channel then. *The Matrix* was the most popular movie.

I zoomed the final pill through the air as Mom finally held out her blue tongue.

Just then Simon burst through the door, glasses askew, hair dripping with sweat. His face was on fire, dark red as a cherry, and he struggled to catch his breath. He locked the door behind him and then closed the curtains in front of all of the windows. In the past few weeks, I hadn't seen him other than in school since he spent all of his spare time at his lab tinkering with the time machine.

"What are you doing?" I asked as he peeked through the curtains and then shut them again.

"I think I'm being followed."

My stomach dropped. We hadn't heard a peep from Omni since Smith was taken into jail. After six months, I began to forget about Omni, but deep down I knew they'd return and go after Simon and the time machine again. I hated to think that they might come back even more determined this time.

"Are you sure you're being followed?" I asked. I left Mom's side to go look out of the window.

"It's inconsequential right now, Miles, because I have some news that will blow your mind."

"What is it?"

"I sent Stinkers back into the past again to a very specific date. I tied a note around his neck that asked someone to write down whatever date it was."

Simon was bouncing around on his tiptoes, a nervous ball of energy, pacing from one end of the room to the other.

"Stinkers came back, Miles! And the date on the note around his neck was exactly the one I sent him to!"

I could hear my heart thumping, an accelerating bass line groove.

"What was the date?"

"Over a year in the past." Simon grinned and then fell onto the couch in shock. "And the changes I made to the time machine brought him back to the present exactly when I wanted. I gave Stinkers twenty-four hours in the past, and he came back right when he was supposed to. Don't you see what this means? We can travel to an era before I created the time machine!"

He jumped up to touch the ceiling and then bent down to touch his toes.

"So, what do you say? You ready?"

"Right now?" I asked. I looked over at Mom, who was working on swallowing her last pill.

"Not this second, there are some final adjustments I still want to make. But yeah, really soon. If I'm being followed again, we might not have too much time to spare."

A bevy of long-ago eras floated through my brain. The Dawn of Time. The Roman Empire. The Renaissance. The Wild West. A huge smile erupted on my face, but then I looked over at Mom again, who was refusing to blink with all of her might and crying bloodshot tears.

"So where do we go?" Simon asked, putting his arm around me. "The options are limitless. We might be able to go anywhere, see anything!"

Mom let out a moan as the final pill worked its way down her throat. All of the eras I had just imagined became replaced by the specific time I knew we should travel to if there was any chance to save her.

"I think we only have one option," I said.

Simon looked over at Mom as well. Immediately, I could tell that he understood when I was talking about, as clearly as if I'd written it in Okoboji.

A Look At: Time Fixers (Miles in Time 2)

Fix the past, save your mom...and don't fall for the enemy.

After solving his brother Simon's murder and rewriting history, 15-year-old sleuth Miles Hardy returns to quiet Frontier, Iowa—where cases are scarce and boredom runs deep. But when their mom's mental health rapidly declines and she's placed in a care facility, Miles and Simon make an impossible choice to travel back to 1999 to rewrite her fate.

In a world of Discmen, JNCO jeans, Britney Spears, and pre-Y2K paranoia, the brothers, alongside the ever-bold Maisie, must navigate high school hallways and family secrets to rescue their teenage mother from the abusive home that sent her down a dark path. But the mission takes a dangerous twist when they discover their grandfather is working for the same ruthless corporation that once hunted the time machine—and he's still after it.

As Simon infiltrates the enemy from within, Miles finds himself torn between two girls: fierce, no-nonsense Maisie, and a mysterious new crush who just might be playing both sides. Every choice in the past risks unraveling the future, and failure could mean losing their mom...forever.

Can Miles rewrite history without erasing what matters most? Or will love and loyalty collide in a timeline beyond repair? Jump back to 1999 in Time Fixers—a heart-racing blend of teen sleuthing, time-travel thrills, and emotional twists you won't see coming.

AVAILABLE NOW FOR PRE-ORDER

About the Author

Lee Matthew Goldberg is the author of the novels THE ANCESTOR, THE MENTOR, THE DESIRE CARD, SLOW DOWN and ORANGE CITY. He has been published in multiple languages and nominated for the 2018 Prix du Polar. After graduating with an MFA from the New School, his writing has also appeared in The Millions, Vol. 1 Brooklyn, LitReactor, Monkeybicycle, Fiction Writers Review, Cagibi, Necessary Fiction, the anthology Dirty Boulevard, The Montreal Review, The Adirondack Review, The New Plains Review, Underwood Press and others.

He is the editor-in-chief and co-founder of Fringe, dedicated to publishing fiction that's outside-of-the-box. His pilots and screenplays have been finalists in Script Pipeline, Book Pipeline, Stage 32, We Screenplay, the New York Screenplay, Screencraft, and the Hollywood Screenplay contests. He is the co-curator of The Guerrilla Lit Reading Series and lives in New York City. RUNAWAY TRAIN and its sequel GRENADE BOUQUETS will be his first Young Adult novels from Wise Wolf Books in 2021.

Follow him at LeeMatthewGoldberg.com